PENG...

# THE DREAMS OF BETHANY MELLMOTH

'Smart, funny and compelling'

*THE TIMES*, BOOKS OF THE YEAR

'Clever and cinematic'

*OBSERVER*

'A skilled and humorous storyteller'

*I*

'Compelling and highly entertaining. One of Britain's
finest living writers'

*SUNDAY EXPRESS*

'Spiky, sparkling and simply brilliant'

*SUNDAY MIRROR*

'One of Britain's most brilliant and versatile authors'

*MAIL ON SUNDAY*

'No one charts the highs and lows of the human condition
like Boyd'

*RED*

'One of Britain's most compelling authors . . . Funny and surprising'

*ELLE*

'A riveting collection of short stories from one of the best'

*WOMAN & HOME*

'You are confronted by the full force of Boyd's undeniable
talent for storytelling'

*STYLIST*

### ABOUT THE AUTHOR

William Boyd was born in 1952 in Accra, Ghana, and grew up there and in Nigeria. His first novel, *A Good Man in Africa* (1981), won the Whitbread First Novel Award and the Somerset Maugham Prize. His other novels include *An Ice Cream War* (1982, shortlisted for the 1982 Booker Prize and winner of the John Llewellyn Rhys Prize), *Stars and Bars* (1984), *The New Confessions* (1987), *Brazzaville Beach* (1990, winner of the McVitie Prize and the James Tait Black Memorial Prize), *The Blue Afternoon* (1993, winner of the 1993 *Sunday Express* Book of the Year Award), *Armadillo* (1998), *Any Human Heart* (2002, winner of the Prix Jean Monnet), *Restless* (2006, winner of the Costa Novel of the Year Award), *Sweet Caress* (2015) and *Love is Blind* (2018). Some seventeen of his screenplays have been filmed, including *The Trench* (1999), which he also directed, and he is also the author of five collections of short stories: *On the Yankee Station* (1981), *The Destiny of Nathalie 'X'* (1995), *Fascination* (2004), *The Dream Lover* (2008) and *The Dreams of Bethany Mellmoth* (2017). He is married and divides his time between London and South-West France.

# The Dreams of
# Bethany Mellmoth

## WILLIAM BOYD

PENGUIN BOOKS

PENGUIN BOOKS

UK | USA | Canada | Ireland | Australia
India | New Zealand | South Africa

Penguin Books is part of the Penguin Random House group of companies
whose addresses can be found at global.penguinrandomhouse.com

First published by Viking 2017
Published in Penguin Books 2018
001

Some of these stories have been published in the *Guardian*, *Notes from the Underground*,
the *Spectator*, *Country Life*, Oxfam's *Water* anthology and in a pamphlet issued by the
Royal Parks of London.

Printed in Great Britain by Clays Ltd, St Ives plc

A CIP catalogue record for this book is available from the British Library

ISBN: 978-0-241-97976-1

www.greenpenguin.co.uk

For Susan

# Contents

PART I

# The Man Who Liked Kissing Women

Ludo Abernathy looked at himself in the mirror – objectively, analytically – and, by and large, liked what he saw.

'You handsome devil,' he said out loud, noting dispassionately that his hair – his full head of hair – was greying very fast for a forty-seven-year-old man. Should he take steps, he wondered? But men who dyed their hair were sad, he thought. Everyone noticed; it was impossible to hide, and even though he happily admitted to a degree of personal vanity he didn't want anyone to *see* that he was vain. No, grow old gracefully was the maxim to adhere to. Anyway, it wasn't as if he was 'on the pull' any more.

As he walked down the stairs to the ground floor of his large house in Kensington a tune came into his head, and with it a line from the song: 'You have to hurt, to understand.' Where was that from? And who sang it? And what did it mean, exactly? So many questions. Tina Turner. Yes. No. Country and Western? . . . James Taylor. No, it was a woman's voice, that much he remembered. Probably from some shop or coffee bar he'd been in. Funny how craftily these songs insinuated themselves into the myriad of impressions that flashed constantly through your brain. 'Ear-worms', that was what they were called.

As he turned into the kitchen he almost collided with his wife, Irmgard. She was in tennis whites and rummaging through the bowl that contained their various keys.

'Who're you playing?' he asked.

'Beate.'

Beate, Beate . . . Yes, he'd kissed her – he remembered now. Thin, blonde, like most of the women he'd kissed.

'Are you sure you should be playing tennis in your condition, darling?' He patted the bump of her tummy. She was nearly five months pregnant. Pregnant with twins.

'We just knock about.'

'Knock up. Run about,' he corrected her instinctively. Irmgard was Austrian and her English was almost perfect, grammatically. She still had quite a strong accent. 'Are you lunching with Beate?'

'Yes. I suspect so.' She found the keys to her 4x4 and pecked him on the cheek. 'See you later.'

'*Wiedersehen.*'

As he drank his coffee he realized that the annoying earworm had returned on its incessant loop. 'You have to hurt –' He sang a few lines from 'The Fool on the Hill' in an attempt to disperse it and was distracted by the sight of his assistant, Arabella, going down the side stairway to the basement office. Ah, yes, work.

After Arkady Lemko and his wife left – Ludo assumed the young woman was his wife, but you should never assume with these types, he knew – he lifted the small Lucio Fontana off the viewing stool and took it back to the strongroom, wondering again, as he slid the painting back into its rack, why anyone in their right mind would spend hundreds of thousands of pounds on a Lucio Fontana. Disloyal thought, he was aware, as Lucio Fontana had been very good to him over the last few years. In fact, you could argue that he owed his entire success as a dealer to Lucio Fontana. Those four he'd bought, right at the beginning, just after he'd married Irmgard – like winning the lottery. He had paid back Irmgard's father, Heinz – old '57 Varieties', as he referred to him – within six months. 57 Varieties had been very surprised: now he had no hold on his son-in-law. Ludo smiled. It had been good to look the gift horse in the mouth. Why should he worry if people wanted to hang Lucio Fontanas on their wall? Their money – their choice, however boringly predictable.

Lemko and his young woman had studied the painting – cobalt blue with four diagonal razor slashes – as if looking for a meaning.

'Is a good one?' Lemko had asked.

'Very good,' Ludo had said. 'Nineteen fifty-nine, you know.' Adding a date always worked wonders.

Lemko nodded, sagely, as if he'd known the date all the time, and spoke some words in Russian to his companion.

'I give you seven fifty.'

'Seven seven five. It's nineteen fifty-nine, after all.'

He had sent them through to Arabella to sort out the tax and transfer details.

A good day's work, Ludo thought, to clear a six-figure profit in half an hour. He locked the strongroom and sauntered back into the front office.

'That all for today?'

'No,' Arabella said, consulting the appointment diary. 'You've got a . . . a Riley Spacks at four.'

'I'm going to pop out for a coffee,' he said, thinking, not for the first time, that he hadn't kissed Arabella, yet. She was pretty in a sulky sort of way. Still, not a good idea to kiss the help, he supposed – a bit too close to home.

'Oh, yes, your son called.'

'Which son?'

'Xan.'

His eldest, twenty, from his first marriage.

'He wants to stay the night next week,' Arabella continued. 'And can he bring a friend?'

'I'll get back to him.'

Ludo sighed. Irmgard didn't like his children: not Xan, not Rory. She didn't like them on principle, she had told him, because they were the children of his previous wives. Tiresome.

He pulled on a coat and strolled up to Kensington High Street, heading for Coffee O'Clock. He wondered if Sinead would be there.

Ludo kissed Sinead gently, his eyes closed, and pushed tentatively at her teeth with his tongue. Her tongue flickered back and Ludo registered the brief lurch in his gut and sensed his erection burgeoning satisfyingly. Now Sinead had a hand round the back of his head and grunted softly as she thrust her tongue deep into his mouth. Ludo sucked at her bottom lip and felt Sinead's other hand going for his groin. He broke off. Sinead was aroused, he could see. She reached for him.

'I've got to go,' he said.

'I get off at six.' *Awf.* He loved her Irish accent. 'I know a place,' she said. 'I've a friend with a flat in Fulham.'

'I can't,' he said. Beginning to realize he'd made a mistake. This was the third time he and Sinead had kissed. He should have stopped at two, as he usually did.

They were standing in a small storeroom near the Coffee O'Clock lavatories. Jute bags of coffee beans slumped on shelves. Shrink-wrapped stacks of milk cartons were piled against a wall.

Sinead straightened her clothes, frowned, touched the corners of her mouth with finger and thumb.

'What's the game, Ludo?'

He liked that. Game/Ludo. Did she realize?

'I'm a married man,' he said. 'My wife's pregnant.'

'So why do you come round here and kiss me?'

'Because I like kissing you.'

'You'd like fucking me better.'

'That would be a betrayal.'

She laughed.

'Come on. What's a kiss like that, then, if not a "betrayal"?' She made the air-quotes with her fingers. She was a small, haunchy woman, in her thirties, he guessed, with dark, bruised eyes and dense auburn hair, cut short. She wasn't married – she didn't wear a wedding ring, anyway.

'Everybody kisses,' he said. 'It's not a betrayal.'

Ludo sat in his sombre, silent office, thinking, staring at the two lit, glowing Howard Hodgkins on the wall, waiting for this Riley Spacks to turn up. Thinking about Sinead. She had tried to slap him but he caught her hand, just in time. Three kisses, big mistake. He wouldn't be going back to Coffee O'Clock for a while. Damn.

Arabella knocked on the door and showed a girl into the room. A second glance told him that she wasn't a girl. She was a woman, a woman as small as a girl. Five feet tall, a little more. She wasn't wearing heels. One of those petite waif-women, girl-women. A third glance made him estimate her age as early thirties. She had long dirty-blonde hair. She held out her hand. He shook it – firm grip, brief hold.

'I'm Riley Spacks,' she said. She had a slight American accent, he thought, or one of those mid-Atlantic European accents that sound American, most of the time. She was tiny and slim but full-breasted, he noticed unreflectingly, as he drew out a chair for her and ordered coffee – double espresso – from Arabella. There was something slightly grubby about her, also, he thought, as he sat down behind his desk again, as if she could do with a good scrub. The idea excited him and he immediately speculated about kissing her. Where, how, when?

'Riley . . .' he said, wanting to concentrate on the real world. 'I was expecting a gentleman. Apologies if I looked a bit blank.'

'You did look a bit blank, actually.'

'Well, "Riley" isn't a female name.'

'Any name can be a female name, surely? I know a woman called James. I know a woman called Morgan.'

'Right. Point taken.'

She had wide restless eyes, always on the move, flicking here and there, checking things out. She seemed nervous, on edge. He would bet serious money she was a smoker.

'Would you like a cigarette?' he said. He opened a drawer where he kept a variety of packs for clients – Gauloises, Marlboro, Seven Stars, Dakota.

'I don't smoke,' she said. 'But, please, do smoke if you want. I'm not an anti-smoking fascist.'

'I don't smoke, either.'

She cocked her head and looked at him, strangely, as if seeing him properly for the first time.

'What's the . . .' She paused. 'We seem to have gotten off on the wrong foot, here.'

She had a small fine nose, with perfectly arched nostrils. Her lips were pale, no lipstick.

'What can I do for you, Ms Spacks?'

'I have a Lucian Freud. I want to sell it.'

Ludo sat in a small pub called the Captain Bligh in Pimlico waiting for Ross Haverley-Grant. Ross was over half an hour late but Ludo didn't care, happy to enjoy the pub-mood: the harmless inertia and mild melancholy. It was a London pub from central casting, Ludo decided. A heavily patterned carpet and moulded maroon Anaglypta walls hung with etchings of the *Bounty* and other ships of the line. Two ancient men sat in a booth nursing half-pints of beer; semi-audible muzak pulsed faintly from little speakers and, parked in the corners, silent flashing gaming machines bulked in a minatory way, Ludo thought. Try me, try me. It was mid-afternoon. The barman, in his grey-white shirt, was absorbed by his fingers, biting and picking dry skin from around his fingernails. Ross liked pubs, Ludo remembered, and the more rebarbative they were, the better. Ludo had suggested lunch at his club, but Ross was barred from most London clubs so they settled for a pub.

Ludo sipped his fizzy water. Irmgard was at the gynaecologist having an ultrasound. She had asked if he'd wanted to know the sex of the twins and he had said he didn't mind either way. Untypically, that made her cry, briefly. Why? Hormones, or had he been unintentionally cruel? Maybe it would be good to know – good to have two girls to match the two boys. He thought about his life and his offspring: three decades, three marriages, three sets of children from three different women. If he carried on like this, and managed to live until he was eighty, say, he might end up the father of eight children, assuming there were no more twins . . . That's why he had taken up kissing. Adultery had always been exciting, more than exciting – sometimes he felt that life was hardly worth living if he wasn't having an affair of some kind – but, at the same time, painful and costly. Xan's mother, Edith, hadn't talked to him since their divorce. His marriage to her best friend, Jessica, had only lasted long enough to produce Rory. And by then he had met Irmgard and had decided to give up his philandering ways. Now he only kissed women and refused to have affairs. Life was less exciting, true, but a little boredom had its particular rewards –

Ross Haverley-Grant stuck his head round the door, saw Ludo and sidled in. He was Ludo's age – they'd both worked at Mulholland-Melhuish and had met there as young trainee auctioneers. Ross was an old acquaintance rather than a friend, Ludo decided, then realized, with something of a pang, that all he had in life amongst the men he knew were old acquaintances.

Ross was very bald with a patchy ginger beard, he was wearing an ochre-green, orange-checked tweed suit and a blue shirt with no tie. Ludo sampled the material of the lapel between fingers and thumb.

'Never brown in town, Ross.'

'Don't be such a snob. I'll have a large gin and tonic, if you please.'

Ludo fetched him his drink and sat down, taking the photograph of the Freud out of his pocket and passing it across the table.

'Twelve inches by twelve inches,' he said.

'Late forties?'

'Nineteen fifty, apparently.'

'Is it "good"?'

'I'm seeing it tomorrow. I'll know instantly.'

'Very nice,' Ross said, and sipped his drink. 'Very nice indeed.'

'Know anyone?'

'I can think of half a dozen. Maybe more.'

Ludo allowed himself to relax and feel some pleasure.

'So,' he said. 'What do you reckon?'

'Two million. Two and a half, possibly.' Ross smiled broadly through his ginger beard. 'I'd want ten per cent.'

'Five.'

'Dream on.'

'Nice seeing you as always, Ross,' Ludo said, standing up. 'Take care. Give me a call one day.'

Ross grabbed his sleeve.

'All right, all right. Mean bastard.' He smiled. 'Where'd you get it? Lucky mean bastard.'

'The less you know the safer you are.'

★

The taxi headed north and soon they were in Hampstead. Ludo thought that Riley Spacks seemed a little nervous. She was wearing a grey trench coat buttoned to the neck and her long hair was wound up under a wide black beret. She looked like a French film star, he thought. They talked safely about nothing – the weather, London's traffic, jet-lag cures – Riley had flown in from Bali, she told him. Then she turned and looked at him squarely.

'I read somewhere,' she said, 'I can't remember where – but this writer said that the art world was more corrupt than the Mafia.'

Ludo took this in and thought about his own skulduggeries over the years – and all the massive fraud and deceit he had witnessed and heard about.

'That's probably putting it mildly,' he said.

She laughed, a low growling instinctive laugh. She was genuinely amused. Ludo knew then that he had to kiss her.

'Why do you ask?' he said.

'It was a test. Kind of a test.'

'And did I pass?'

'With flying colours.'

The taxi pulled up in a crescent not far from the High Street, outside a Victorian brick villa, divided into flats. There were half a dozen assorted bell-pushes by the front door. Riley rang a bell several times and eventually the door buzzed open. They went into a dark hall with a table full of unopened mail and free magazines scattered over the floor. Dead house-plants lined the one windowsill. They tramped downstairs to the basement and Riley banged on the door, loudly, shouting, 'Lily, Lily – it's me! Lily, open the door.'

Ludo heard a key in the lock and the door opened to reveal a tiny ancient lady with thin dyed-black hair, wearing a sequinned evening dress and heavy make-up. She had a cigarette in one hand. She and Riley hugged strongly for a long time.

'Darling, this is Ludo Abernathy – he's come to look at the painting. Remember, I told you. Mr Abernathy, this is Lily Daubeny.'

Ludo shook her hand. Light, almost weightless, like something made out of paper. He smiled his welcoming, friendly smile.

'How do you do,' he said.

'How dee-do-dee,' she said in reply and gave a mad, bronchial chuckle.

They followed her into the ramshackle flat, furniture everywhere, as if it was being stored, photographs, books stacked, piles of yellowing newspapers and an overriding odour of carpet deodorant that failed to hide the tang of cat urine.

'I used to have cats,' Lily Daubeny said. 'But I got rid of them all.'

'Liar,' Riley said.

Tea was offered and declined. Whisky was offered and accepted.

Riley went in search of the bottle. Ludo looked at the pictures on the walls. Nothing financially interesting, he thought. A big Mark Gertler, an awful Duncan Grant, a lot of Josef Herman. He spotted an Alan Reynolds and a couple of Keith Vaughans. Post-war English. Cultured, intelligent good taste – but nothing his clients would want.

'Now what exactly are you doing here, Mr Aberdeen? I'm very busy.'

She lit another cigarette and Riley glanced over at him, as she came in with a bottle of whisky.

'We want to see the portrait, darling. The one Lucian gave you.'

*

It was always strange being back at Mulholland-Melhuish, Ludo thought. To think I spent almost twenty years of my life here . . . Nothing had really changed. The discreet entrance off Dover Street and then the huge staircase, the vast emerald green rooms giving off each other – a kind of volumetric subterfuge, a spatial illusion. And below there were storerooms and packing rooms and accountancy services and, above, two floors of cramped offices. And all this produced an auction once or twice a month. How did they survive in the face of all the competition? Sotheby's, Christie's, Bonham's and the others? He'd never really found out. 'Old money', was the best explanation he had received. Someone had said that the firm owned half of Derbyshire. Someone else had said the first Mr Mulholland made a fortune in Victorian coal mines. And yet here it was, unchanged, seemingly thriving. He looked at the smart, suited young men and women of Mulholland-Melhuish and he knew how little they earned, their tiny, meagre salaries. That's what had driven him out, finally, after the divorce with Jessica. He was broke. And so he found independence in the arms of Irmgard and the generous line of credit from old 57 Varieties. Ludo Abernathy Ltd was born. Best deal you've ever done, Ross had said, enviously. He'd been sacked by then, anyway.

He wandered around, looking at the art on the walls. *Important Modern European Paintings*, the catalogue in his hand said. Where was the obligatory Fontana? – ah, yes, there it hung. And the Vasarely. Check. The Yves Klein. Yes. Serge Poliakoff, Valenti, that fraud Blancmain. And the prices! How could there be a market for this stuff? He knew the answer – because of people like you, mate, he said to himself. You and your ilk keep this whole tawdry show on the road.

To distract himself he thought of Riley Spacks and the afternoon they had spent with Lily Daubeny. The Freud had been brought out for his inspection and he knew within five seconds that it was genuine. Genuine early-phase Freud. Flat paint, the mannerism, the immaculate detailing, the careful distortion. A portrait head of a young woman, bare-shouldered, overlarge almond-shaped green eyes, with a pearl necklace, about nine inches square in a flaking white wooden frame. Signed. He had turned it over. There was a scrawl on the brown canvas: 'Hampstead, June 1950'. He had held it in his hands, thinking. £2 million. Play this one right and I'll never need to sell another painting again –

'Ludo, I don't believe it!'

He turned. It was Suki Goodman. Big and brazen in cherry silk, jewels flashing, a wave of ash-blonde hair. They kissed – *les bises* – and he smelt the musk of her perfume. Had he kissed Suki? Yes, he had. Two years ago, he thought, he remembered, outside some other *vernissage* in a shop door-way in Bond Street. They talked platitudes – Irmgard, the impending twins, skiing, New York, more skiing. He picked a glass of champagne off a passing tray and offered it to her. He thought of Riley Spacks and suddenly wanted to kiss her. Suki would have to do.

They went and stood in front of a Tàpies. He let his arm touch hers.

'You're looking fabulous, Suki,' he said, quietly.

'Thank you, darling. You're not looking so shabby yourself.'

'Have I ever told you that I think you're a stunningly attractive woman?'

She turned her knowing brown eyes on him.

'You have, actually. Many times.'

'I'd love to kiss you. Properly, I mean.'

It nearly always worked. It was a simple wish expressed – heartfelt, genuine – and one hard to be offended by. It was a compliment, of sorts, though risqué. Sometimes the women said, 'Well, thank you, but no thanks.' Or else, 'Not here, not now.' Sometimes they looked at him, smiled, said nothing, and moved away. But, mostly, they were intrigued, and soon, after a while, after some more conversation, they found a way and a location and a time where the kiss could take place.

'You've already kissed me,' Suki said, sardonically. 'If I recall.'

'That's why I want to kiss you again.'

'Peter's picking me up in half an hour.'

'You see that door . . .' Ludo knew it led to a stairway, down to a floor of offices, and a kind of glassed-in counter where payments were made. 'I'll go through it. You follow in a minute.' He smiled. 'If you want.'

In the semi-darkness downstairs they kissed, for quite a long time, and almost tenderly, holding each other close, her breasts flattening against his chest, Ludo's lips on her neck, tasting the sourness of her perfume on his tongue, feeling her hands roving his back, squeezing his buttocks. She broke it off, saying that Peter would be looking for her.

As she reapplied her lipstick she said, 'We have a little flat, you know, in Chelsea. It's empty most of the time.'

'Wonderful,' Ludo said, unexpected tears in his eyes. 'I'll call you.'

'So, what's your best estimate?' Riley Spacks said.

'I think I could get you eight hundred thousand, easily. Possibly eight fifty.'

'I was thinking a million.'

'That might be harder.'

'Someone said that at auction I might get even more.'

'At auction it's public. You're in the public domain. Everybody knows the figures.'

She thought about this.

'What's in it for you?' she asked.

'Ten per cent.'

'So you'd do better if I got a million.'

'That's true.'

'What about more than a million?'

'Then I'd want twenty per cent.'

'A million,' she said. 'Deal?'


Irmgard was playing patience. She loved card games, but he didn't and so, she would rebuke him teasingly, she was thrown back on patience – some consolation for the solitary card player. The gender of the twins was still a secret, Irmgard had said, having elected not to be told. Healthy babies, happy mother, that's all I want, Ludo had said, smiling, considerate. All was well.

Ludo thought about his kiss with Suki Goodman and wondered how he could contrive to kiss Riley Spacks. He felt his chest fill with excitement as he sat with his wife and pondered this recent little infidelity and this new, putative one. That was his flaw, he knew. Dalliance. He fooled around, he 'played away from home', as they said, because it made life more interesting. He didn't excuse it or condone it – he was just being honest. Without that current in his life he became bored and the world and its ways lost its allure.

He stood up, went to the kitchen and poured himself a glass of wine. But, whatever the attractions of dalliance, he was going to stay married to Irmgard, come what may. Three wives were more than enough for one man's lifetime, he reckoned – that's why he was never going to have an affair again. Never again. All his infidelities would be stolen kisses. When he had made that decision, on marrying Irmgard, he wasn't sure if it would work, but it had, and here they were, five years on, babies impending, and he hadn't slept with anyone apart from his wife. He had kissed forty-two women in the past five years, however, according to the running tally that he kept. And, paradoxically, those kisses had kept him faithful, had saved his marriage. In the old days, when he was married to Edith and then to Jessica, he had slept around compulsively, to make himself feel alive – and had duly been caught out and had paid the price, emotionally and financially. No, he was a happier and wiser man now.

He wandered back into the drawing room and sat on the arm of Irmgard's chair as she studied her cards. He kissed the top of her head and she squeezed his thigh. They were a funny thing, kisses – his kisses – he thought. As intimate, in their way, as lovemaking. An act of oral fornication. The touching of lips against lips, the softness of the contact, mouth to mouth, the penetration of tongues, the conjoining of tongues, the yielding, the feelings provoked, the messages that were sent in that illicit coming-together . . . He strolled back into the kitchen and texted Riley Spacks.

They were at the rooftop bar of his club and it was very quiet, half a dozen hardened smokers huddled under the glowing heaters around the wintering pool. They were sat at the bar, their cocktails just placed in front of them, marvelling.

'Did you ever smoke?' he asked.

'No. Did you?'

'No, funnily enough.' He smiled. 'I've found your buyer. One million.'

He sensed the relief surge through her. Like an invisible blush. What problems had been solved by this announcement, he wondered? What new doors opened for her now?

'Good,' she said. 'Excellent. Thank you.'

'Everything is fine with Mrs Daubeny, I trust,' he added carefully.

'She's left the painting to me. In her will. It's mine.'

'Good.' He gave her the necessary instructions. She was to bring the painting to his house at a specific time. While she was there she would be able to verify the money transfer to her stipulated bank account. Then she could leave and he would deliver the painting to its new owner.

'As simple as that,' she said. 'Who's buying it?'

'The buyer wishes to remain anonymous.'

Ludo called for another drink. Ross Haverley-Grant had found a buyer prepared to pay £2.2 million. He wouldn't tell Ludo who it was, but Ludo suspected the buyer was another dealer, known to Ross, the conspiracy multiplying. More profits would be made down the line as the Freud was sold on but they wouldn't equal his profit. He did the sums quickly: five per cent to Ross; his own ten per cent finder's 'commission' from Riley, and then the hidden extra – his own secret over-£1 million profit. £1,190,000, to be precise.

'What made you come to me?' he asked.

'I did my researches. I was told you were very good, very reliable.'

He felt a little shiver of bad conscience but then he told himself: *caveat venditor*. Riley had wanted a million and she had it, thanks to him. Whatever understanding, or not, that existed between her and Lily Daubeny was her business. It was a transaction and everyone was entitled to their profit. He'd have to do a little sleight-of-hand accounting himself – pay some tax, certainly – but it was, without doubt, the sale of his dealing life. In fact it might mark the end of his dealing life – that would be a relief. He looked at Riley as she stirred the olive in her martini, thoughtfully. Yes, she was a very beautiful young woman. She raised her glass and they toasted each other.

'As long as you're not cheating me,' she said with a smile, narrowing her eyes suspiciously. 'Are you?'

'Nobody's cheating anybody,' he said, with maximum sincerity. 'It's a simple transaction.' He changed the subject. 'So Lily Daubeny is your aunt.'

'She says she's my aunt but I think she's my mother. That's why she's leaving me the painting. I think she "gave" me to her sister when I was born. She was in her early forties . . . I was a bit inconvenient. I've no idea who my real father was.'

Ludo felt a little shocked at this revelation, these dark family histories, fleetingly revealed. He didn't want to know any more about how Lily Daubeny begot the daughter who became Riley Spacks.

'Do you mind if I say something to you?' he said, lowering his voice. 'Something personal.'

'No.'

'I find you exceptionally attractive. Exceptionally. You're one of the most beautiful women I've ever met.'

She didn't seem perturbed by his statement.

'Thank you.'

'I'd very much like to kiss you. May I?'

She looked at him, cocking her head in that way as if she was focussing on him anew.

'No,' she said. 'I don't want to kiss you. Not at all.'

It all went smoothly enough. All the arrangements were made. Riley came to the office with the painting, wrapped in brown paper. Ludo called Ross. Ross transferred the £2.2 million to Ludo's Channel Island account. Once the money had arrived Ludo transferred £900,000 to Riley's account in Djakarta. Riley called her bank there who confirmed the deposit had been made. Ludo took the Freud, wrapped it in a sheet and locked it in the big safe in the strongroom, then called Ross who said he would come and collect it personally the next day.

They stood outside in the gathering dusk on the gravelled forecourt of his house between the 4x4 and the Bentley and shook hands. She was wearing boots with high heels and he found it odd, her being four inches taller than usual.

'Are you sure I can't call you a taxi?' he asked.

'No, I'd like to walk for a bit,' she said. 'Come to terms with it all. What it all means.'

'Of course. All the ramifications.'

'Exactly. All the various ramifications.'

He smiled at her.

'Great day,' he said. 'Congratulations.'

'I'm staying at the Oberon Hotel in Mayfair,' she said. 'Room 231.'

'Room 231. I know the Oberon.'

'Would you like to join me there at eight?' she said. 'In my room. I think we need a real celebration of some sort.'

Ludo lay in bed, naked, spent, in room 231 at the Oberon Hotel listening to Riley taking a shower. He felt increasingly strange and was aware of an unfamiliar and deep uneasiness building inside him. Of course, he hadn't slept with another woman in over five years. He'd forgotten what it was like, the feelings and sensations it released . . . He looked at his watch – nearly midnight. Jesus. He'd been cavorting naked in bed with an equally naked Riley Spacks for almost four hours. He checked his phone. Irmgard had texted: 'When are you coming home?' Was he insane? He sat up, rolled out of bed and began to put on his clothes.

Riley came out of the bathroom, in a dressing gown, as he was searching for his tie.

'Leaving so soon?' she said.

'Ha-ha. I was meant to be at a gallery opening,' he said. 'I'll have to think of some elaborate excuse.'

'I bet you're good at that.'

He slipped on his jacket and she stood at the door, opening it for him, just an inch or two. He kissed her gently. Their tongues touched.

'Thank you,' he said.

'See, you got to kiss me. That was what you wanted, wasn't it?'

'We've done more than kissed, my sweet.'

'No, but the point is, the thing to remember is, that a kiss isn't ever enough.'

'Riley, I wanted to say –'

'I'm here for another week,' she said. 'Before I have to leave. Will you come and see me again?'

He thought for a second. No. Bad idea. He rubbed his eyes. Very bad idea. Breaking all his rules tonight.

'Of course. When?'

'I'll text you.'

'Good idea. Send me a text.'

She opened the door wider so he could leave.

'Thank you, Ludo. Be good.'

When Irmgard confronted him with the texts, the dates, the actual hotel, the precise contents of the brief messages he and Riley had exchanged, he didn't bother to deny anything. Riley Spacks had gone by then, gone by a few days. Back to Bali, she had said. She'd be in touch – he should visit, she'd said. But he knew it was over.

Except it wasn't over. He apologized to Irmgard and admitted his guilt in full. Then he apologized to her coldly furious father – Heinz. Ludo Abernathy hung his head and accepted the vituperation, the assassination of his character, as the financial consequences of his adultery and the ensuing divorce were made very plain to him by old 57 Varieties. At least he had plenty of money stashed away in Jersey, he thought. At least he had the money from the Freud – at least he could pay for the damage.

The old saw, the old cliché – that the whole thing seemed as if it were happening to somebody else – appeared never more true, never more apt, he felt. One afternoon, returning in a taxi from his lawyers, in a fiscal daze of figures and demands and counter-demands, iron-clad guarantees and swingeing penalties, he saw they were driving through Pimlico and he recognized the Captain Bligh as they motored past. He told the driver to stop, paid him off and went in. It was early evening and he was glad to see more clients than the last time he had been there. As long as Ross Haverley-Grant doesn't suddenly appear, he thought, as he ordered a large whisky and water and found a seat as far away from the gaming machines as possible.

He sat there for a while sipping his whisky, indulging in the familiar pub-mood: the inertia, the melancholy – the melancholy tinged with some deserved self-pity, he thought. The whisky was helping as he contemplated the meandering rocky road that was his future. The twins – when would he see them? How would he get to know them properly? There was already talk of Irmgard's return to Vienna for the parturition . . . What if she stayed in Austria? . . . Bloody hell. He was aware of something intruding into his muddled speculations. That song again, the ear-worm, plaintively yodelling through the pub's ceiling-high speakers. 'You have to hurt, to understand.' What was that singer's name again? A woman, he'd been right about that. Nice voice.

Yes, he was hurting – but did he understand? Some truth was out there, lurking in the darkness, beyond the firelight of his intelligence – but it was too dim for him to see, just too far off for his intellect to grasp it. Something Riley had said to him . . . 'A kiss is never enough'. What cryptic message was she sending? Was that it? But there were other things she had said to him, as he thought further about the times they had spent together, that seemed to resonate more significantly now. The idea struck him, and he almost instantly dismissed it, that – possibly, conceivably – it was Riley who had betrayed him to Irmgard . . . No. Madness! There had been something between them, that night, and those subsequent nights when they met in the Oberon . . . A closeness, something truly special. But, then, Irmgard had all the dates, the times, testimony of the staff . . . It was the texts – the texts had done for him. But why had Irmgard looked at his phone, anyway? She never did that . . . He frowned, thinking of Riley. Riley couldn't have known, couldn't have guessed at the secret profit he'd made, could she? He'd been very careful but what was it she'd said to him? . . . *The art world was more corrupt than the Mafia*. Why had she said that? And they'd only just met. Was it a warning? She'd said it was a 'test'. No, fantasy. Paranoia. It was just rotten luck, filthy rotten luck.

He went to the bar to order another whisky and decided to sit there. The barmaid delivered up his golden whisky and a small jug of water. He thanked her. She was a black girl, with many strands of thinly plaited blonde hair. He noted also that she had a small silver ring implanted at the left corner of her upper lip. Pretty girl, slim, blue beads attached to the ends of her plaits. She smiled at him and asked him if he wanted some ice. London accent. *Oice*. Whisky is best drunk warm, he said.

She laughed, turned to serve another customer and Ludo looked at her from the rear. Blue jeans, torn everywhere, heavy mountaineer's boots. Pretty girl, though. I wonder, he thought – tentatively, tenderly – I wonder what it would be like to kiss a girl with a ring through her lip? That would be a first.

# The Road Not Taken

## Today

Meredith Swann is driving in her new car under the M40 flyover checking on her GPS system to see if she's following the flowing arrows correctly. She has switched off the woman's voice – 'Turn left in two hundred yards' – because it reminds her, uncannily, of her mother, all calm, quiet advice with a subtext of disapproval. She turns and turns again. Now she is on a road of towering glass office blocks. Is she lost? No, there it is – Sainsbury's Homebase.

She parks, steps out of her car and pulls down her T-shirt to cover the neat dome of her pregnant belly. The car, magically, locks itself as she walks away, its lights giving her a knowing wink of acknowledgement.

In the vast Homebase she is daunted and diminished by the size of the place. Aisles stretch away in front of her, hundreds of yards long, it seems. She walks into the immense grid of stacked shelving feeling lost – why has she come here to buy a pair of secateurs? She wanted to leave the house, is the answer. Then she thinks: maybe it's a pregnancy thing – a strange craving for secateurs . . . She wanders down the corridors of shelves, turning at random. The place is quiet, it's eleven o'clock on a Monday morning. She seems entirely alone. No – look – there's a man pushing a trolley loaded with plastic sacks of earth. She looks at him as he effortlully turns his loaded trolley round a corner and out of sight. She sees a sign – 'Gardens and Gardening' – that's where she needs to be.

*

Faced by a selection of over twenty secateurs Meredith feels flummoxed. She reaches for one as the man with the earth heaves his trolley round the end of the aisle and heads towards her. He's grey-haired, wearing a baggy maroon corduroy suit and what look like hiking boots. She turns away. Maybe kitchen shears would be more practical –

'Meredith?'

The man with the earth has called her name. She looks at him.

'Max! My God!'

They go to each other. She kisses his cheeks and feels the brush of his stubble. He steps back, his hand on his forehead, theatrically stunned, as if he can't believe what he's seeing.

'You look amazing,' he says. 'And in pod. Amazing.'

'You look – different. What're you doing in that fancy dress? Are you wearing braces?'

'I'm a landscape architect now,' he says, spreading his corduroy jacket, showing her his wide navy braces. 'I have to look the part – it's a uniform, sort of. Let's have a coffee. There's a café in here. I insist on knowing everything. It's over here, somewhere.'

He takes her hand and she follows him, trustingly, and they turn down another long aisle.

'I'm worried about all your earth,' she says. 'Abandoning it like that.'

'It's fine. It's mature earth.'

In the café she tells him briefly about herself, what's happened in the intervening years, tells him about Jean-Didier, her husband, who works for BNP Paribas.

'What's that?' Max asks.

'A French bank.'

25

'*Formidable.*'

'I can't quite get used to you as a landscape architect. Bit of a transformation.'

'Bit of a euphemism. I design small urban gardens.'

'Are you happy?'

'Define "happy".'

'Ha-ha, I remember that trick.'

'Can I?' He reaches forward, before she can answer, and places his hand on the dome of her belly.

'It's surprisingly hard,' he says.

'Isn't it? Yes . . .' She's a little flustered that he's done this. 'Where's our coffee?' she says, looking round and seeing the waitress approaching.

Max rips open three sachets of sugar and stirs them into his cappuccino. He holds his cup out to her as if he's going to toast her.

'How amazingly completely wonderful to see you after all this time,' he says, staring at her. 'I can't quite believe it.'

Meredith doesn't know what to say and feels a prickle of tears in her eyes. She clinks her coffee cup against his and smiles.


### Five Years Earlier

Meredith clinks her mojito against Max's Diet Coke.

'I think I'll get mullered tonight,' she says.

'You mean "mulled".'

'I mean "mullered". It's my birthday. You're not twenty-five every day.'

'Well, you are for a year. Every day for a year – before you turn twenty-six.'

'Pedant. Pedantic pedant.'

'Alcoholic.'

'Why don't you have a drink?' she says, looking round the pub. 'Celebrate with me.'

'I'm driving,' he says. 'I'll have a glass of wine at the restaurant.'

'You're becoming very middle-aged in your middle age,' she says.

'I'm not middle-aged,' he says.

'You're forty,' she says. 'Forty is the beginning of middle-agèdness, everyone knows that.'

'But does everyone know that the expression "mullered" is named after the diminutive but solidly built German striker, Gerd Müller?'

'I don't know what you're talking about,' she says, draining her mojito. 'Anyway, I hate sport.'

In the car driving to the restaurant she smokes a cigarette, enjoying the slight head-reel that the two mojitos have induced, and knowing that Max doesn't like her smoking in the car.

'How can you say "I hate sport"?' he says. 'It's like saying "I hate mountains". "I hate music". Ridiculous statement.'

'Give it a rest,' she says. She can sense he's spoiling for an argument. Something she said must have got to him – probably about being middle-aged. He was getting very prickly, these days, in his middle age.

'You're getting very prickly, these days,' she says. 'Very chippy.'

'Fuck you. Turn left or turn right?' Max asks.

'Ah. Right. No, left.'

'Precise as ever.'

'Fuck you.'

'You chose the restaurant. I don't know where it is.'

They drive along a street in Notting Hill, saying nothing.

Meredith peers out – she doesn't recognize where she is – suddenly wishing they weren't off to a restaurant to celebrate her birthday. It's going to end in a fight, she knows.

'We should have turned right,' she says.

'Jesus Christ.'

Max turns right, abruptly, drives down a street and turns right again. Meredith looks out of the window as they drive past a parade of shops.

'That's it, turn left, here.'

Max wheels the car left and they enter a narrow street. At the end, a row of concrete bollards blocks off the exit. Max stops the car, takes his hands off the wheel.

'You know that sign – T-shaped – the top of the T red?' He turns and looks at her, furious. 'It means "Dead End".'

Meredith looks at him. Something snaps in her. She looks back at him with cold eyes. 'Pretty much sums up our relationship, wouldn't you say?'

She gets out of the car and walks away without shutting her door, striding through the concrete bollards so he can't follow her. She doesn't look back but she hears his door open.

'Meredith!' he shouts. 'I'm sorry! Come back!'

She turns a corner out of sight.

Max stands by his car. He walks round it and closes her door, muttering swear words to himself. He slips back into the driving seat and slams his door shut.

## Two Years Before That

Max opens the door to the gents' lavatory. There's a printed sign on the cubicle door – 'Out of Order. Please use other Facility's.'

He shakes his head despairingly – the curse of the apostrophe – and steps back into the corridor. He's in the basement of the club and the lighting down here is a murky dull red – like a nuclear bunker, he thinks. He walks along the corridor heading for the stairs. A chef clatters down and Max asks him where another toilet is. The chef tells him to go back down the corridor, turn left, go up the stairs and he'll find the brasserie. There's another toilet there. Max sets off.

Max returns to the roof terrace of the club, where the smokers go, and sees that in his absence Meredith and her friends have been joined by two more people – there are seven of them now and they all seem to be smoking.

'Where've you been?' Meredith says. 'We were about to send out a search party.'

Max sits down on a square padded plastic box.

'Try finding a loo in this place. Nightmare.'

'A "loo"?' someone says.

'He went to boarding school,' Meredith explains.

Max reaches for his beer – it has warmed in his absence.

'This is Zack and Moxy,' Meredith says, introducing the newcomers. Max glances at them and smiles. Zack seems to have managed to smear his hair over most of his face. Moxy is small and dark – she has a ring through her lower lip.

'Hi,' Max says.

'Cool,' says Zack.

They say nothing more. Meredith and her other friends are laughing stupidly at some joke, rocking back and forth. Max seems to have been left to entertain Zack and Moxy.

'So, what do you guys do?' Max asks.

Zack and Moxy look at each other in amazement.

'What is this? Some kind of interview?' Moxy says.

'Just a question. You know – idle curiosity. How you fill the diurnal round.'

'It's not what you do, it's who you are, mate,' Zack says.

Max sighs and stands up. 'Nice meeting you.' He turns to Meredith. 'We'd better go. We'll be late.'

'Late for what?'

'You know.' His eyes are signalling – let's get out of here. 'We said we'd be there at –' he looks at his watch. 'Ten. It's twenty past.'

'Be *where*, for God's sake?'

'Better go, Meredith,' one of her friends says, knowingly.

'Yeah.' She stands. 'See you around, *mes amis*.'

Max is already heading for the door to the roof terrace. Meredith makes a rueful face and pops a peanut in her mouth.


### One Year Before That

Meredith pops a grape in her mouth and passes the remains of the cheese board on to the person sitting next to her. She's staring at Max who seems very involved in some discussion.

'But don't you see,' he's saying to a man with a beard and black glasses. 'If John Smith hadn't died of a heart attack we'd never have had Blair. Brown was the dauphin – not Blair.'

'Happenstance,' the beard says. 'It's irrelevant.'

'More wine, Meredith?'

Meredith looks up. It's Eliza, the woman who's hosting the dinner party, Max's editor. Meredith wonders why Eliza is not wearing a bra. Bad idea.

'No thanks,' Meredith says. 'I'll fall over if I have another.'

Eliza doesn't listen and tops up her glass.

Max looks round and catches Meredith's eye. Meredith inclines her head towards the door, ever so slightly. Let's go, please. Max smiles, and stands.

'We'd better split,' he says.

See, Meredith thinks, we don't even need words to communicate.

At the door Max kisses Eliza goodbye.

'Thanks so much,' he says.

'Congratulations again.' Eliza gestures at the pile of Max's new book. 'Do you want to take these? I could bike them over tomorrow.'

'I'll take one,' he says reaching for it.

Eliza whispers in his ear. 'I like your little gallerina. Bit young, isn't she? Jailbait.'

'She has wisdom beyond her years,' Max says in a deep voice.

'Sure. It's her wisdom that turns you on.' She lets her hand rest on Max's bum for a second and kisses him goodbye again, on the corner of his mouth.

Out in the street Max and Meredith kiss.

'I saw her,' Meredith says, as they walk off, Max's arm tight around her, 'hand on your bum. Outrageous.'

'She gets a bit amorous when she's had a few, old Eliza,' Max says.

'If looks could kill,' Meredith says.

'No, she liked you, really. She said so as we were leaving.'

'Bollocks.'

Max kisses the top of her head. Pauses.

'Hang on, where are we?' He looks around.

'You said we could walk back to your place.'

'I've only been living there a week. Let's go down here.'

They walk down a street with a church at the end.

'I can see that church's spire from my flat,' Max says.

'Let's take our bearings from the church spire and circle round it, Captain Scott.'

'It's definitely a few streets away. I checked.'

Meredith holds up her hand and a passing taxi stops.

'I want to go to bed,' Meredith says, opening the door. 'Urgently. Tonight. Get in.'

In Max's bed, Meredith lies in his arms.

'Well, it was good for me,' she says.

'Ditto. Did anyone ever tell you that you were incredibly beautiful?'

'No.'

'You're incredibly beautiful.'

'Thank you, kind sir.'

Max kisses her gently.

'Happy?' Meredith asks.

'Define "happy",' Max says.

'Happy being here in your flat in bed with me.'

'I'm happy.'

He touches her face with his fingertips.

'Don't go away, I've got a present for you.'

He slips out of bed and leaves the room. Meredith rolls over and picks up his book from the bedside table. A hardback, just silver lettering on the navy cover. *Dark Labyrinth: sexuality and duplicity in the poetry of T. S. Eliot.*

Max slides back into bed. Meredith puts the book down.

'Are you astoundingly clever, or just clever?'

'Astoundingly clever.'

'Where's my present?'

'Hold out your hand.'

She holds out her hand and he drops two keys on to her palm.

'The keys to the door,' he says.

## The Beginning

Meredith takes her keys out of her pocket and locks her bike to the railing. She lifts her rucksack out of the front basket and goes into the building, checking her watch. She's in good time.

Inside on a noticeboard she sees that the American Literature module is taking place in seminar room 3B/Level M. Level M? She asks a couple of students but they can't help her. She wanders down a corridor and goes up a flight of stairs and sees a sign: 'Floor 1'. She goes back down the stairs again. There's a man swabbing the lino with a mop. She asks him where level M is and he tells her it's on the mezzanine level above the concourse at the other side of the building. He gives her precise directions.

Meredith arrives at 'Mezzanine Level' and wanders along the corridor looking for room 3B. She finds the door – on it is a handwritten sign: 'American Literature. Dr M. Bassman'.

She pushes open the door and steps in. She's the first – no she's not. There's a young guy standing at the back in a T-shirt and cargo pants looking out of the window. He turns.

'Hi,' she says. 'You here for the American Literature module?'

'I certainly am,' he says.

He wanders over to her as she dumps her rucksack on a desk at the front and takes out her laptop. He's looking at her intently. Not so young, she thinks – mature student. His hair is cut short and he has the shadow of a beard. Fit, she thinks. Yeah.

'I'm Meredith.'

'I'm Max.'

They shake hands. He's looking at her very intently.

'Have we met before?' he says.

'No.'

'Why not? Life can be so unfair.'

'We've met now.'

'So we have.'

He goes over to the white plastic board on the wall and picks up a magic marker and writes in large letters, 'ROBERT FROST – 1874–1963'.

'Ah,' Meredith says. 'Dr Bassman, I presume.'

Before he can answer a couple of students come in, soon followed by others and the room fills up. Max takes some sheets of paper out of his bag and walks around distributing them. Meredith looks at the paper. A poem – 'The Road Not Taken'. Not very long.

Max goes to the front and sits on his desk.

'Right, everyone,' he says. 'I hope you're ready for this because I'm going to change the way you read poetry for ever.'

There is a faint susurrus of paper as the class looks at the poem he's handed out. Like a whisper, Meredith thinks, like a wind has blown through the room.

'Let's have a listen, first,' he says, and looks straight at Meredith.

'Meredith. Why don't you read the poem out to us?'

Meredith doesn't reply immediately, lets a little pause develop.

'All right,' she says, clears her throat and begins.

> Two roads diverged in a yellow wood,
> And sorry I could not travel both
> And be one traveler, long I stood
> And looked down one as far as I could
> To where it bent in the undergrowth;
>
> Then took the other . . .

# Camp K 101

It's ironic, Jurgen Kiel thought to himself – and then wondered if 'ironic' was the right word. It was 'unusual', certainly; 'unforeseen' definitely. Because when Jurgen Kiel joined the German army he never expected to be posted to Africa, far less the medium-sized provincial town of Min'Jalli in the Democratic People's Republic of Douala. Yet here he was sitting in a watchtower five metres above the beaten-earth compound of Camp K 101, three clicks out of Min'Jalli, guarding, to the best of his ability, some 5,000 tonnes of rice, powdered milk, millet seeds and assorted other cereals. He sighed, took off his pale blue UN helmet, and rubbed his short hair vigorously. Of course he was not alone: the squad of UN German soldiers was supported by squads of UN Spanish and Pakistani soldiers. They took turns to guard the camp and provided armed escorts for the convoys of NGO lorries that went out to the food distribution centres in other parts of the DPR of Douala. They were well fed, the civil war was taking place many hundreds of kilometres away and the local population was more than pleased to have a UN base in their town. He was doing good, he supposed, in a vague kind of way, though guarding sacks of rice wasn't exactly the main reason why he had joined the German army. Perhaps it *was* ironic, after all.

The African dusk was beginning its short but spectacular duration, the light becoming first a heavy, tarnished gold and then swiftly a muddy orange before the darkness arrived like a door slamming. Already the perimeter lights of Camp K were glowing brightly in the gloom and Jurgen stood and switched on the powerful searchlight in his watchtower overlooking the main gate and the road to Min'Jalli. The road ran alongside a small creek that also formed the boundary to the forest. Jurgen swung the beam across the creek and ran the white circle of light along the treeline. If anyone was coming to pilfer they would arrive from the forest. The creek was low – you could wade across it. Cut the barbed wire, slip into the camp, steal a sack or two of rice. It didn't happen very often but as Colonel Kwame, the commandant of Camp K 101, regularly insisted it was the 'ostentation of vigilance that is our best defence'. Hence the two watchtowers with the .50 calibre machine guns and powerful searchlights. Hence the randomly timed intra-perimeter patrols through the night. Sometimes they caught pilferers – a terrified boy from the bush, naked and starving; three women with their babies looking for powdered milk – but Camp K 101 was new, the barbed-wire fence was dense, taut, tall and well lit. It was very hard to get into.

Jurgen ran the searchlight beam back again. This banal vista of a little corner of African landscape had become as familiar to him as the view from his back bedroom in his mother's house in Waldbach: there was the bamboo grove, there was the footbridge, there was the giant Mungu fig tree, then trees, more trees, more trees. He switched his light off and called up Stefan in the other watchtower at the other end of the camp on the walkie-talkie. 'K2 all clear,' he said. 'Copy that,' Stefan said. Jurgen could imagine him writing it down in the logbook for Colonel Kwame. Operation Ostentatious Vigilance was underway.

Two hours later, Jurgen climbed down from the watchtower, unslung his Koch-Noedler PMG and clicked off the safety, and wandered through the camp amongst the sack-mountains and the corrugated-iron warehouses. When he reached the fence he flipped down the night-vision device on his helmet and looked out at a world turned green. The open ground between the camp and the creek glowed a fuzzy pistachio, the creek was olive and the trees of the forest beyond were dark, shadowy emerald, shifting and pulsing as the branches moved in the night breezes. Jurgen switched on his walkie-talkie and reported in to Stefan. All clear.

Jurgen walked up the wire to the western corner of the camp – ostentatiously – and thumbed-up the cover of his PMG's night-sight. Arms had to be carried visibly, practically flourished, Colonel Kwame had insisted. Yeah, yeah: flourish, brandish, waggle, show . . . Jurgen froze. Something was moving in the trees on the other side of the creek. He ran to the watchtower and climbed up. He had powerful night-vision binoculars there, mounted on a tripod. He swivelled the lenses, focussed. There, flitting amongst the pale lemon branches of the bamboo grove was a figure, crouched over, hesitant. Jurgen zoomed the lenses, and chuckled. A goddam monkey! Jesus!

He watched it for a while as it searched the leaves under the Mungu fig. Too large for a monkey – this was a chimpanzee. A chimp with a limp, Jurgen said to himself, as he noticed that one leg was shorter than the other, minus a foot, in fact – no right foot, just a short stump under the knee. The chimp slung itself up into the fig looking for fruit. Jurgen thought about switching on the searchlight and frightening it away but, what the hell, he thought, if he can find any figs left in that tree, good luck to him.

He kept the binoculars on zoom and after a minute or two watched the chimp lower itself to the ground. He was a big shaggy beast, Jurgen saw, and the hair on his chin was lighter, as if it was grey. A grey goatee. Like Ludger, his mother's fat boyfriend. So he christened the chimp 'Ludger', there and then. It made him smile – he'd look forward to telling Ludger this story when he went back home to Waldbach at Christmas on leave. Hey Ludger, I called a big old chimpanzee in Africa after you. Why? I wonder: perhaps something about him reminded me of you, fatso . . .

The next night, Jurgen watched as Ludger the chimp returned to the Mungu tree. There must be the odd fig remaining or fallen, Jurgen thought, to draw him back. Ludger spent hardly any time in the tree, he seemed to find a few figs or remains of figs in the leaf-fritter on the ground. Jurgen zoomed in on the leg stump. How did you lose your foot, Ludger? A snare? Maybe he stood on a mine? The rebels had laid the odd minefield around their forest camps when they held the territory here a couple of years ago. Jurgen noticed Ludger never put his weight on the stump – maybe it was still sore.

Two days later, when Jurgen knew the rota had come round again for him to be on guard all night in the watchtower, he took six bananas and an old enamel cooking pot and crossed the creek by the foot bridge, making for the Mungu tree. He put the bananas on the ground and upended the cooking pot on top of them, checking that he would have a clear sightline from his watchtower. Ludger was in for a treat, tonight.

And sure enough, an hour or so after dark, he saw Ludger limp out of the bamboo grove and head for the Mungu tree. He went straight for the cooking pot – the bananas must have smelt good – and threw it brusquely away. Jurgen zoomed in, watching him eat the bananas, skin and all. You'll be back, Jurgen thought, now you know how to play the game.

And so it progressed, nightly for the next ten days, whether Jurgen was on watch or patrol or not: at some stage in the day he placed a cache of bananas under the cooking pot beneath the Mungu tree and each morning the bananas would be gone. Jurgen didn't see Ludger retrieve his bounty every time he was on duty in the watchtower but each day's return to the Mungu tree made it obvious that the nightly gift had been discovered.

And then on the eleventh day Jurgen lifted up the cooking pot and saw that last night's bananas had been untouched. He frowned, added the new supply and moved the pot to a slightly more prominent position, kicking away the leaves around it so that it sat in a patch of clear ground. That night he was in the watchtower but saw nothing. The next morning he checked – the bananas had been untouched again. He left them there, just in case. He and some of the Spaniards had been assigned a two-day NGO run up to the northern provincial town of Kitali. Maybe Ludger was unwell – or had moved on. He found himself obscurely troubled, as if the relationship had been unwittingly compromised in some way. Maybe Ludger had become sick of bananas and had been hoping for some figs? . . .

All the way up to Kitali and back he found himself wondering vaguely what could have happened, running through various uninformed scenarios. Was Ludger part of a nomadic tribe of chimpanzees? Had his injured leg made him a pariah figure? Had his leg become worse? . . . It was pointless speculating. The empty convoy stopped in Min'Jalli before returning to Camp K and the soldiers were allowed to go to the market. Jurgen was looking for some carvings or knick-knacks he could take home to his mother and his sister in Waldbach – souvenirs of his African tour of duty. The six UN soldiers, big in their packs and helmets, their PMGs slung across their fronts, wandered grandly through the market stalls handing out sweets and chewing gum to the hordes of kids who surrounded them. Their interpreter, Jean-François, swore at the children, spat in their faces, slapped and kicked them away, but the crowd never diminished, and the soldiers kept giving away sweets.

Then Jurgen stopped. He was in the butchery area of the market. Hacked thin bony joints of meat hung from the rafters of low shacks. The butchers – all women – waved palm fronds to keep the flies off. Three kids in ragged shorts sat in front of some liana and cane cages containing small deer and in another cage was a large potto, blinking uncomprehendingly in the sunlight. Jurgen called Jean-François over. This was another problem. The lingua franca of the PDR of Douala was French – you had to speak English to Jean-François (nobody spoke German, let alone Spanish) then he would translate into French for the locals.

'These boys, they go catching this animals?' Jurgen said in his best English.

Jean-François asked the boys and they replied.

'This bush-pig,' Jean-François translated. 'He tasting very good. Yum-yum. For you one dollar.'

An idea was forming in Jurgen's mind.

'They catch him?'

Yes, came the eventual reply. They were experts at catching wild animals. Very, very good hunters.

'Tell them,' Jurgen said, drawing Jean-François to the side. 'They go catch me one chimpanzee. Bring him to Camp K.' He pointed to the cage containing the potto. 'Put him in cage like this.'

Jean-François explained. The boys all nodded eagerly. '*Pas de problème, chef,*' one of them said, giving Jurgen two thumbs up.

'I give them ten dollars,' Jurgen added, and then explained about Ludger, the bamboo grove, the Mungu tree, the bananas and the nightly visits. Jurgen watched Jean-François relate the key details to the raggedy boys. He was thinking: there was a small zoo in Victoireville, Douala's capital, a day's journey away. He could ship Ludger down to the zoo on one of the NGO convoys, his wounded leg could be examined and treated and he could spend the rest of his days in captivity, true, but in comfort and safety. He conjured up to himself an image of the label set on the bars of Ludger's capacious cage: ' "Ludger". Male chimpanzee. *Pan troglodytes*. Gift of Mr Jurgen Kiel.' He would have done something good, Jurgen reckoned, pleased with himself, pleased with his initiative – his three months in Africa would have amounted to more than just guarding sacks of rice.

Three days later he was shaving in the wash house when Severiano said that Jean-François was asking for him at the service gate. Jurgen sauntered over to the small gate on the west side where the camp-workers came and went. Jean-François had been charged by Jurgen to purchase him 4,000 American cigarettes on the Min'Jalli black market – twenty cartons of 200 cigarettes – the price was unbelievably low if you paid in American dollars. He was heading back home on leave in a week and he planned to hand out these cartons around Waldbach as Christmas gifts to his friends and acquaintances. Jean-François was standing by the checkpoint with his hands in his pockets. Jean-François gestured him over with a covert twitch of his chin. No cigarettes, obviously, Jurgen reasoned, displeased. He followed Jean-François a few yards down the path. Three kids stood there with a wheelbarrow, a coloured cloth thrown over the contents.

'They get him for you,' Jean-François said with a knowing smile.

Jurgen knew at once but he felt he had to pull the cloth back just the same. Ludger lay there on his back, dead, blood from the big gash on his brow had trickled down to stain one side of his grey goatee. Apart from that he looked calm, Jurgen thought – his eyes closed, as if he were taking a lengthier nap than usual. Jurgen swore under his breath and felt a wave of strange emotion wash through him. He exhaled and looked up at the sky, veiled with a thin nacreous sheen of cloud. He looked down again and noticed that Ludger's stump was raw, alive with small beige maggots feeding. Ludger – lost in translation. Perhaps he'd done Ludger a favour – inadvertently saved him from a lingering gangrenous death . . . He would hold on to that thought – it would help.

'I wanted him alive,' Jurgen said emphatically, suddenly remembering the French word. '*Vivant.*'

'You never say,' Jean-François replied. 'What you do with one big chimpanzee? You crazy man?'

One of the kids spoke.

'He say very good to eat. Good food,' Jean-François translated, rubbing his stomach. 'Yum-yum.'

'They can have him,' Jurgen said. 'I don't want to eat him.' He turned and began to walk back to the camp. Jean-François caught up with him, touched his elbow.

'Jurgen, *mon ami*, you owe these boys ten dollars.'

Jurgen paid.

The train to Waldbach from Straubing was cancelled, Jurgen saw from the noticeboard. The next one left in a couple of hours. Two hours in Straubing, Jurgen thought, wonderful, just what I was hoping for. His mood was bad because when he'd arrived in Munich he had telephoned his mother to let her know he was home from Africa. She said that she'd arranged for him to spend his leave at his sister's house. Ludger was going to be staying with her. 'It'll be easier,' his mother had said. 'You know how you and Ludger don't get on.'

Jurgen deposited his kit bag in the left-luggage office and walked into Straubing. He didn't get on with Jochen, his sister's husband, either. A jazz musician, Jochen played the trombone in a casino nightclub. An annoying, opinionated man, he practised on his trombone two hours a day, seven days a week.

The handsome, wide main street of Straubing had been transformed into a Christmas market, full of small wooden huts selling food and drink and articles of woolly clothing. There was some sort of funfair also, Jurgen saw, strolling through the crowds, moving through successive aural zones of competing styles of music, and feeling a little self-conscious in his uniform, aware of the curious glances coming his way.

He went into a bar and had a few beers, trying to raise his mood, rebuking himself for his irritation and selfishness. His sister would make him very welcome, he knew, and he could easily go out for a walk when Jochen practised his trombone. Then a young girl – seventeen or eighteen – a bit drunk, he could tell, came and stood by the bar next to him to buy a drink. 'How many babies did you kill in Afghanistan?' she said, and then swore at him. Jurgen sighed, wished her a Happy Christmas, and left the bar.

'Welcome home,' he said to himself bitterly, standing by a wooden stall that was selling some kind of powerful and warming glühwein. Here the music was traditional, folk songs and Christmas carols that Jurgen could remember from his schooldays. He drank another couple of glühweins, feeling marginally better. The drink was strong with some kind of aromatic schnapps in the mix. He flexed his shoulders, rolled his head: it was good to be back home, after all, one stupid drunk girl wasn't going to ruin his leave.

He saw that the traditional music was coming from an elaborate barrel organ, brightly painted, encrusted with carved wooden figurines from folk tales – witches and wizards, bears and foxes, lost boys and girls and gingerbread houses. He ordered another glühwein and wandered over with it to hear the music better. He dropped a couple of euros in the felt hat that dangled from the front. The man turning the handle of the barrel organ smiled and said thank you.

Then Jurgen saw the monkey sitting on the top. It was small and grey-furred but it had a white wisp of goatee on its chin, like Ludger, only miniature. There was a chain around its right leg attached to the barrel organ. What kind of monkey was it? What were they called? A macaque? A gibbon? Jurgen whistled softly at it and it turned its head, its big round black eyes staring at Jurgen and it made a plaintive staccato cheeping sound and bared its sharp yellow teeth.

'What's this monkey called?' he asked the organ grinder.

'Mo-Mo.'

'Mo-Mo? What kind of name is that?'

'You want a different name – get your own monkey.'

'Okay,' Jurgen said, thinking. 'How much do you want for him?' Jurgen turned and smiled at the man.

'He's not for sale.'

'Everything's for sale,' Jurgen said. 'Just depends on the price. I'll give you a hundred euros.'

'He's not for sale, man,' the organist said, his faint smile fading. 'He's part of the act.'

'I'll give you two hundred euros.'

'Go and sober up somewhere, yeah? Leave me alone. Do me a favour.'

Jurgen emptied his pockets of money.

'Three hundred and twenty-three euros,' Jurgen said, showing the man the money in his hands. 'You can buy six monkeys for that.'

'*You* buy six monkeys, you stupid, big moron –'

'I want this monkey. Only this monkey.'

'Why?'

'He reminds me of someone.'

'He's not for sale.' The organist stopped turning the handle. He came closer, and lowered his voice. 'If you don't stop bugging me, you cretin, I'll call the cops.'

For a second Jurgen thought about smashing the man in his self-satisfied face, of knocking him to the ground and kicking the shit out of him, but suddenly he had a better idea. He looked back at the little monkey, then back at the man.

'You think about that three hundred euros when you count your takings tonight. Asshole,' he said, and wandered off, casually.

The wire cutters cost eighteen euros. They had thick orange rubber handles and a capable-looking system of levers that quadrupled the pressure applied, so the assistant in the hardware store told him. Jurgen paid and walked back on to Straubing's main street.

He circled the organ player for a while, waiting for a few people to gather and claim his smiling attention. Then, with a couple of long strides, he came up swiftly behind the organ, grabbed the chain and cut through it, about three inches from the monkey's leg. It was like cutting string, it was so easy. The monkey turned and looked at him.

'Go, Mo-Mo,' Jurgen said softly. 'You're free.'

He stepped back and clapped his hands. And the monkey leapt off the organ and on to the roof of the next-door shack that was selling alpaca hats and scarves.

'Hey!' the barrel-organist shouted. Jurgen darted off into the crowds of the funfair. He looked back. The monkey was sitting on the roof of the alpaca shack, and then suddenly it scurried along the looped electric cables attached to the wall of a nearby house and shimmied up a drainpipe to the guttering on the roof.

Jurgen felt a sense of ineffable happiness warm him, almost making his head reel. The last he saw of Mo-Mo was as he made his way daintily up the stepped gable of the house to the rooftop. Then he climbed on to a television aerial and disappeared in the darkness. The whole of Straubing was out there, waiting for him, the whole of Bavaria, of Germany, Europe . . . Jurgen looked at his watch. Mo-Mo was free. He felt good. And it was time to catch the train to Waldbach.

# Humiliation

London is the first city of humiliation: London does it better than anywhere else. I should know, its latest victim. First my divorce – you would think, what with war in Korea and the death of King George, that *The Times* would have more news-worthy events to report than my decree absolute from my wife of eighteen months. 'Novelist Yves Hill divorces, con-fesses to adultery.' Of course I confessed – only to spare myself the further wounds, the death by a thousand cuts, of admit-ting to Felicity's adultery with that zero, that *nul*, that parvenu nonentity Gerald Laing-Turner.

Yet after the humiliation of the divorce came the further humiliation of the publication of my fourth novel, *Oblong* (Dunn & O'Leary, 10s 6d) and the sudden, brutal auto-da-fé of my long-nurtured reputation. Does it seem crass to admit that I felt this last humiliation more keenly than the first? I am still an artist, after all: I have stopped being a husband. The pain I felt, the physical pain in my belly, as I read review after hostile, bile-charged review (why do they hate me so, these strangers?) still lingers. What is an artist to do in this ghastly situation? Why, go to Paris, city of artists, city of Degas, Proust, Larbaud, Jean-Paul and Simone. I took the boat train that night, played records in my solitary compart-ment, dreaming of Paris and the Paris-cure. But the city was slow to work its magic, this time. First, there was the flaccid and embarrassing session in the *maison de tolérance*, followed by a melancholy meal and far too much drink. Crapulous, angry with myself the next morning, I sat in the Café de Flore contemplating a spitting glass of mineral water (liver salts fizzing within) and wondering vaguely about my life. Why do they call that potent liqueur *eau de vie*? *Eau de mort* is more apt. Why are paid women so understanding of a man's temporary physical inadequacies? (Answer: relief.) What was I to do? What was Yves 'Humiliated' Hill to do with his miserable life? Halfway through my fourth decade and all was ashes around me. Felicity and Gerald – good God – to be cuckolded by Gerald Laing-Turner . . . How had *The Times* reviewer described *Oblong*? 'A turbid, horizonless sea of utter tedium.' And what had possessed George to give the book to Raleigh Maltravers, of all people? . . . Somehow, one of Maltravers' sentences came unbidden to my mind: 'A talent so nugatory it casts not the faintest shadow.' 'Casts not'? 'Casts not' – what middle-class pretension. How could George let that go by?

I looked around the Flore and signalled for the waiter: time for some hair of the dog – a Fernet or a Dubonnet, I thought. Early June in Paris and the place seemed full of English tourists: what a loud harsh unpleasant tongue we have. And they were all reading English newspapers and magazines, no doubt containing further humiliating notices of my failed marriage and failed novel. I knew at once what I had to do: I had to work. I had to get out of Paris immediately and write something, anything. Anything that paid, that was. Rio, the Atlas Mountains, Shanghai – far away. I asked the waiter (a surly fellow) for some *jetons* for the telephone. He replied in English even though my French is fluent and colloquial. I had decided to call my agent, Findlay McHarg. Get me a job, Findlay, I would say: one that will take me away from here and will recompense my literary abilities handsomely.

Sainte-Radegonde is a modestly sized provincial town and is the ideal starting point for one's peregrinations in this most verdant and delightful of the south-western riverine valleys. It sits on the Dordogne a few miles east of Sarlat and is serviced by the autorail from Bordeaux (trains for Paris may be had at nearby Brive), contains three excellent garages, an adequate hotel (Hôtel de la Gare \*\*\*) and two large brasseries on the charming central square, La place de la République.

'By automobile through the Dordogne Valley' by Yves P. Hill, *The English Motorist*, July 1952

I was cross with Findlay. No, that is unfair. I appreciate his bluntness, his northern candour, I need it. But, really, *The English Motorist*? A twenty-guinea fee and expenses of no more than £10. Plain robbery: my fee would go to pay my extra expenses while I researched the article. 'It's the best I can do at this short notice,' Findlay said. 'The *Oblong* fiasco is still the talk of the town.' He does not pull his Caledonian punches, dear Findlay.

I checked into the Hôtel de la Gare and asked for their cheapest room. I was working out a clever, developing plan. You are a writer of fiction, Yves Hill, I told myself, so why don't you write some fiction? My room deserved its low rate: under the eaves with slanted ceilings, it was graced with a sagging bed squeezed between a chest of drawers and a table with a jug and ewer. The small dirty window was three feet from a chimney crowded with cooing doves (and crusted with dove shit) and a distant view of a washing line. On my way downstairs I noticed a maid airing out two grand rooms on the first floor: wide beds with padded headboards, panelling, painted armoires. I questioned the receptionist: I thought you said the hotel was full? It is – we await the arrival of the English guests, monsieur, he said with an odd sheepish, conniving smile as if I were party to his conspiracy.

I investigated the two brasseries on the place de la République: the Café Riche and the Café Couderc. To my seasoned eye it seemed that the Riche had the better situation (its *terrasse* warmly illuminated by the evening sun), while the Couderc had the better menu. The Café Couderc even had a makeshift seafood stall where a burly young lad with a first moustache performed the duties of the *écailler* and was shucking oysters with frowning concentration – flair and nonchalance would doubtless come with time.

I took a Pernod on the *terrasse* of the Riche and let the setting sun warm my face. For the first time in a year I felt myself relax, forgot about the ill-named Felicity and her beau and their hideous new union, forgot about the savaging that my poor brave *Oblong* had suffered, and felt the balm of France seep through me. I sauntered across the square to the Couderc and engaged the young oyster-shucker in conversation. Do you have oysters every day? Nearly, he said with an expressive shrug, they come from Arcachon – it depends on the trains. I went inside, was shown to a perfectly acceptable table, ordered a dozen *fines de claire*, a bottle of the local Sauvignon Blanc and began to think about my next novel.

What is the essential nature of the Dordogne? It rises in the Massif Central and flows west to join the Garonne near Bordeaux. The vegetation is northern; the light and air recall more southern climes. Travelling this meandering cusp of northern and southern Europe is a true delight, and surprises await the enterprising motorist at every turn.

The next morning I rose early and caught the local bus to Brive, where the sheepish desk clerk had told me there was a good bookshop. There I bought three different guidebooks, all in French, that dealt with the Dordogne department. I had an abominable lunch (people forget how easy it is to eat badly in France), and caught the bus back to Sainte-Radegonde. I read my guidebooks on the way, plotting my course from Sainte-Radegonde down the River Dordogne to Bordeaux. What need of a noisy and noisome motor car, several nights in dreary provincial hotels, the bother of going up by-ways to seek out allegedly charming villages? These paths have been trod before – send your imagination, Hill, on your behalf, steered by your French guidebooks. Stay in your mean room, enjoy your aperitif at the Riche and your simple, hearty meals in the Couderc, have your fee and expenses cabled to the post office. You deserve a paid holiday. If *The English Motorist* is that tight-fisted what more can it expect?

> From the arid, rugged high Causses and sombre gorges the river descends and civilization begins as it starts to wind through flat water meadows, walnut orchards and dense, thick woods. Its character changes as we enter the Périgord Noir, so called because of the truffles found there, those knobbled, dark, delectable parasites – not to everyone's taste, so muskily redolent of the earth – that grow on the roots of sturdy oaks.

In the Couderc that evening, Benoît, the young *écailler*, brought me my dozen oysters, open on the half-shell, nestling on a gleaming bed of ice. He arranged the plate of bread, the cold butter, the little bowl of chopped shallots and red-wine vinegar neatly around them. He topped up my glass with chill Sauvignon Blanc. *Bon appétit*, Monsieur Hill, he said, with a tiny bow. I felt the seduction of France surround me again, its effortless, complex civilization. '*Merci infiniment*, Benoît,' I said and discreetly slipped him a hundred-franc note.

What is it about the oyster and its curious, subtle narcosis?

I drizzled lemon juice over them, added the tip of a teaspoon of shallots and vinegar to one, scraped the meat clear of its restraining muscle and forked it into my mouth, where I chewed the oyster, two or three bites (chewing is absolutely essential – the true oceanic taste is not otherwise released) and swallowed. A corner of bread, a swig of chill wine: it is a drug, and powerfully addictive, one could eat a hundred, two hundred – some people do – but I always stop at twelve.

I laid down my last shell. Closed my eyes for a moment, masticated. That taste . . . I opened my eyes to see a tall man in a pistachio tweed suit entering the Couderc and looking around. He saw me and strode over. I recognized him instantly and felt a kind of falling, a nausea, as if I had driven too fast over a humpback bridge.

'Yves Hill?'

'Ah, yes?'

'I'm Raleigh Maltravers.'

'I'm sorry?'

'Maltravers, Raleigh Maltravers.'

I allowed myself a baffled smile while my guts writhed like eels in a pot. 'The name is vaguely familiar,' I said, dabbing my mouth with my napkin, 'have we met?'

'We're both in the same hotel,' Maltravers said.

'Simple but comfortable.'

Maltravers stroked his chin. For the first time I noticed he had a near-transparent blond half-goatee, a gesture at a Van Dyke beard but, oddly, no moustache. He gave a great exhalation, as if he had decided something very important.

'I reviewed your novel *Oblong*. For *Illuminations*. George asked me.'

'Really? I don't take *Illuminations*. I hope you were kind.'

'I was very severe.'

I shrugged, as if I had been told my train was five minutes

late. This is what you must do: utter indifference is your best weapon. I thought my throat would close but I managed to say, 'Oh, well, *c'est la vie.*'

'That's very white of you,' he said, and offered his hand. 'Professional standards, professional courtesies.'

'What?' I said, shaking his proffered hand, limply.

'Men of letters. English men of letters. So I know I can ask you this particular favour.'

I was wordless. Maltravers leant forward and thrust his face at me. I saw he had a pliant, mobile, upper lip, covering an overbite. I realized the half-goatee was an attempt at hirsute facial ballast to hide his weak chin.

'The thing is, Hill,' he said in a deep, confiding voice, 'I'm not here. You've never seen me. We have not spoken. I am, so to speak, invisible.'

Oxen are still in general use in the fields and farms of the Dordogne, and many a shock awaits the daydreaming motorist as he rounds a corner and comes upon an ox cart with its pair of oxen, apparently immobile, in the middle of the roadway. The ox cart moves more slowly than a walking man but a good pair can plough as well as horses.

'*Oblong* is an expense of spirit in a waste of shamefully useless reading time . . . Mr Hill's laboured symbolism, his banal profundities, engender a fatigue the like of which . . . Toiling efforts at attaining a European philosophical dimension provoked hoots of incredulous laughter in this reader . . .' Raleigh Maltravers' long two-page review of my novel in *Illuminations* came to me, as I lay sleepless in the hot furrow of my bed, almost as if dictated. How could I recall every word? I listened to the doves shifting outside my window as the first lemony dawn light penetrated my thin, too-narrow curtains and I felt a form of pure sensation shiver through me – one that I had not experienced since early childhood. It was hate. I recognized it: unadulterated, grade 'A' hate. I hated Raleigh Maltravers, and I wanted to kill him, slowly and with agonizing pain.

I slipped out of bed and washed my face in the ewer. Calm down, Yves, I said to myself, bide your time, everything will be revealed. Maltravers clearly needs your complicity, your absolute discretion – he must be very unhappy to ask a favour of a man whose book he has so recently destroyed. What is going on?

I spent the day in the Café Riche with my guidebooks writing up my vicarious journey down the Dordogne valley. I finished my article for *The English Motorist* by mid-afternoon, went back to the hotel, had a snooze, some sort of a bath, changed my shirt and crossed the square to the Café Couderc for supper. Benoît was shucking oysters with a panicked, panting energy.

'The Englishman,' he said, gesturing at the new tray. 'Now it is thirty-six in ten minutes.'

Maltravers had the oyster-need, the oyster-craving, clearly, but far worse than me. He was sitting erect at a table under the big clock, waiting for his next dozen. But he was with someone, a woman, her back to me. I sat on the other side of the big room, half obscured by a pillar. When Benoît brought Maltravers his third plate I saw the woman excuse herself, stand and go to the *toilettes*. She was tall, in her thirties I would say, with a fine clear face and thick dark-blonde untidy hair. I found myself immediately and powerfully attracted to her, and that had nothing to do with Maltravers. I watched him eat his oysters. Everyone has their oyster foibles, and Maltravers liked to swallow his directly off the shell, freeing the meat first, dousing it with a liberal spoonful of shallot-vinegar and then slurping the oyster down whole, giving a little jerk of the chin, flipping his small pointed beard as he swallowed. There was something unpleasant – carp-like, lamprey-like – about the way his long upper lip seemed to enfold the oyster-bearing shell. He ate the dozen in astonishing speed, in under a minute, like a refugee frightened his meal was going to be snatched away.

The woman returned and they began talking, leaning intimately towards each other across the table. Like lovers . . . Of course. Everything was clear and fell into place – suspicions now confirmed – and I almost laughed out loud. Maltravers had handed me my revenge. 'Thank you, mighty Zeus,' I said softly to myself, composing the short deadly letter in my head: 'Dear Mrs Maltravers, Last week, your husband was in Sainte-Radegonde, Dordogne, accompanied by a woman. Sincerely, a Friend.' There *was* a Mrs Maltravers, that much I knew for sure, and, as far as I could recall from some newspaper article, there was quite a sizeable litter of Maltravers children, also. I felt a warmth spread through me, an inner calm, as I looked across the room at them. Maltravers ordered more oysters. Forty-eight – of course, the legendary aphrodisiacal qualities of the bivalve. What did that really very – not to say extremely – attractive woman see in the faintly repulsive, saurian Maltravers? Why should that man have her as his mistress? . . . Still, I was about to ruin his life. Let him enjoy the last few days of the affair. But then another idea began to take hold of me, far more subtle and satisfying than a simple anonymous letter. My piece was written, my fee was telegraphically on its way to me, why not stay on in Sainte-Radegonde and enjoy a well-deserved holiday while I dallied with Maltravers and considered whether I could elaborate a more intriguing outcome to this unhappy encounter?

In the Dordogne valley sudden storms driven inland from the Atlantic can erupt even in summer: the rain pelts down but we know the deluge will not last, the darkness will not endure. Look, the sun is out again, the hedges steam damply, and we can happily resume our journey.

It took me the rest of the meal to configure the details of my plan and I decided to let twenty-four hours elapse before I put it into practice. Maltravers and his lady friend drove off in a large Citroën the following morning. I went for a stroll on the banks of the Dordogne as it flowed smoothly beneath the handsome old bridge that linked Sainte-Radegonde with the northern bank. At lunch I went to the Couderc and spoke with Benoît. We talked idly about oysters and the excellent quality of those that came from the *bassin* at Arcachon. He had asked the *patron* to order more, he said, Monsieur Maltravers' extraordinary appetite had to be taken into account. As I left him I picked, unnoticed, a large oyster off the pile he was ready to shuck and wrapped it in my handkerchief before slipping it in my pocket.

In my mean room I laboured to open the oyster with my clasp knife. Abominably difficult – wedging the tip of the knife in the hinge, I levered and swivelled the blade, gashing my knuckles badly on the rough surface of the shell, before the beast yielded and I separated the two halves. Beads of blood swelled on two of my knuckles and I watched a ruby drop fall from my finger on to the pewtery flesh of the oyster. For a moment it sat there glistening unpleasantly before the saline fluid in the half-shell dissolved it. I placed the semi-closed oyster on the windowsill, covered it with a flat cap and went for an extremely long walk.

I was already established at my table behind the pillar, my meal over, when Maltravers and his lady friend came in after their day trip. Something about Maltravers' manner made me think he was in a state of some excitement. He called for champagne, an ice bucket, and of course he ordered a dozen oysters from Benoît. The first dozen went down in the usual minute, champagne was poured and I thought I detected a hand-squeeze between the lovers below the level of the tablecloth.

I paid and wandered outside. Benoît was in his usual semi-panic shucking Monsieur Maltravers' next dozen. He laid the half-shelled oysters on the round tray of ice, like the hour markers on a fishily themed clock. I said, by the by, that I thought the *patron* wanted him, and as he darted inside, I removed the oyster that was at three o'clock and replaced it with the one that had been cooking in the sun on my windowsill all day. I glanced at the tray and I dribbled some ice-water on my oyster – it looked as plump and glossy as the rest. I sauntered across the square to the Café Riche where I ordered a Calvados and smoked a soothing cigar.

> The motorist drives on, past Bergerac, and the lazy river widens as its journey nears the end. Here we are at the lower river, fertile and rich with its neat vineyards on the steep bluffs on either side. It was Delacroix who said, contemplating the Dordogne valley: 'How shall I describe my pleasure in this place? It is a mixture of all the sensations that are lovely and pleasant in our hearts and imaginations.'

Like everyone in the hotel I was awakened by the clamorous bell of the ambulance at around two o'clock in the morning. I went back to sleep almost immediately.

At midday, wandering over to the *terrasse* of the Riche for my pre-prandial Pernod, I spotted Maltravers' lady friend, sitting alone at a corner table, her back to the window, her eyes obscured by sunglasses.

I introduced myself. 'Yves Hill, I'm a friend of Raleigh.'

We shook hands. 'Parker Fitzgerald,' she said, her slight American accent immediately evident. She invited me to join her.

Poor Raleigh: he had excelled himself in his high carnal excitement – five dozen *fines de claire*, before the magret and the cheese and the tarte tatin. Then in the night, agonizing stomach pains, copious vomiting. Parker (it was indeed her Christian name) heard his frantic beating on the adjoining wall. The concierge was raised, a doctor called, an ambulance summoned. Raleigh was in the hospital at Brive, his stomach pumped empty, a full twenty-litre enema, immobile, a saline drip in his arm, not to stir for at least another three days.

I winced and tut-tutted as I looked at Parker's strong and elegant features as she related, with great expression, the various diagnoses and prognoses the doctors had given her and I wondered if it were possible to have an affair with a beautiful woman who shared a first name with the pen I wrote with every day. I decided, on balance, that it was. We agreed to meet for dinner at the Couderc later, after her trip to Brive to see poor Raleigh. Do give him my very best, I said.

We did not eat oysters, that night, needless to say. We talked about books, plays, films, cities we knew. She was a young widow, intelligent and cultured (Raleigh had known her late husband, a composer), rediscovering her place in the world. I felt that honour – or professional standards, professional courtesies – obliged me to tell her about Mrs Raleigh Maltravers and the Maltravers brood and she disguised her evident shock with admirable indifference, though I saw a tear well momentarily in her eye. After our supper we walked down to the *quai* by the old bridge and stood under the elms and watched the black oily river slide by, limned by the lights of the town behind us. I knew I could have kissed her if I had wanted to and thought that she would have let me, but I decided to wait until tomorrow (we had made plans to go to Périgueux – shame to waste the hired car). As we stood there I conjured up the image of a pale and voided Raleigh Maltravers, groaning quietly in the hospital at Brive as his body tried to subdue or expel the remaining toxins lingering inside him. Was it my sun-stewed oyster that had done for Raleigh, I wondered? Or was it that bitter drop of my humiliated blood? No matter: perhaps he would prudently chew his oysters in future – if he ever dared let another one down his throat – the only certain way to tell if an oyster is bad. Parker and I walked slowly back to the Hôtel de la Gare. I kissed her hand in the lobby and climbed the stairs briskly, like a boy, two at a time, to my attic room.

# Unsent Letters

1 March

Dear Meryl,

We haven't met but, as you can see from my letterhead, I am
a film director and producer (Flaming Terrapin Productions
Ltd). I thought I would write an old-fashioned letter rather
than email, if only to show ~~how much an admirer I am of
you~~ how much importance I attach to this communication.
In fact, we have a mutual friend in the shape of Tarquin
Wolde, my co-producer – whom I believe you worked with,
or were about to work with, on *Jezebel* – before the whole
thing collapsed. What a business!

Anyhoo, I wanted to send you the script of my latest film,
*Oblong or Triangle*, in the genuine hope that you'd consider
playing the co-lead role of 'Ernestine' – above the title, of
course. If you were interested, at all, I'd be prepared to travel
the world to meet you (I'll be in New York next month, as it
happens). Nothing would give me greater pleasure than –


2 March

My darling Jadranka,

How I miss you, my sweet girl. I miss you so much I thought
I'd write to you, rather than call. Set things down in black
and white, not rely on those transient, shifting things that are
words, spoken. How are matters in sunny Pietermaritzburg?

I hope that bastard Tim Whatsisname is treating you well. He's a lecherous swine, so be careful – and don't make him force you to do night-shoots. He deliberately tries to exhaust his actors, so I've been told, to make them more vulnerable to his advances. And don't be alone with him. ~~He flashed his cock at Paula Vanni in a script meeting~~. Just keep your distance – and keep mentioning my name – he absolutely knows who I am. Call me your 'fiancé' (well, I am, sort of!). Darling, I wanted to write because it looks very much as if the shoot of *Oblong or Triangle* isn't going to happen in June, after all. The usual boring financial issues. We will definitely be going in the Fall so I want you to keep yourself available – if anyone can pull this off, I can, don't worry. I have hopes that Meryl (!) might play 'Ernestine' – negotiations are underway. What do you think about a week in Capri when your shoot ends? Let me know and I'll book a suite in –

7 March

Dear Marty (if I may) –

I'm sure you won't remember, but we met fleetingly in Cannes on the terrace at the Majestic a few years ago (my film *Ten And A Half Grand* was screening). I'm writing to you in your capacity as producer – very cognisant of your relationship with the studios, of course! My new film, *Oblong or Triangle*, is in pre-production, aiming to shoot in the Fall (in Lisbon and Prague). I am directing, Jadranka Juranic is attached and we are in negotiations with an A-list star to play 'Ernestine' (script, herewith). It goes without saying that your name would add immeasurable lustre to the project – and, dare I say it, I think the subject matter is something very close to your –

15 March

Darling girl,

No! You can't do reshoots in October. No, no, thrice no! Tell that arsehole Tim Hopkins-Hughes to fuck himself. That's when we're filming *Oblong or Triangle*, you know that. Look at your contract; get your useless manager to look at the contract. Anyway, why do you need reshoots? You've been in South Africa for eleven weeks already – what's he been doing? My film is ninety per cent financed, everything's looking very positive, all sorts of people are interested. If I say you're not available we'll have to push back to next year. ~~Everything will fall apart.~~ Let's not jeopardize a project that's already been five years in the works. It must happen this year – and this is your moment, my darling, I wrote this film for you. You can't possibly let me down at this –

20 March

Dear Geraldyne Vaux,

You don't know me – but you know my name. I am the director of *Claustral*, the film that you have decided not to release. Actions have consequences, my dear. And the consequences of your disgusting betrayal – we have a contract, by the way – is that I have lost almost all my financing for my next film. Yes. Does that make you feel good? Feel happy? My producing partner, Tarquin Wolde, said that your sudden absurd decision – how did you get your job, by the way? – is the single salient cause for this new shortfall. ~~With *Claustral* released as Video on Demand it will be impossible~~ Do you ever think about the consequences of your whims, you losers? You 'eunuchs at

the orgy' (I'm quoting Richard Burton – ever heard of him?).
If you had any idea how difficult it was, in the current
climate, to make a film of any remote artistic merit you
would die of shame ~~at what reasons you gave of my – of~~
~~what farcical judgement you display~~ – at your utter
ignorance, your utter stupidity, your depthless inanity. Yes,
actions have consequences, 'Geraldyne' (no 'y' can make you
any more interesting, darling) and the consequences of your
insane, baseless destruction of *Claustral* will be this: I know
where you live, I will be waiting for you outside your
house – one day, one night – and I will follow you to
whatever place you are going and I will make sure that you
are never going to ever be able to ever –


1 April

Dear Mr Macfarlane,

I thought I would write, personally, to you, my 'Personal
Banker' to alert you to the fact that I am in urgent need of
an extension of my overdraft. Unforeseen circumstances
have meant that my new film, *Oblong or Triangle*, has had to
postpone filming until the autumn. We will be shooting in
Lisbon and Prague, we are fully financed and I am in final
negotiations with a major Hollywood star to play the lead,
but I currently need to cash-flow this crucial period of
pre-production. I have to fly to New York to meet this
particular actress (I'm not allowed to divulge her name,
alas) and I would greatly appreciate it if my overdraft could
accommodate a further expenditure of £20,000. As and when
the film is made I'd like to invite you and Mrs Macfarlane
(or your significant other) to our premiere. I'm most grateful
for your attention to this matter and fully appreciate the –

2 April

Dear Ned,

Fuck you and the horse you rode in on. I'm sorry, but no, dream on, there is no way you can claim back that 'money' you lent me. You were actually *repaying* me the loan I made to you, you total idiot – a loan provided so you could make a deposit on a flat you were going to buy (whatever happened to that flat, as it happens?). In fact, your call reminded me, inconveniently for you, that it was a partial repayment and you still owe me another £5,000, thank you very much, you dickhead. Make sure the cheque is in the post. And don't ever do that deplorable brotherly love act on me again, it makes me want to puke. You may be my brother but that doesn't stop me from seeing what a useless human being and waste of space you happen to be. Have you any idea what I'm going through? Have you the slightest notion of how difficult it is trying to forge a career as a film director of integrity in a culture of crass philistinism and money-obsession? Do you ever give any thought – even a moment's thought – to what I may be up to, other than to sponge off me or touch me for another loan? Did you ever thank me for paying five years of Emily's school fees? Of course not. No. Take, take, take. When it comes to solipsistic self-absorption you really are the absolute master, no one can hold a –

23 April

Dear Tarquin,

Perhaps you might read a letter as you don't seem to be able to reply to emails or listen to your voicemail. Where the fuck are you? What's happening with *Oblong or Triangle*?

I got a call from Terry Muldoon saying I would have to get
another DOP. He said you hadn't paid his retainer for months
and he was only staying on board because of me. You know I
can't shoot a film without Terry. Get him back, mate –
pronto. Jadranka is still attached and free for an October
start. Her film in S. Africa has run over by four weeks for
some mystifying reason. For 'some mystifying reason' read
the self-regarding, raging incompetence of Tim Hopkins-
Hughes, I mean. Anyway, Jadranka is still solidly there,
wonderful human being that she is. And I've written to
Meryl again. I can't believe some pretentious critic could be
causing us such problems. Who in the name of Zeus reads
film/e.com? Anyway, call me, email me, write to me, you
bastard. You're giving me sleepless nights and I'm beginning
to worry that the whole thing might be –


3 May

Jadranka – I can't call you 'darling' any more, after what
you've told me, what you've done to me. Don't you see
everything is ruined, everything? Not just 'us', but
everything that was 'us', that world of 'us', and more.
Our plans, our films, the life that we were going to have
together. How can I tell people that *Oblong or Triangle* isn't
going to happen because of your affair with Hopkins-
Hughes? I may be a fool – a lovelorn, blind fool – but I
don't want to be a public fool, laughed at by my peers,
mocked, pitied, the subject of salacious industry gossip.
No – you've destroyed everything. You say 'we can still work
together' – and I wonder: are you completely insane,
totally out of your mind? How can I even see you – let alone
work with you – when I know what you and that nonentity

(that hideously ugly nonentity, by the way) have done together? To think of his thin cracked lips on your lips, his blunt hands on your breasts, his tiny –


9 May

Dear Mr Macfarlane,

You call yourself a banker, you sad little man. Worse, you call yourself a 'personal' banker and yet you hide and cower behind the faceless law. As a banker you are meant to offer fiscal support – not withdraw it. And to send a writ, like that, with no warning . . . It defies belief. Or rather it doesn't defy belief – a second's thought makes one realize that it is the nasty little bureaucrats, the creepy apparatchiks of the financial state like yourself, who are the true enemies of people like me. People with ambitions, with dreams – artists, in other words. ~~Someone, some worm like you, some vile money-lender in Renaissance Italy, would have closed da Vinci's line of credit.~~ I herewith terminate my account with your bank. I herewith counter-sue you for incompetence and negligence. I herewith warn you that I will write to every consumer website on the planet and inform them of –


15 May

Tarquin, the despicable, Tarquin, the vile,

Yes, you truly are a deplorable sham of a human being, a miserable excuse of a man. A nothing, un nul. Imagine my astonishment when I opened my *Hollywood Reporter* and saw that the 'executive producer' of Tim Hopkins-Hughes's next film, *Inflammable*, was to be one Tarquin Wolde. No wonder you were hiding from me, you cretin, you hypocrite. What I marvel at – no, what dismays me to the core of my being – is the fickleness of friendship. How can you treat such a bond so lightly, be so cavalier? We have made three films together. I was best man at your second wedding. Where did you run to when that ended? You lived with me for nearly eight months – eight long months – while you 'got your mojo back'. And now this brutal betrayal. ~~Maybe you are unaware of this but Tim Hopkins-Hughes is having an affair with Jadranka.~~ And now Jadranka isn't available for the *Oblong or Triangle* shoot in October. Just when I need you, you desert me. Well, I won't forget this, my ex-friend. You'll come crawling back to me one day, asking for forgiveness (or money) and do you know what I'll do? I wouldn't piss on you if you were on fire, I wouldn't –

2 June

Dear Granville,

This is a difficult letter to write – and it had to be a letter because of that very difficulty – but I'm afraid I sadly have to let you know that you are, henceforth, no longer my agent. I will take up one of the many other ardent suitors who so keenly wish to represent me. You know of my personal issues with Tim Hopkins-Hughes (though I have to say I now regret sharing them with you – please regard them as absolutely confidential) but how – how in the name of reason – could you take him on as a client and expect me to happily remain with you? It defies any credence. We have been associates – I cannot use the word 'friends' any more – for seventeen years, since my first short film, *Wild Flowers*. Remember that? Remember the audience award at the San Sebastián Film Festival? It was the beginning of everything. The world, as you so memorably put it, was our lobster. And we were a team – or so I thought. But I suppose, in your game, money is everything – or rather ten per cent of everything. And so you sacrifice an old friendship for ten per cent of Tim Hopkins-Hughes's lamentable but lucrative career. Shame on you. Shame on your life. You deserve nothing but the worst of ill fortune and I heartily wish you that. In fact I wish you nothing but –

13 July

Dear Mr Macfarlane,

This has been a burdensome time for us both, or so I sense. I would like to apologize for my last telephone call to your office, and to the young lady who had to endure my unkind words. I was under a great deal of stress, owing to the failure of a film that I had spent some five years bringing to fruition only to see it fall apart at the last moment through no fault of my own. I am only human – a plaint made since time immemorial, I am aware – but it is worth remembering: sometimes we know not what we say or do. I am convinced, also, that you are an understanding man. Please find enclosed a cheque for £200. This is to open a new business account (Flaming Terrapin Entertainment Ltd). Might I take this opportunity to ask for overdraft facilities of £10,000? This will enable me to get the new company up and running and cash-flow the production of my new film *Circle into Square*. We have already approached an A-list Hollywood star to play the principal role. I would like to thank you for your shrewd financial guidance of my affairs over the years and I want to reassure you there will be no repeat of my egregious –

25 July

Dear Tarquin,

This is an apology. A letter of apology. An apologetic letter
to apologize for the series of texts I sent you some weeks
ago. They were extreme, shrill and totally uncalled for.
The collapse of *Oblong or Triangle* affected me more than
I thought it could, coupled with Jadranka's betrayal.
I was a little unhinged as a result of that double whammy,
as I suspect you, of all people, will understand. Films have
collapsed under me before and I've never reacted this way so
I can't really understand why I was so sideswiped by this
one. Perhaps because I had written it for Jadranka and I felt
in my bones that this was 'it', the one. When will we ever
learn, us dreamers? . . . Congratulations also for the new
job – my God, Filmzilla – hot, hot, hot. No one better
than you, my man. Great fit. However, if this doesn't seem
too snidely opportune, I have something I think you may
be interested in and, moreover, that will fit the Filmzilla
slate to the proverbial tee. I've written a new script, *Circle
into Square*, for me to direct. Nothing like *Claustral*, you'll
be glad to hear. True indie fare but with a commercial spin
(all right, erotic!). Can I bike it round? It would be great to be
back working together. We were always a –


10 August

Dear Dr Manakulasuriya,

Your secretary asked me to list my symptoms before she
would give me an appointment with you. I've been a
patient at the clinic for some five years and this bizarre
demand has never been made before. I'm not going to tell

some unqualified stranger – a secretary or receptionist – what's wrong with me! No, these personal problems are for a doctor's ears alone. I'm sure you understand – hence this missive. I have to admit I have been under some stress these last weeks and months – nothing new, as I work in a highly stressful industry (the movie business). However, I have to say I've never experienced such a collection of ailments. Let me list them in no order of importance: extreme lassitude, intermittent nausea, a sense that my skin on my face is being stretched to ripping point, light-headedness, occasional vertigo and loss of balance, acute hunger followed by a sudden detestation of food, chromophobia (especially the colour red), incipient migraine, unexpected attacks of weeping, leaden depression that can last for several hours, racing of the heart, neuralgia, a conviction that the earth is rotating faster than normal, a fear of leaving my house, short-term memory loss. Have you any idea what might be wrong with me? Is there any medication that you –

23 September

Darling Jadranka,

Yes, it's me. I hope this has arrived safely. I hand-delivered it to a runner on the set and told him to take it immediately to your Winnebago. How wonderful that you're shooting in London – you should have told me. I wanted to make contact with you ever since I heard the news that Hopkins-Hughes had married Paula Vanni. He is a complete bastard-shit, my darling. Unadulterated, grade 'A' manure. I warned you about him. But, paradoxically, even though I hate him even more for what he's done to you, I'm grateful

to the deplorable scumbag that he is: he has brought us
back together (I hope). I have news. I have a new job. I am
Professor of Film and Media Studies at the University of
Shoreditch. Here in London, East London. ~~Quite a good
salary, long holidays, moderate teaching load.~~ I am living
in a very nice two-bedroomed flat in Hackney owned by
my brother, Ned. Rent-free for a year (he owes me money).
I miss you, my darling. I realize I've never loved anyone in
the way I loved you. I've been physically ill since we split
up – I won't go into details – but it was a bad time. But now
my life has stabilized. No more movies – never again, all in
the past, that door locked and barred. It's astonishing how
equilibrium returns as soon as you make that decision.
Let's meet up. Let me show you my little flat in Hackney.
Come and stay with me for a few days when you finish
shooting – or if you have a weekend off. Softly, softly. ~~There
never was a couple like us, darling one, you know that.~~ Let's
rebuild what we had. I say I've abandoned the movie
business but I have to confess I have written another script.
It's called *Circle into Square*. Very cool, edgily erotic. There is
a perfect part for you. Shall I send it round to –

# The Things I Stole

I stole a BOAC Speedbird lapel badge from my friend Mark Pertwee. I was eight years old and it was the first act of conscious larceny that I can remember. BOAC – British Overseas Airways Corporation – that dates me; and the 'Speedbird' logo is now long gone, also. I can see the small badge in my mind's eye: a ten-pence piece would cover it – navy blue, edged with silver, a cross between a notional bird-shape and an arrowhead – modern, thrusting, stylish, everything that the 1960s, BOAC and its fleet of mighty, navy blue and white, four-engined, turbo-prop planes were meant to embody . . .

Mark Pertwee's mother was a travel agent and she was a source of all manner of travel-agent freebies – timetables, small desktop models of planes (KLM, Pan Am, Air France), little plastic pennants of national flags and their carriers – and she generously shared this bounty with me as well as her son (I was his best friend), but she pointedly did not give me a Speedbird lapel badge. Perhaps she was only provided with one, herself, perhaps it was valuable – silver plate and enamel – it now strikes me. And perhaps this was why I coveted it so.

I planned my theft well. First of all, I hid it in the Pertwee house, in the cupboard under the sink in the guest toilet. I waited a fortnight (Mark seemed oblivious to its disappearance) before I pocketed it one day and took it home. I never showed it to my parents or my three older sisters – indeed I never wore the Speedbird lapel badge in my lapel. It was, in a way, a pointless theft – Mark Pertwee never knew he had lost it and I was never able to sport it. Was it, even, a bona-fide theft, worthy of the name, given it had never been registered as stolen in the theft-victim's mind? I think I lost it in one of my parents' many house moves. I wonder why I stole it at all.

I stole cigarettes from my mother – never money, I want to make that absolutely clear. She smoked heavily, two packs a day, and favoured a brand called Peter Stuyvesant, a cigarette with a somewhat astringent, throat-warming taste, as I recall (and much enjoyed by raffish, square-jawed, Caucasian airline pilots, if the advertisements were to be believed). I would steal four or five cigarettes a week and she never spotted they had gone.

I ask myself again: is this an example of another non-theft? What category of genuine theft have we here? In my teens I must have stolen hundreds, possibly thousands, of cigarettes from her. She would buy cigarettes in cartons and, as I grew more bold, I would steal entire packs from the drawer in her bedroom where she kept her stash. My father was a pipe-smoker, with a penchant for fragrant, aromatic tobaccos (until he died in his fifties from lung cancer). Our house reeked of smoke, like a pub. I smoked in my bedroom and no one noticed; my three sisters smoked. It was like that in those days.

I smoked regularly through my teens, even after my father died, and only gave up when I married my first wife, Encarnacion. She detested smoke and smokers to a neurotic degree – I would not have managed a kiss had I not forsworn cigarettes. I think back to all that subterfuge – opening my mother's handbag, rifling through its contents looking for the Peter Stuyvesant soft-pack, checking to see how many were left – always risky to steal if there were under ten. Then a few heart-thumping seconds watching her fish in her bag to light up herself, and, later, the furtive, head-reeling inhalation with my friends down the lane, under the railway bridge; the subsequent needless deodorizing of the mouth – chewing gum, Listerine – and clothes and body (Brut aftershave was particularly masking). For years I must have walked through my house leaving in my wake a pungent, invisible contrail of chemical perfume. Nobody noticed, ever.

I stole food at my boarding school. We were allowed a modest food parcel once a week (like POWs) from a local grocer: a few bananas, a box of dates, mini packs of cornflakes – no buns or cakes, no chocolates, nothing that could be purchased from the school tuck shop where fizzy drinks, colas, biscuits and every tooth-rotting sweet the confectionery industry could serve up were on offer.

In my house there was a very rich Greek boy whose food parcel might have come from Fortnum & Mason, such was its size and magnificence. I and my coevals pillaged this boy's food with no compunction (he was plump and cried easily). It was thanks to Stavros's food parcel that I developed my enduring taste for Patum Peperium, The Gentleman's Relish, a dark pesto-like spread made from anchovies. It is my Proustian madeleine – it summons up all my early pilfering. I can taste its earthy, farinaceous salinity now.

I stole other things, as well – everyone stole at my school – it was tacitly understood that we all stole from each other, all the time. We stole food, drink, deodorant, shampoo, clothes, pornography, pens, stationery, books . . . We also shoplifted shamelessly and efficiently in the local town and villages. Only stealing money from your schoolmates was the ultimate sin, which brought permanent pariah status on the perpetrator and earned him, for the duration of his school career, the nickname of 'Fingers' – his personal badge of iniquity, his mark of Cain.

\*

I stole a pair of Ray-Ban aviator sunglasses from a department store in Bath where I was at university doing a degree in Architecture. I tried them on, then tried on a dozen others, replacing some back on their little racks, taking them off again and, halfway through this elaborate process, putting on my own spectacles and slipping the Ray-Bans into my spectacle case. I wore them all summer to much acclaim. I was probably wearing them when I met Encarnacion (my future wife, the one who hated smoking) who was working as an au pair for a solicitor's family in nearby Bristol. I look back on my university years as my thieving pomp. I stole at will, whenever I felt like it. Nothing grand, nothing exceptional, just things I wanted and didn't feel like paying for. I stole newspapers and magazines (the *New Statesman*, *Mayfair*, *Men Only*, *Flight*, *Gramophone*); I stole hardback books (I still remember some titles: *The History Man*, *Keats and Embarrassment*, *The Metropolitan Critic*); I stole food – Mars bars, sandwiches, fruit. I once stole a haunch of venison from a delicatessen. One day I stole a tin of cherry pie-filling – I've no idea why I did so: I don't particularly like cherries and had no intention of making a pie. The man who ran the corner shop, where I casually lifted the tin from a shelf on my way out, saw me and gave chase. I lost him after a couple of streets – I ran fast – but I have never since experienced such a pure rush of emotion: an atavistic fear followed by an adrenaline-fuelled exhilaration that made me sway as I stood there catching my breath.

I stole nothing for several years – I simply stopped stealing for a while. Perhaps it was marriage to Encarnacion, the swift arrival of the twins (Lolita and Bonita) and the responsibilities that went with my job. I was an architect working in a large and prestigious firm – the Freedlander, Cobb Partnership – I was a married man and a father of two lovely little girls. Stealing in these circumstances would seem demeaning, despoiling, almost filthy. All right, like everyone else in the firm I fiddled my expenses but no one in their right mind would call that theft. However, it was over a fractious and unpleasant formal query about my expenses that I met the managing partner of Freedlander, Cobb – Margaret Warburton, FCA, and my life changed.

I stole my daughters' happiness. Perhaps that's too strong: I stole Lolita's and Bonita's right to a stable family life with two parents, a father and a mother. To this day I don't know how Encarnacion discovered my affair with Margaret Warburton but when she presented the evidence of our liaison (her father José and her brother, Severiano, also sternly present, their dark eyes shining with implacable loathing) it was compendious and irrefutable. We separated, she took the girls back to Valladolid, we divorced and I moved in with Margaret.

I missed the girls but I did not miss Encarnacion much, I have to confess. There is a problem marrying someone who speaks your own language imperfectly – all nuance is lost: and with nuance goes humour, irony, sarcasm, subtext, secrets. All these were present with Margaret Warburton – a clever, sly and salacious mind operated beneath that perfect accountant's exterior: the lean, pale, expressionless face, the deliberately too-tight, well-cut suits, the coiffed dark helmet of hair, the black-framed officious spectacles – swiftly removed and swiftly replaced to make forensic points in meetings. Indeed it was exactly this juxtaposition that made my adulterous sex life with her so energetic and alluring. I didn't take enough care – I didn't take any care, I now realize – all I wanted and waited for was the covert rendezvous, the snatched weekend, the airport hotel, the meeting of two cars, nose to nose, in some rural lay-by.

*

I stole £985,622 from Freedlander, Cobb over a period of seven years. Margaret Warburton, the managing partner, supervising the burgeoning accounts of the firm, saw the opportunity, especially as more and more of our projects were abroad – the desalination plant in Saudi Arabia, the new terminal at Calcutta airport, three office blocks in Shanghai, and so on. She needed a senior partner in the firm to collude – and why wouldn't I collude with my clever wife? (We married shortly after the divorce, but told no one, not even my mother and sisters – Margaret's idea.) I signed wherever she told me – overruns, unforeseen expenses, delays, extra hours worked at night in London because of global time differences – the opportunities were manifold. In a $100 million contract do you notice an extra $80,000? No, not if it's all properly accounted. We were careful, we took our time, we weren't greedy. Small amounts on almost every job were hived off and banked in the Cayman Islands. Sometimes we deliberately admitted to our mistakes, apologized and reimbursed the client. Everything appeared above board. We lived well, holidayed discreetly but at considerable expense (Margaret bought us a permanent suite on one of those floating cruise-ship hotels) and we maintained separate houses for form's sake. When we were arrested together, in Margaret's office in the new Freedlander, Cobb headquarters in Southwark – the one that looks like a hand grenade – it came as a massive shock. I felt like an innocent man, wrongly arraigned on a trumped-up charge.

I stole tobacco from my fellow prisoners in the austere but not intolerable open prison where I was sent to pay my debt to society for my shameful white-collar crime. For some reason, I received a sentence of six years and Margaret three. Tobacco, cigarettes – is this the thieving leitmotif in my life? . . . I stole tobacco – I'd given up smoking years before, remember – to buy alcohol. Prisoners who worked in the allotments made a virulently potent hooch from potatoes and other tubers. I would pinch fingerfuls of roll-up tobacco from casually set-down plastic envelopes of the stuff and when I had enough accumulated (a fistful, say) would exchange it for half a pint of moonshine and a few hours of oblivion. It was like drinking some sort of burning, ruthless, liquid toxin, you sensed small ulcers forming in your stomach almost immediately. You felt it could have de-iced aeroplanes in the Arctic Circle, stripped layers of paint from antique cars. It was marvellously strong. My drink problem became more acute after Margaret left prison and quickly divorced me. She moved abroad, to Latin America, and I never heard from her again, of course. How much had we really stolen? I had no idea. The prosecuting counsel came up with the £985,622 figure but for all I know it could have been double. It was entirely Margaret's plan, the whole operation – she was the thief, the real thief, not me. Old Julius Freedlander himself took the stand to destroy my character, claiming only to be 'sadly disappointed' with Margaret's betrayal. Margaret was demure, only rarely weepy – I think I seemed some brutal mastermind who had dumped his nice Spanish wife to manipulate this blameless accountant. Both Margaret and I were advised by our briefs to plead guilty, advice we took – it seemed to work for her.

I stole three and a half pints of bitter, a near-full gin and tonic and a Bacardi Breezer in the Richard the Lionheart in Cromer, Norfolk, last night. It's laughably easy – a legacy of my prison-induced alcoholism. I steal drinks in crowded pubs at weekends or, better still, pubs with beer gardens in the summer. I sit nursing my bitter lemon or Diet Coke waiting for the bar staff to emerge and start clearing up empty glasses. I just follow them around and in the bustle that their progress creates more often than not can help myself to an unguarded drink, take it as far away as possible and consume it quickly. Crowds of young men and women, always leaving their drinks to go out and smoke, are very fair game. You'll see five or six glasses on a ledge or a table – nobody knows whose drink it is, nobody pays attention. Solitary drinkers who leave their drink to go to the lavatory are also useful prey. It's amazing how many people buy a pint or a glass of wine and leave the pub without finishing them. I discreetly help myself to these unwanted drinks – but then again that's not stealing. If you read a discarded newspaper on the train have you stolen it? Of course not.

To go into prison a successful, highly trained, middle-class professional and emerge a semi-functioning alcoholic was hardly what I planned and naturally, after the disgrace, the profession no longer allowed me to call myself 'Architect'. I managed to buy a small cottage in South Runton near Cromer and set myself up as a 'Designer'. In the first years I was commissioned to do a few jobs – a cricket pavilion, a conservatory in a nursery, a wing of a doctors' clinic in King's Lynn – and managed to live quietly, respectably. But the jobs seemed slowly but steadily to diminish – I wonder if word had leaked out somehow about the Freedlander, Cobb scandal. I wouldn't be surprised if Julius Freedlander himself wasn't quietly blackening my name around East Anglia . . . In any event I haven't worked in eighteen months and I'm seriously behind on my mortgage repayments. I recently sold my car and bought a bicycle.

My great pleasure, apart from drinking, are my daughters, Lolita and Bonita – rather, I should say 'Lola y Bona'. They are a pop sensation in Spain and other Mediterranean countries – Greece, Croatia, Cyprus. They have a website: www.lolaybona.es – check it out, their fame is local but huge. I cycle into Cromer once a week and buy all the foreign celebrity magazines, you know the ones – *Calor!*, *Proximité*, *Peep'L*. I cut out the pictures of Lola y Bona and stick them on a huge pinboard that covers one wall in my kitchen. My wall of celebration, I call it, at least something turned out well.

Last week when I was in Cromer I took my pile of magazines into the Lionheart and flicked through them looking for pictures of my babies. I found a couple of them at a film festival in Dubrovnik. Tanned, lithe, sexy girls with black, black hair, like their mother. Identical twins, that's the catch, you see – the songs they sing seem entirely ordinary, bouncy, rhythmic, heavy on percussion, thumping drums – but those girls, eighteen years old, impossible to tell them apart.

A man I vaguely know wondered if I'd like a drink and so I asked for a large vodka and tonic. I think he's a novelist, very curious about my stint in the open prison. I tell him colourful anecdotes about 'doing time' – I suspect it's all going into a book. After he'd gone I managed to procure a couple of half-pints and most of a large glass of red wine. I wandered out on to the front. I like Cromer, perched on the edge of England, on the edge of England's plump, round bum. I think of continental Europe out there, across the North Sea, and I wonder where Lola y Bona might be: Majorca, Zagreb, Larnaca, Tel Aviv? It makes me feel I'm not that far away from them – not close, but not far away.

There's a large bric-a-brac antique shop in a side street by the pier and I wandered in to kill some time. I was stunned to see, in a small display of badges and brooches pinned on a velvet cushion, a BOAC Speedbird lapel badge. I asked to have a look at it and enquired about the price. The owner – he has mutton-chop whiskers and wears loud checked suits and coloured waistcoats – told me it was £150. There was no price ticket, of course – what kind of fool did he take me for? 'Very rare,' he added, 'extremely.' I asked him his best price and he said he couldn't go lower than £130. I laughed, I scoffed – I told him I'd had one of those BOAC Speedbird lapel badges when I was a boy. Should have hung on to it, mate, he said, smugly: very rare, much sought after by collectors of airline memorabilia. I said I'd think about it and then stuck the badge back on the cushion but was careful not to fully close the securing pin. I'll come back next weekend.

# The Diarists

PRUNELLA LAING

Everything seems fine, under control – I can't believe I can write this but it is a tribute of sorts to my forward planning. The two marquees are up at the end of the garden. The catering team have installed their mobile kitchen. The champagne is already on ice. Fernando Benn is coming this afternoon to hang Brodie's portrait. Fernando asked – sweetly, I thought – if he could bring his girlfriend, Gill John, to the party. Gill John, he repeated – I must have looked blank – the sculptress. Oh yes, I said, wonderful stuff. Brodie is happy, pleased, I think, that his sixtieth is being celebrated so grandly, in such conspicuous style – protesting that I fuss too much, but happy all the same to be fussed over. Two little flies in the clear gelid ointment remain, however. I told Brodie that I was a little puzzled: Tim Sundry had called to accept, very late. Yes, Brodie said, I invited him. I like Tim and his wife, whatshername, you know. I reminded him that Tim's wife, Lizz, used to be the – what is the term? – common-law-wife, mistress, paramour? – of his oldest friend, Hugh Seeger, and that perhaps the presence of Hugh, Tim and Lizz at his birthday celebration might be a tiny teeny little bit combustible, no? Hugh is married now, he said (I'd forgotten – the Filipino girl, of course, Pamora, Sayonara? . . . ) and, Brodie went on, they're all grown-ups, as if that dealt with the matter. Doesn't he realize that grown-ups often behave far, far worse than the littlest children? The

82

other fly is Inigo – or 'Joe' as I must now learn to call him. I asked him if he was coming to the party and he said he would make an appearance, under duress, but his fee was £200 plus expenses. It's your stepfather's sixtieth birthday, darling, I protested, what do you mean your 'fee'? He said he would have to miss an important lecture, the return trip from Bristol was expensive, general inconvenience engendered and so on. I sighed and moaned for form's sake but inevitably agreed. I've decided to put two Portaloos behind the rhododendrons – his and hers (I shall style them carefully) – to ease traffic from the marquees to the house.

### JOE REED

Mother acceded quickly to my demand for 200 quid. Perhaps I should have asked for three? Why should I pay homage at the court of King Brodie, unremunerated? He doesn't like me – he tolerates me. I never forget when I told him I had got grade 'A' at German A level, he said in all seriousness: Why do you want to learn German? It's a dead language. Subconsciously I now realize that remark must have made me want to read German at Bristol. I want to become a Professor of German Literature to remind Brodie Laing of his ineffable, small-minded foolishness. I want to be a little bit of Germany in his placid neo-modernist English landscape. I shall marry a German girl and have monoglot children called Wolfgang, Edeltraud and Anneliese. I wonder if Lizz Sundry will be at the party – funnily enough, of all my parents' hundreds of friends, the only one I'd like to fuck is Lizz Sundry. Maybe because she spells her name with two zeds . . . Talking of names, I must remind Mummy to tell everyone that I'm to be addressed as 'Joe' – not Inigo, not any more, never again.

### GILL JOHN

I drove past Brodie Laing's new building on the Embankment some sort of office block it's disgusting made me laugh when I remembered what Fernando called it – a smoked-glass food processor – it's exactly what it looks like so I called Fernando when I got home and said where are you? At Brodie Laing's he said hanging the bloody portrait where do you think. Has he seen it yet I asked no way said Fernando still the cheque's in the bank though fifty grand. 50K. I hate the portrait it stinks terrible. Fernando says it's '*faux-faux naïf*'. '*Naïf*' painting is crap but charming he says '*faux naïf*' is good painters trying to paint in a crap but charming way and '*faux-faux naïf*' is just crap but everyone will think it's amazing. I said you can't sell that for fifty grand but he said you're wrong baby the whole point is that it's SO bad it's good – it's the way ahead – bad art. Not looking forward to the party tomorrow I think I'll just get shit-faced. I hate it when he calls me baby.

### HUGH SEEGER

Memories of important men avoid the specific. The specific is for the quotidian hero. Memories of great men flash, irradiate, blind, overwhelm. Describe a sunset in five words – impossible. The great inflict their own vagaries, their genius, upon the world. A moth flits through the garden at dusk, hither, thither, all eyes upon it. A moth has passed, yet its trace is immutable, uncancellable (is there such a word?). *The Flight of a Moth* – good title for the next novel? Prunella Laing called to ask if we were indeed coming to Brodie's party. Did you not receive my RSVP, I enquired? Samsuna and I are looking forward to it immensely. Just triple checking, she simpered, you know me. How could Brodie have married such a *nul* (should that be *nulle*?). Then the real purpose of her call emerged. Tim Sundry's coming, she said, grotesquely disingenuous.

How lovely, I said, I look forward to seeing him again. And Lizz too, she added. Lizz too, I said, I'm immensely fond of them both.

Who was it who said: 'Mediocrity is the one true daemonic force'? I detest London in summer. When the temperature rises above 20 degrees the city becomes insupportable. English houses are designed to combat cold, not heat: the hot air rises through the house to become trapped beneath the layers of fibreglass insulation in the loft and so we slowly bake. Last night in bed I lay in warm rivulets of sweat, unsleeping, cursing my perennial failure to buy a simple electric fan. Must go to John Lewis tomorrow. Lizz relishes the heat. From my study now I can see her sunbathing topless on the terrace below, overlooked, if my calculations are right, by three potential voyeurs' windows. I pointed this out to her: I said a man in the back bedroom of no. 42 Woodland Street could spend all day, with a pair of powerful binoculars, looking at your breasts, wanking. She said, with some justification I admit, that I hadn't objected when she had gone topless on various Mediterranean beaches over the years, nor did I remonstrate, she further reminded me, when she'd eaten lunch topless at Dino's villa last summer, nor when we'd all gone skinny-dipping in Barbuda at Xmas – so what, suddenly, was the problem with a bit of discreet nudity in the privacy of our own home? I surrendered. Still there's something about a sooty terrace in North London that isn't quite right: it seems brazen here, sleazily decadent. Rather dreading Brodie's party tomorrow. Apparently that fraud Fernando Benn has painted his portrait. Maybe I can get a piece out of it. I sit here sweating in my boxer shorts looking at my half-naked wife wondering where it's all heading. For the moment the end of episode five of *Accident & Emergency* should be preoccupying me. I said to Sam, the producer, what if the proctologist got bowel cancer, and then the cardiologist had a heart attack and so on – every specialist getting their own special disease – we'd have two years' worth of gripping telly. He wasn't amused. Too dark for Channel Ten, I suppose – our universe is not malign.

### Thursday Night

#### PRUNELLA LAING

The only thing that went wrong in the entire evening was when Hugh Seeger fell in the rose garden and cut his lip. He said the stone path was wet but I know he was drunk. He was very peculiar, very hostile, when I said did he want me to put some Dettol or ointment on the cut. He just said – 'Get me Samsuna, we're leaving' as if I were some kind of flunky. I felt quite upset for a moment, almost tearful he was so abrupt, but went and found his wife (a tiny person, sitting alone, abandoned, small as a nine-year-old girl, hardly spoke English) and delivered her up to Hugh. Something will always go wrong, however hard you try: you cannot legislate for the selfishness and irresponsibility of your guests. Inigo/Joe was strangely quiet, kept himself to himself. Everyone spread out into the garden after the supper and the presentation. Lovely sunset.

#### TIM SUNDRY

I have to admit, as fights go, it was rather inept. Still, I landed one full-on blow, right in Hugh Seeger's complacent mush. I gashed a knuckle on one of his teeth and jarred my hand. His head snapped back – satisfyingly – and he went down at once, his lip bleeding. I stood over him and said, 'You've never forgiven me, have you, you sad fuck? Never forgiven me for taking Lizz from you. Keep your hands off her or I'll kill you.' He started to mumble some sort of protest but I turned and marched off, fizzing with adrenaline. I don't think I've hit anyone in the face since I was fourteen. The fact that it was now Hugh Seeger makes it all the more satisfying, yet the odd thought struck me, as I stood above him as he sat struggling on the ground: his grey hair had fallen over his forehead in two bangs and his lip was fat with blood – so that he looked uncannily like Virginia Woolf in the Man Ray portrait that graces volume four of her collected essays (slightly portlier than VW, of course, and far more agitated and disturbed) that I've just taken down from my shelf to verify. I can hear Lizz crying in the bedroom. When I saw her stumbling out from behind the rhododendron shrubbery, her clothes awry, her face shiny with tears, I felt some awful news was about to be announced – everyone you love has died, or something similarly apocalyptic. I was terrified. I said: what is it, what's happened, what's wrong? And she blurted out – 'Hugh' and then pushed me aside and ran off into the dark. I went looking for Seeger, couldn't see him in the marquee and headed for the house. I found him wandering back from the house, drink in hand. Can I have a word, Hugh, I said, and led him into the rose garden. Then I punched him. Lizz was waiting for me in the car, still crying (she's actually been crying for three hours steady by my calculations). I didn't tell her what happened. I'll tell her in the morning. My hand is throbbing. I might have fractured a knuckle. Who was it who said: 'Only intelligent people are stupid enough to fall in love'?

GILL JOHN

It was so embarrassing some partner from Brodie Laing Partnership made a speech saying what a great man Brodie was and pulled back the curtains on the portrait there was silence though I thought I heard someone's snorting laugh then Brodie shouted 'Bravo!' and began to clap and then everyone went mad laughing and cheering. I hadn't seen the portrait for weeks and went up and had a proper close stare. If you had taken a really bad right-handed painter and asked him to paint a portrait with his left hand he would have done a better job. *Faux-faux naïf* works I said to Fernando: well done, mate. It's so bad it's good he said that funny knowing smile on his face I tell you it's the next big thing the new wave just you watch and wait baby you read it here first. I said nothing went out into the garden lovely soft light on the horizon dark warm duskiness thought I might smoke my joint now just to keep me calm. I wandered round behind the rhododendrons and came upon the Portaloos then a girl no a woman burst out of one and practically knocked me over. I found some kind of shrubbery and stayed there quite happy thank you smoking until I heard Fernando drunk as a skunk stumbling around shouting for me to go home.

JOE REED

I should note this down, this is what I saw. I was standing by the bar and I had ordered a Campari and soda. The barman went back to the store area to see if they had any Campari and as he flipped back the flap of the tent I saw Brodie kissing Lizz Sundry – really kissing her, and she was really kissing him. The painting had been revealed in all its inverted glory and people were milling around, the party in its end-game. I slipped round the side of the tent and I saw them again, kissing, touching and talking. What in God's name does a woman like Lizz see in my stepfather? He pointed to the rhododendrons and they split up, walking 'unconcern-edly' away from each other. Brodie looked suddenly in my direction but I had ducked back behind the side of the marquee. This was my moment to run up to Lizz and tell her what a horrible human being Brodie Laing is, what a *verkolning aschloch* he happened to be. But she had slipped away, heading for the Portaloos. You go your own way and you make your own mistakes. I went back and picked up my Campari. I seem able to drink as much as I like of the stuff, it has no effect on me at all. Lizz Sundry – I must have been mad.

### HUGH SEEGER

The feeling is not so much one of humiliation, too strong a word, nor of disgust – disgust is wasted on someone like Sundry. I feel I have been watching an ape in a circus performing elementary tricks – throwing a ball in the air and catching it – and yet people are cheering and at the same time throwing rubbish, rotten fruit, small sharp stones. The ape turns towards the cheers, flinches from the stinging gravel. I feel something like that, I feel the ape's confusion. 'Bring me poppies brimmed with sleepy death'. Samsuna asked me, please what is wrong (I was very brusque). How to begin to explain to her? I can't explain it to myself. The green-eyed monster, of course – sad Tim Sundry. Poor Lizz with that moron and his 'Doc show'.

## Friday

### GILL JOHN

I went into Fernando's studio this afternoon and found him painting a still life – three oranges and a pineapple. I said Neville what the fuck's going on? – he hates being called Neville even though it's his real name but I couldn't help myself I was so shocked. It was even more shocking that he was painting it with the brush held between his teeth as if he was some kind of quadriplegic. What do you think? he asked me be honest – I said it's brilliant keep it up fabulous. He said I've got two commissions as a result of that Brodie Laing portrait. Brush in the teeth it's the way ahead baby. So bad it's good you read it here first.

## JOE REED

I was just leaving the house to catch the bus back to Bristol when Brodie asked me to come into his study. He said he wanted to thank me for coming to his party: he was very touched and grateful that I had taken time off, appreciated the inconvenience and so on – all very avuncular and friendly. I said: don't mention it. Then he handed me a cheque for £1,000. What's this for, I asked? It's for doing so well in your finals, he said. My finals are next year, I reminded him. Well consider it a vote of confidence, then, he said, smiling, completely unfazed, completely unperturbed, have yourself a good time, my pleasure. I realize he must have seen me last night, that's what's happened – perhaps when I came round the side of the marquee as he was giving Lizz his instructions and he sensed that I had seen something. He couldn't be sure what, though – but some important silence would have to be bought, all the same. I folded up the cheque and pocketed it, thanking him and saying I had to run to catch the bus. We shook hands in a firm, manly, confidential way. I felt the burden of my financial anxieties – present and future – fall from my shoulders like a cloak. That's what I call a good party.

## HUGH SEEGER

I find it hard to explain Sundry's hatred of me, his banal paranoia. Yes, I have written many successful novels to his solitary unsuccessful one. Yes, I have an OBE and other honours from

Italy and Greece. Yes, I am married to a young and beautiful
Filipino woman and he has married my former research assistant. Can that explain his violence and his incoherent rage? I
think his blow loosened a crown. I shall invoice him once Mr
Tennyson of Harley Street has worked his expensive dental
magic. Was it Brodie's fiftieth where we first encountered
each other? Full circle, then, a decade on. I was kind to him,
Tim Sundry, I recall (though I did ask him how his name was
pronounced – to rhyme with 'wry'? or as in 'all and'?): he was
very much the young tyro, keen to learn about the weird and
demanding world of letters. That's where he would have met
Lizz for the first time too, of course. Lizz was cooling on me,
I could tell, that look of *envie de voyager* in her eyes should have
alerted me. (Though, I remember, Brodie rather colonized
her that day, funnily enough, very taken with her.) Who was
Tim Sundry a friend of? Brodie? Prunella? Some publisher?
Why was he there? Why is he here in this world, sad little
man? Too much reading has played him false and still he cannot write. What does it matter? A wind has blown and stirred
the trees and prompted untimed manoeuvres of clouds that
vanish and melt and touch without concussion. Tim Sundry
struck Hugh Seeger and yet the rain falls, the earth spins, all
is chop and change and bright and breezy motion – space lies
between us tranquil as a deep sea never to be ruffled by
further acquaintance. Some sort of blessing from a truly
unforgettably ghastly evening. Samsuna is calling: supper is
ready.

#### PRUNELLA LAING

Wasn't it Virginia Woolf who said there's nothing quite so
pleasing as a successful party? Someone like her anyway. The
marquees were down by ten, the caterers had cleared up in
the wee small hours and the lorry's just come to take away

the Portaloos – didn't seem much demand for them, I must say. I picked some roses, put them in a vase and took them into Brodie's study. He was on the phone: I heard him say, yes, thank you so much, goodbye and he put the phone down rather quickly. Who was that, I asked? Lizz Sundry saying thank you for a lovely party, he said, nice enough person but she does go on a bit. I put the flowers on his desk. He took my hand and said thank you for everything, darling, he kissed my fingers and said let's go off for a few days, let's go somewhere mad – Cape Town, Buenos Aires, Hawaii – get away from horrible old England. I didn't know what to say and I think he was a bit hurt that I didn't respond with wild enthusiasm immediately. It was an odd moment, not really like Brodie at all. I walked out into the garden and wandered around. I looked at the bruised, flattened grass where the marquees had been, the cigarette ends in the borders, the deep holes made by the stanchions of the Portaloos, and the mess where someone had clearly fallen into my choisya bush. But it was a wonderful party and everything would have been perfect apart from Hugh Seeger. Not a nice man, I think. Brodie was pleased, that's the main thing.

### TIM SUNDRY

Lizz didn't surface until lunch: eyes like cherries and her face both puffy and slumped with misery. We sat in the kitchen over beer and bread and cheese like a couple in a Sickert painting steeped in our boredom and resentment. Then I told her: I don't know what he did to you but, if it's any consolation, I knocked Hugh Seeger flat on his arse. Cleaned his clock. Bunch of fives. Punched his lights out. I showed her the cut on my knuckle, now rather angry and inflamed. She stared at me: why would you hit Hugh? Because you told me he had hurt you in some way, for God's sake – grabbed you, made a pass at you, tried to ravish you. I didn't say any such thing, you insane lunatic, she said. I kept calm, did not point out the redundant adjective, took a sip of my beer. I repeated our exchange of the night before word for word, as we had stood by the rhododendrons. You were weeping, distraught, I said, I asked you what had happened to you, who had done this to you and you said 'Hugh.' The look of utter incredulity and then disgust that crossed her face was rather disturbing. She stood up and walked to the kitchen door. What's wrong, I asked, a bit too plaintively. 'No I didn't. I said *"You."*' she spoke both emphatically and softly, 'You, you, you.' Then she left. Ah. Right. A blunder – a simple error. Who was it who said: 'Disillusion is mankind's natural and happiest state'? I heard her crying in the bedroom as I came into the study to write this down. Now I've just heard the front door slam.

# PART II

# The Dreams of Bethany Mellmoth

## One . . .

Bethany can't take much more of Bob Dylan. Her boyfriend, Sholto, listens endlessly to Dylan tracks while simultaneously watching twenty-four-hour rolling news – Sky News or CNN or BBC News 24 – with the sound turned completely down. He flicks between these silent channels looking for footage of unspooling news events. He seems to have every track Dylan ever released, and bootleg also, tracks that he plays at just-above-tolerable volume – the music score to his mute images of large and small wars, sporting triumphs or humiliations, press conferences, celebrity appearances and natural disaster after natural disaster. He claims it is an endlessly variable, unique, 365-day movie, a new art form that he has invented, available to anyone with a source of music and a television. The contrast between random image and random Bob Dylan is completely mind-blowing, he says, interminably stimulating, tragic or uplifting, funny or surreal, 24/7, as long as there is documentary footage and Dylan's accompanying soundtrack: all you need are these free images, free music and a vaguely attentive brain.

A little goes a long way, Bethany thinks, as she pulls on her coat and leaves the reverberating flat – Sholto is watching scenes of cows in a blizzard in the north of England to the sounds of 'Like a Rolling Stone'. It's cold outside and a thin sleety rain is falling. She walks fast to her usual sushi bar in Meard Street and orders the scallop sushi and the tuna sashimi and a glass of Thames water. She eats sushi all year round, even in winter: no cholesterol in rice and the otherworldly, spooky taste of raw fish somehow kills the urge for anything else.

There is a young English girl wearing a kind of black forage cap working with the other Japanese chefs in the luminous steel kitchen. She is severe and unsmiling with dense, dark eyebrows. Suddenly, Bethany sees her future: she too will become a sushi chef and prepare beautiful, clean, healthy food and open a sushi bar in London.

After her lunch as she leaves the restaurant she sees the English girl-chef on a cigarette break huddling out of the drizzle in the meagre shelter of the back door. Bethany takes out a cigarette and asks her for a light. They smoke and talk. How long does it take to become a sushi chef? There's a two-year apprenticeship, the girl-with-the-eyebrows says.

'Cool,' Bethany says. 'Do you have to go to Japan?'

'If you're serious about it.'

Even better, Bethany thinks, pondering her new life in Tokyo. It would be warm in Tokyo, wouldn't it?, she considers, liking the idea of some city-warmth.

'What exactly do you have to do?' she asks.

'Well,' the girl-chef says, 'for the first two years all you do is watch.'

'*Watch*?'

'Yes, you simply stand and watch a sushi master at work and then, after two years of watching, they give you a knife and let you begin to cut fish.'

Bethany goes back to the flat.

'Bloody freezing outside,' she calls, noticing that Sholto has moved off the sofa on to the floor. He's watching images of Bangladeshi air-force personnel pushing sacks of rice out of a hovering helicopter to swarming flood victims below. He doesn't reply. Bob Dylan is singing 'It's All Over Now, Baby Blue'.

## *Two . . .*

Bethany crosses Piccadilly and enters the park, sensing the palpable chest-filling inhalation of pleasure that she always experiences as she leaves the noisy and noisome city behind and confronts the neat, contained, leafy landscape in front of her, the clipped, undulating grass and the great shifting masses of the crowded plane trees stretching all the way up to Hyde Park Corner. She walks down towards the 'bullring' trying to resist the temptation of smoking her one lunchtime cigarette immediately. Work then reward, she says to herself. Stick then carrot.

The bullring is a wide circle of tarmac at the east end of the park with a lamp post in the middle and four equidistant benches on the rim facing inward, as if marking the quadrants on a compass. She was sitting on the north-west bench with Sholto when he told her their relationship was over and that he was going travelling – to Namibia, to Laos and Alaska, he said – alone. She stands by the lamp post now, feeling the Sholto vibrations in the bullring very strongly today – sometimes they're good; sometimes they're overwhelming and make her cry. She selects the south-west bench and takes her notebook out of her bag.

When Bethany dropped out of college (English and American Literature) and then failed to find a place at drama school (there were six annoyingly unsuccessful auditions) she decided that there was nothing for it but to become a novelist instead. She realized that she'd need a job to subsidize her novel-writing and reluctantly asked her mother to help. Bethany knows her mother can achieve almost anything she's asked – given a little time. Consequently, Bethany now works in a small narrow shop in the Royal Arcade called Pergamena that sells antique pens and parchment paper. The shop's owner (who has some mysterious connection with Bethany's mother), Mrs Donatella Brazzi, pops in from time to time and spends many hours on the phone in the tiny back office talking loudly to her family in Italy. Sometimes three days can go by without a single customer crossing the threshold. Still, Bethany reasons, she is earning money and she has plenty of time to think about her novel.

Bethany writes her novel in the park during her one-hour lunch break – weather permitting – as she finds being outdoors more inspiring and of course the memory of her and Sholto's last, anguished exchange makes the bullring one of the special places in her personal geography, a trig point on her autobiographical map. Green Park will resonate for her all her life, she realizes, even when she's an old lady she will think of this park, the bullring's wide circle of tarmac with its central lamp post and that innocuous wooden bench in a unique, unforgettable way.

Bethany smokes her lunchtime cigarette – early, guiltily – waiting for inspiration. The day is sunny and breezy with a few chunky white clouds passing swiftly overhead. She sees that the old man is at his bench as usual, in his beret and tweed coat, his notebook open on his knee, his head cocked as if he's scenting the air itself. Hardly a day goes by without her seeing this old man. One rain-lashed Saturday, as she was hurrying to a coffee shop, splashing through puddles, she spotted him from Piccadilly, sitting in the bullring with an umbrella above his head.

She opens her notebook, pausing at the title page: 'QUEEN OF A SMALL COUNTRY – a novel by Bethany Mellmoth'.

She always relishes the frisson these simple words give her. It makes everything seem real, a wish fulfilled.

Meredith Crowe is the central character in *Queen of a Small Country*. She is approximately Bethany's age and the novel charts the minor nervous breakdown she is experiencing following her break-up with her boyfriend – Mungo, Cosmo, Aldo (the name keeps changing). Aldo and Meredith separated, with acrimony and tears on both sides, in Green Park one evening, Aldo confessing he was returning to a former love, a childhood sweetheart.

In her misery Meredith haunts the park, finding it impossible to stay away and – to console herself – in her imagination she transforms the place into a small central London kingdom of which she is the benign ruler. Meredith knows every feature of her realm's few acres, knows its highways and monuments (the war memorials, the decorative fountain), its two wooden snack bars, its leafy avenues, its gentle hills and dales, its various portals (grand or merely practical) and its small well-tended copses. The park attendants, in their olive and Lincoln green livery, are her loyal retainers. She happily tolerates and licenses the safe passage of foreigners, as they wander to and fro across her territory, opening her borders at 5 a.m. and closing them firmly at midnight. She bows her head in quiet acknowledgement as the Scarab Sweepers rasp by, their revolving brushes dutifully scouring her roadways, and she wonders if, one day, her neighbour, the other queen of a larger country, in her palace across Constitution Hill, will come and pay her a visit.

Bethany is pleased with the start she has made to her novel: the scene is set – the park and its dream-life in Queen Meredith's head are well established, precisely recorded – and the context for Meredith's delusions and burgeoning emotional crisis is clear . . . She's just not sure what exactly is going to happen next.

The next Monday Bethany takes her seat on the Sholto bench and opens her novel. It's warm: a hot, still day. Tourists and office workers are spread out on the grass, prone and supine, sunbathing, reading, picnicking. She hears the regular flat thump of drums as the soldiers march up The Mall towards the palace for the changing of the guard. Perhaps Meredith should meet a soldier, she wonders, and take him for a lost prince . . .

She notices that the old man is not in his usual seat but she almost immediately spots him in the grove – a circle of a dozen or so ancient plane trees planted opposite the bullring across the main thoroughfare that runs down the east side of the park. He is standing in the central clearing looking intently up at the leaves as if he's seen something trapped there. He makes a note.

'Could I trouble you for a light?'

Bethany looks up, momentarily lost in her plot. Meredith Crowe has just spotted Aldo in a group of tourists, has run up to him, slapped his face and caused shock and offence to a perfect stranger.

The old man stands there, an unlit cigarette in a stubby holder between his thin fingers. Bethany fishes in her bag and hands him a book of matches.

'May I?' he says, sitting down, lighting his cigarette and taking a theatrical puff and, as he exhales, flexing his arm, holding his cigarette holder away from him and then study- ing intently the way his exhaled smoke is dispersed by the slight breeze. He takes out his notebook and jots something down. He has a seamed, gaunt face and his white hair is long at the back, resting on his collar.

'I notice you're always writing,' he says and Bethany tells him about her novel.

'How extraordinary,' he says. 'I'm a novelist as well. Yves Hill.' He holds out his hand 'Y, V, E, S – French. *Yves.*'

They shake hands – his grip is firm – and Bethany introduces herself, intrigued to meet another writer for the first time in her life.

'What novels have you written?' she asks.

'Oh, a good few,' he says. He mentions some names: '*The Parsley Tree, Oblong, A Voice Crying, The Astonished Soul, Trembling Needle . . .*' He tails off. 'Almost impossible to find these days. All out of print. You'd need to go to one of the better antiquarian booksellers.' He looks at her with sympathy. 'It's a difficult trade, being a novelist, making a modest living. Very much the long haul.'

Now that she and Yves Hill have introduced themselves they often smoke a cigarette and chat for a while at the end of Bethany's lunch break. Yves Hill smokes a pungent French cigarette called Gitanes. Beneath his overcoat he wears a suit and a shirt and tie. The suits are shiny with use and sport many small, neat repairs. One day he asks her how old she thinks he is.

Bethany looks at him. 'I don't know. Sixty?'

'I'm eighty-seven,' he says with a discreetly triumphant smile.

'You don't look eighty-seven,' she says. Spontaneously, she tells him about Sholto and their break-up, and why she comes to the park to write.

'Let me give you some advice,' Yves Hill says. 'I've been married four times and have had many, let's say, amorous liaisons. When a lover or a wife leaves me I concentrate on a habit they had that I found tiresome. Sadness and self-pity are soon replaced with relief.'

Bethany thinks about Sholto and his many annoying habits. She chooses the fact that he watched television all day with the sound off and music playing as perhaps the most irritating. But then she also found the way he was constantly fiddling with his thick hair – raking it with his fingers, pushing it about to form clumps and tufts, dragging it here and there – was almost intolerable. He whistled, also: she can't abide people who whistle.

Bethany finds that this self-generated, virtual irritation with Sholto is working. Even though she hasn't seen him for weeks she realizes she's increasingly annoyed with him, like a persistent itch that no amount of scratching can dispel. The unfortunate literary side-effect is that Meredith Crowe is also ceasing to pine for Aldo and, without that narrative motor, *Queen of a Small Country* is not going smoothly any more. She asks Yves Hill what she should do.

'Something totally surprising and unforeseen,' Yves Hill says, confidently, at once. 'That's what I did when I ran out of steam or ideas. Something out of the blue.' He thinks for a while. 'Queen Meredith gets run over by a Scarab Sweeper and has a leg amputated . . . Or a plane crashes in the park – dozens killed and mutilated.' He smiles. 'You'll find you'll be off and running again, no trouble at all.'

She considers this, somewhat sceptically, and to change the subject asks Yves Hill if he is writing a novel.

'No, no,' he says. 'It's a work of non-fiction. A little monograph, you might say. It'll be my last book but I suspect it will make my name.'

Bethany lies alone in her bed in her flat at night trying to convince herself that she's glad Sholto has gone, that she's thankful the caper and flicker of light from the permanently-on mute television is no longer visible in the gap beneath the door that leads to the sitting room. Yves Hill asked her why Sholto had decided on Namibia as his destination and she had told him that it was as a result of watching the silent images of a documentary on Namibia that Sholto had seen on television while simultaneously listening to *The Dark Side of the Moon* by Pink Floyd. 'A very *bad* lie,' Yves Hill had said, sternly. 'I'll wager he's not yet left the country.' This idea both upsets and angers Bethany: the thought that Sholto could still be in the country, still in England, pretending to be abroad . . . She tries to move her mind away from this topic, thinking of something surprising that could happen to Meredith Crowe, something to kick-start her novel, stalled for more than a week now on page 43.

The next day the newspapers announce a bona-fide heatwave. London swelters, London melts. In Green Park the lunchtime tourists and sunbathers seem stupefied by the sheer weight of the heat, flattened and immobile. Bethany and Yves Hill sit on their bench smoking.

'Do you feel that?' Yves Hill asks her.

'Feel what?'

Yves Hill points to the climbing grey thread of his cigarette smoke; suddenly it judders, ripples, bends and breaks. Bethany feels her long hair stir on her bare, damp shoulders.

'How would you describe that?' he asks.

'A very faint breeze? The slightest current of air?'

'How inadequate is that? How vague? How inaccurate?' Yves Hill says, his voice reedy with frustration, and points up towards the thin cobbling of milky cloud, motionless in the washed-out blue of the sky. 'The most insignificant cloud has a proper name – cumulo-cirrus-nimbus, or some such.' He looks sharply at her. 'Why can't we do better than "a very faint breeze"?'

'I can feel it just stirring my hair,' Bethany says.

Yves Hill takes out his notebook and jots something down.

The next time Bethany sees Yves Hill the weather has changed: cool and overcast with a nervy, blustery wind, more like autumn than summer. Bethany sits in the bullring wearing a fleece, her novel open on her knee. It is her last day at work as Donatella Brazzi is closing Pergamena for the month of August while she returns to her home in Brescia. Bethany is wondering what she will do with all the spare time on her hands.

'Ah, Bethany, hoped I'd find you here,' Yves Hill says, coming over and sitting beside her. 'Any news of that rascal, Sholto?'

'No, I'm very glad to say,' Bethany replies, firmly. 'I think I may have met someone else, in fact. He's called Kasimierz.'

'That's the spirit,' Yves Hill says. 'A good kingly name,' and he hands her a small packet wrapped in brown paper and tied with string. 'A present,' he says. 'My little monograph. My work is over now.'

## A NOMENCLATURE OF BREEZES AND WINDS
### by YVES HILL

> Odilon – dead calm
> Bethany – stirs hair
> Arnaud – cools sweat
> Marius – grass moves
> Valentin – leaves rustle
> Modeste – branches shift
> Honorine – grass is combed
> Isidore – fallen leaves blow
> Anselm – whips hair
> Solange – hats blow off

Blandine – windows rattle
Prosper – thrashes branches
Hippolyte – lifts sand and dirt
Fabrice – birds fly with difficulty
Gontran – umbrellas blow out
Norbert – loss of footing
Zoltan – trees uprooted

Yves Hill's little monograph is bulked out with an introduction that contains a ferocious attack on the Beaufort Scale method of describing winds – 'a clumsy, primitive tool, incomprehensible to laymen, based on air speed that must be measured with an instrument' – an analysis of his seventeen categories of breeze and wind that can all be simply and instantly evaluated by a normal human being's functioning senses and an explanation of why he has chosen – by and large – French saints' names for his notional taxonomy ('no Anglo-Saxon baggage or associations'). He has inscribed the flyleaf with a dedication that reads: 'For Bethany – now there is no excuse for not being precise. Good luck. Spread the word. Fondly, Yves Ivan Hill'.

Bethany opens it at home and is very touched – not least because she has a type of gentle breeze named after her, but also because now she knows what Yves Hill was doing all those days in the park, in all weathers, evolving his classification of the winds. She wants to write and congratulate him on his achievement, to assure him that she will describe breezes and winds from now on using his patent system – whether exhausted by an odilon, refreshed by a marius, made anxious by a norbert – and to thank him for his kind words and thoughtful advice at a difficult personal time. To her annoyance she realizes she doesn't have his address.

\*

Bethany goes back to Green Park at lunchtime every day for a week but there is no sign of Yves Hill. The phone book and the Internet provide no address and those few books of his she finds in a second-hand bookshop in Cecil Court are all published by long-defunct publishers. 'Try the Society of Authors,' the bookseller suggests, so she writes to Yves Hill care of the Society and waits for his reply.

Green Park is showing its first signs of autumn: a few yellow leaves on the plane trees, the longer grass bleached and dry. Bethany sits in the bullring hoping, willing Yves Hill to appear. Tomorrow she goes to Norfolk where she has a two-week job as an extra in a film about the poet John Milton. She is playing a serving maid in John Milton's household and the director says there may even be the possibility of a line or two. Once again, Bethany's mother has sorted her daughter's life out. The director is a friend of a friend, a meeting was arranged, he offered her this small role almost immediately. For reasons she can't really explain, Bethany very much wants to tell Yves Hill this news – to tell him that she has decided not to become a novelist, after all, and that being an actor is what she dreams about. But no sign of him. She looks at her watch: she has to go – Kasimierz is going to meet her in a pub in Covent Garden. A bethany stirs her hair and she shivers.

## Three . . .

Just because she has a small part in a low-budget, independent film – a very small part, slightly better than an extra – Bethany Mellmoth has been strictly telling herself not to get any grand ideas and to stop fantasizing, in her many moments alone, of this project as a film 'starring Bethany Mellmoth'. Only bitter disappointment lies that way, Bethany repeats to herself, wondering what the poster will look like.

One of the reasons she finds herself thinking about the poster is that the title of the film keeps changing. When she was first sent the script in London it was called *Paradise (Lost)*. When she was met by the unit runner at Norwich station and handed the new much thinner draft it was entitled *God v. Satan*, as if it were a horror/action movie. Now she sees from her call-sheet for tomorrow that it is known as *JM@PL.com* – most off-putting. When she first read the script it was the story about a young schizophrenic called John Milton, living in contemporary London, who believes he is possessed by the spirit of the seventeenth-century poet and that answers to all his mental problems are to be found in the text of *Paradise Lost*. Now all the contemporary scenes have been withdrawn while they are rewritten and they are only shooting the period flashback sections. Bethany supposes that Gareth Gonzalez Wintle, as he's both the director and the writer, knows what he is doing.

She looks at her watch – only 2.45 – a long time to go before she can cook her frugal supper and even longer before she can decently go to the pub. There is only one thing for it – another walk on the beach. She takes three paces to the end of the caravan and feels it tip slightly under her weight, like a boat, and rummages in her suitcase (never fully unpacked) for her book, *Paradise Lost* by John Milton. There's no point in taking her script because her character has no lines – even though she was promised lines – just stage directions that bear no relation to the set or location or what she is ever asked to do by Gareth Gonzalez Wintle. She checks her bag – phone, purse, cigarettes, lighter, lip-salve, notebook, camera, peppermints, Buddha-mascot. She pulls on her red wellington boots, coat, scarf and beanie, finds the keys to the caravan and steps out the door, locking it behind her – a merely symbolic gesture, she thinks, as the door seems so flimsy and thin even she would be able to punch or kick a hole in it if she had burglary on her mind.

She pauses and lights a cigarette, noting simultaneously that she only has three left – she'll have to buy some more – and that she's smoking too much on this film. Her mother has promised to give her £1,000 if she stops smoking before her twenty-fourth birthday but the sum seems unreal, a chimera, unobtainable. She exhales, audibly, feeling her mood darken, angry at her weak will, frustrated at how everything seems to be going wrong in minor, aggravating, inconsequential ways – such as the caravan and its disadvantages – not significant or provocative enough to generate the key decision to leave and start again, she considers. She has small, nagging grumbles, not real complaints or problems and she would feel ashamed turning up at home having left the film for such footling, silly reasons – squandering this amazing opportunity, this once-in-a-lifetime chance to really make it as a film actress. Or at least start to make it.

The caravan park at Faith-next-the-Sea in Norfolk sits midway between the town with its small inland harbour and the sea itself, almost a mile distant. Faith-quite-far-from-the-Sea should be its name, Bethany thinks, as she plods along the road to the beach beside the narrow-gauge railway towards the shuttered, brightly coloured beach cabins and the vast, endless stretch of sand that low tide has revealed. She already feels her spirits lifting as she approaches the beach and the distant sound of surf begins to whisper in her ears. It's a grey blustery day for September, more like February or March, she thinks, glad of her coat and scarf. One hour up the beach, she says to herself, one hour back, telly, beans on toast, drink in the pub, early to bed ready for the six o'clock call for hair and make-up. An actor's life has its compensations, she decides – and she's getting paid, she must remember, £50 a day plus free accommodation.

Bethany stands in the middle of the enormous, apparently endless beach surrounded by square miles of damp sand, the surf still some hundred yards off, the light pearly and uniform, the horizon a blurry, darker grey line shading into the clouds. Turning, she sees the black-green jagged stripe of the pines behind the dunes and, beyond that, more unchanging grey sky. A kind of dizziness afflicts her – she senses her insignificance, a small two-legged homunculus in the midst of all this space, a mere speck, a tiny crawling gnat in this elemental simplicity of sand, water and sky.

She squats on her haunches, worried she might fall over, and to distract herself takes out her camera and frames a shot of the beach, the sea and the packed clouds – it looks like an abstract painting. Click. It looks like an abstract painting by – what was his name? Colour-field paintings they are called, the three layers of colour-fields in this case being broad, horizontal bands of dark taupe, slate grey, nebulous tarnished silver. It is rather beautiful. She stands up, feeling equilibrium return – maybe she was hungry and felt faint for a second or two or maybe, she wonders, maybe she has experienced an actual existential moment – an epiphany – and has seen clearly the reality of her place in the world and has felt the nothingness, the vast indifference of the universe . . .

Gareth Gonzalez Wintle rehearses the scene in front of camera. Harold Duke is playing John Milton with primitive small dark sunglasses, like black pennies mounted on a simple wire frame. These glasses are Duke's idea, Bethany knows, as she overheard the argument Gareth had with him, trying vainly to persuade him that they were anachronistic. Duke is also playing Milton with a thick cockney accent – his idea as well. 'He was born in Cheapside, for fuck's sake, Gareth,' Duke said. 'He's a Lahndaner, mate.' Gareth had conceded the point. If she is honest, Bethany is a little frightened of Harold Duke. Out of character, he has a deep, plummy voice and an impassive, immobile face, hardly moving his lips when he speaks. He refers to Bethany, whenever he rarely has to, as 'Sweets'. Bethany affects a feigned cool around him – as if unimpressed by his reputation, indifferent to his fame – that possibly explains why she is smoking so much.

Bethany is baffled by this scene. She is playing a maid in the Milton household called Amy Coster and she interrupts the great poet as he is dictating the opening lines of *Paradise Lost* to Andrew Marvell (the singer-songwriter Wayne Hutton, no less). Milton suppresses his huge irritation, looks up and says, 'Is that you, Amy?' At which point Bethany simply nods and, in response to Milton's next question – 'How is the day, my child?' – still says nothing. The problem Bethany has is that Milton then responds, 'Aye, you're right, methought there was rain coming. It'll be here by noontide.' Then Bethany/ Amy leaves and Milton carries on with his epic poem.

At lunch – curried eggs and chips – Bethany wonders whether she should bring this matter up with Gareth. She sees him scraping his uneaten eggs into the bin liner hanging on the rear of the catering van and seizes the moment.

'Gareth? Got a sec?'

'Yeah, hi, Melanie, cool, how are you?'

'Bethany.'

'Sorry. Sorry – fuckwit. Nightmare day. Bethany, Bethany,

Bethany.' He repeats her name a few more times like a mantra. He does look tired, Bethany thinks, his eyes red and sore, his face unshaven. He would be quite a good-looking guy if his chin wasn't slightly weak. Bethany explains her dilemma. If Milton is blind how can he see her nod when he asks if it is Amy? Furthermore, shouldn't she say something when he wonders what the weather is like? His answer seems to imply that she's said something she shouldn't –

'Don't worry, Bethany. We'll sort it out in post.'

'I could just say, "It looks like rain, sire," or something.'

'We've finished that scene. It's in the can.'

'But it seems stupid –'

'Stupid?'

'Well, illogical.'

'Details, Bethany. Don't bother me with fucking *details*! I've got a fucking movie to make, here!'

To her annoyance, Bethany then has a brief cry in the Portaloo. Gareth had thrown his plate and cutlery into the bin liner and strode off muttering to himself. She could see how angry he was and she knows that he is under pressure – this is his first feature film. It doesn't matter how many commercials or rock videos you've made, a full-length period feature film is a different animal – a snarling, hairy, unruly beast longing to create mayhem. There's a knock on the door and she hears Harold Duke's drawling voice.

'Is there a cholera epidemic going on in there?'

She steps out, trying to manufacture an ironic smile.

'Sorry.'

'You all right, Sweets?'

'Yeah. Absolutely fine. How're you?'

It's at moments like these, at the end of the filming day, that Bethany misses Layla, her erstwhile caravan co-dweller.

Layla Gravell played Milton's wife Mary, a role with a few lines. She and Bethany shared the caravan at Faith-next-the-Sea for four days before Layla walked off the set, packed and went back to Swansea, where she lived. Before she left she advised Bethany to quit also. 'Of all the half-arsed, sad-sack, loser films I've worked on this one takes the biscuit,' she said in her husky sing-song accent. So she went away and Bethany moved into her slightly more comfortable divan bed. Milton's wife is written out of the film.

Bethany comes back from the pub a bit drunk. She played pool with two Faith lads and beat them, to their incredulous chagrin. They bought her two double vodkas and cranberry juice – the bet – and she feels their effect now as she bangs around the galley kitchen trying to fill the kettle, light a cigarette and plug in the toaster. There's a knock on the door. It's Gareth, he has a bottle of red wine in his hand and Bethany lets him in. He's here to apologize, he says, for losing his temper at lunch. He's really sorry – it was unprofessional and, worse, uncool.

'No worries, Gareth, I know you're under a lot of pressure.'

'You wouldn't believe it, mate,' Gareth says pouring out a glass of wine and beginning to list the astonishing pressures he faces, 24/7. The more wine Gareth drinks the angrier he becomes and the more candid. Bethany learns that the film is being financed largely by Harold Duke and a few of his wealthy friends. Gareth wrote the script but now Duke is having it rewritten by a writer he knows called Chaz Charles.

'I don't mind being rewritten,' Gareth says, lighting one of Bethany's cigarettes, 'don't get me wrong, Bethany – that's the movie biz, the nature of the beast. But I do mind my film about John Milton being torn apart by a pillock who writes sketches for washed-up comics and talk-show hosts.'

'Hence the title changes.'

'Exactamundo.'

'Why does Harold Duke want to play John Milton?' Bethany asks.

'Because he's sick of playing cops. He's sick of being Chief Superintendent Daniel Speed. He wants to prove he's a genuine thesp. So we meet and I pitch him my John Milton *Paradise Lost* idea. He loves it, I write the script and then it all goes down the toilet.'

Gareth starts to rant again, standing and pacing up and down the short length of the caravan. Gareth being heavier than Bethany the tilt and drop as he reaches the unsteady end is more marked. Bethany instinctively realizes that this is a monologue not to be interrupted, so to pass the time she writes down – on the notepad she uses for her shopping lists – all the words Gareth employs to illustrate his troubles. Harold Duke and Chaz Charles are the targets for most of his bile, and also a man called Terry Arbuthnot whom Duke has brought in as a producer. Amongst the many adjectives Bethany writes down she sees that 'dull' is a particular favourite – also banal, mulish, vapid, nauseating, suburban, drab, gutless, mediocre, ugly, trivial, futile, odious, provincial, petty, constipated, lazy, infuriating, stale and stupid – as well as many assorted swear words. Gareth empties the bottle of wine.

'I sit there listening to these ghastly, trivial nonentities, trying to conceal the wracking *spasms* of contempt I feel for their drab little *turnip* brains as they mumble on about John Milton and *Paradise Lost*. It's Kafkaesque. I mean, I went to Cambridge and got a perfectly acceptable degree in English Literature, and I have to kowtow to Terry Arbuthnot, a property developer who made his money from, from, from, I don't know . . . shopping centres and multistorey car parks, suggesting that it would be "sexier" if Andrew Marvell was a woman.'

Bethany feels a form of supernatural exhaustion creep over her as he talks on, grateful that she has a day off tomorrow. Gareth eventually asks if she has any more drink and, when she says no, he decides he'd better be on his way. He kisses her on both cheeks and gives her a hug as he leaves. He steps out into the caravan park and looks around him in astonishment, as if he's noticing the caravans for the first time.

'Why the hell are you living here, anyway?' he says.

'This is where they put me.'

'No, no, no, we've got to get you into the hotel with the rest of the cast and crew. Leave it to me.' He wanders off into the night.

The next day, keen for it to pass as quickly as possible, Bethany takes a bus from Faith-next-the-Sea along the coast to Hunstanton. 'Hunston,' the bus driver corrects her pronunciation when she pays for her ticket, 'Sunny Hunny.' She wanders around the town and buys herself a sandwich and a can of Coke. She takes a photograph of the curious striped cliffs with their horizontal bands of white and red chalk making them look like some kind of giant cake.

It is a cool hazy day and she peers across the Wash failing to make out the Lincolnshire shore. Given the weather conditions she decides against a boat trip to Seal Island to seal-watch and finds herself a sheltered corner where she sends texts to various people. To her mother; to her father in California ('Movie going great!'); to her girl friends – Moxy, Jez and Arabella. She also sends a blunt text to her so-called boyfriend, Kasimierz, who has promised to come and visit her on set but seems to be the busiest man in London. She has been looking forward to them playing house (and making love) in the tilting Faith-next-the-Sea caravan but he seems determined to disappoint her. 'Two days left. The clock is ticking. B' is all she sends him. Everyone else replies over the course of the afternoon except Kasimierz – which casts her down somewhat. It's drizzling when she reaches the bus stop and she smokes two cigarettes as she waits with four old ladies for the bus back along the coast. They stare at her as if she's some kind of alien.

It's dusk when she reaches the caravan park and as she's walking towards her caravan she meets Gareth Gonzalez Wintle coming the other way.

'Hey, Bethany,' he says. 'I've been knocking on your door for five minutes, I was convinced you were inside. All the lights were on.'

They decide to go to the pub for a quick drink. Two hours later Bethany is still listening to Gareth's complaints ('horror', 'arid', 'maggoty', 'cock-crowing egomaniacs', 'repulsive', 'mental dwarves', 'jaded sense of futility' are some of the words and phrases she logs away). Eventually she asks him.

'Gareth, was there something you wanted to tell me?'

'Ah . . . yeah. You are a fantastically beautiful young woman.'

'Not that.'

'I love your long hair, your lips, your green eyes. Blueish-grey eyes.' Gareth has had four gin and tonics by now.

'Not that. Why did you come to my caravan?'

'We wrapped early. Felt like a chat. You're a very easy person to talk to, Bethany. No, I was just feeling kinda . . . down, low. Yeah? I'm thinking of chucking it all in after this piece-of-shit film. Clearing out.'

'To Spain?'

He looks at her, baffled.

'Why would I go to Spain?'

'I don't know. Your name, I suppose. I assumed you were half Spanish – Gonzalez.'

'Oh. No, I'm English. I'm from Surrey. I just stuck Gonzalez in to make me sound more interesting. "A Gareth Wintle film", "A film by Gareth Wintle" – doesn't work. No way.'

'What's wrong with being called Gareth Wintle?'

'Because I sound like . . . like a weather forecaster. Like a children's TV host. An ink-stained clerk in a Dickens novel. Gareth Gonzalez Wintle – whole different ball game.'

Bethany says she has to get back. Gareth suggests buying a bottle of wine and having a nightcap. Bethany is firm.

'No thanks, Gareth. My big day tomorrow.'

'What? . . . Oh, yeah . . .'

Bethany sits in her costume on the lower floor of the double-decker cafeteria bus where they eat their meals waiting for the second assistant-director (a harassed girl called Frankie) to come and fetch her on set. Bethany is wearing a shapeless grey coarse-wool dress with an apron, wooden clogs and her hair is coiled and pinned up under a cloth bonnet, her face plain and scrubbed.

She is remarkably calm, she thinks, given that she is about to play her one big scene in this film. In it she enters John Milton's study with a basket of logs for the fire. Milton is asleep in his armchair. The complete manuscript of *Paradise Lost* is placed on a stool by his side. A small coal from the fire spits out and lands on the manuscript, where it smoulders, smoke rising. Amy Coster steps forward and plucks it off, burning her fingers in the process. She stifles her cry of pain and tiptoes out of the parlour, so quietly that Milton snoozes on, unaware. Amy knows she's saved her master's work from burning – we, the audience, realize how close posterity came to losing the greatest epic poem in English literature, but for the quick thinking of an illiterate chambermaid, or so it says in the script. Bethany wonders how Gareth will film it – something tricksy, no doubt, she supposes – the coal spitting from the fire in slow motion, a whip-pan round to see Amy enter, the sizzle of burning flesh as she picks up the ember –

She stops herself, Gareth has come in. He puts on what she can only describe as a sickly smile.

'Hey, Bethany. Bit of a slight change of plan . . .'

Bethany would have liked to leave at once but by the time she has changed out of her costume, been to the accountant to be paid and is ready to be driven back to the caravan she is told by Frankie that the unit car will pick her up at nine the next morning to take her to Norwich station.

She packs her things away in her suitcase and goes to the pub where she drinks two double vodkas and cranberry juice and eats a steak and kidney pie with chips followed by apple crumble. She's pleased that not once has she felt like crying, even at the moment when Gareth told her that her scene was cancelled. The whole film is changing, he said – bullishly, unapologetically – yeah, Harold isn't happy, isn't a happy camper. Chaz Charles has come up with a significant rewrite. The young schizophrenic John Milton is changing to Detective Inspector John Milton, a charismatic cop following up a serial killer who leaves clues taken from *Paradise Lost* on the bodies of his victims – the whole flashback-period part of the film is being majorly reduced. The title is now *Lost Exit to Paradise*.

Bethany, feeling very full, walks back to the caravan park from the pub analysing her mood – cold anger, she would say. Mature resignation. A certain cynicism. A worldly acknowledgement about how easy it was to be let down in this life.

Her cold anger intensifies when she sees Gareth 'Gonzalez' Wintle waiting outside her caravan.

'I don't have anything to say to you, Gareth.'

'I want to apologize, Bethany. Just five minutes.'

She lets him in and they sit facing each other across the scratched Formica of the fold-down snack table.

'It stinks, this business,' he says with what seems like real bitterness. 'That's why I'm getting out. I'm taking your advice.'

'What advice?'

'I'm going to Spain.'

'Great. Anyway, no hard feelings, Gareth. I just wish you'd told me last night instead of letting me come in, go to wardrobe and make-up, then sit around like a complete prat preparing myself when everybody knew – except me. This is my first film.'

'I know, I know. I'm weak, Bethany. Weak. Craven. And I was distracted. By you. I was enjoying being with you.'

'Yeah, well, I've got to pack,' Bethany lies.

'Listen. You'll be in the film. I'll make sure of that. I'll make sure you get a credit as well.' He gestures out the names, horizontally, with thumb and forefinger. 'Amy Coster – Bethany Mellmoth. You'll get your Equity card, it'll look good in *Spotlight*, put it on your CV.'

That would be something, at least, Bethany thinks, reaching for her cigarettes – but Gareth intercepts her outstretched hand, taking it in both his.

'You won't have wasted your time, Bethany,' he says. He brings her hand to his lips, smiles at her, kisses her knuckles. 'Can I stay the night?'

Bethany can't sleep. Her crowding thoughts won't let her. So as soon as she sees it growing light outside, she dresses, pulls on her wellingtons and coat and scarf and goes for a final walk on the beach.

The tide is out and she walks hundreds of yards down the wet sand to the surf's edge. The light is ghostly, monochrome, almost as if she's in a black and white photograph – the black sea, the silvery grey clouds, the beach shining, nacreous, softly gilded by the shrouded, rising sun. When she told Gareth to get out and told him how pathetic, suburban and nauseating she thought he was, how gutless, vapid and maggoty, he had sneered at her at first, laughed and then, to her alarm, had teared-up and turned away, then sniffed and tossed his head and said in a small, suddenly hoarse voice that he just wanted to be with someone he liked, how he hated everyone on the film except Bethany, no big deal, no sex required, just company. She held the door open for him and he asked if he could kiss her goodbye. So she let him kiss her cheek, shook his hand, said she would see him in London once the film was over and he walked away.

Bethany sets off, heading north up the beach, allowing the foamy wavelets to wet her boots. My God, she thinks – get real, girl. '*Paradise Lost* starring Bethany Mellmoth'. She pauses, turns to face the black, restless sea and spreads her arms, shouting at the top of her voice:

> Of man's first disobedience, and the fruit
> Of that forbidden tree, whose mortal taste
> Brought death into the world, and all our woe . . .

Her voice sounds small and lonely, she thinks, so she stops, hearing only the wave-crash and the distant cry of gulls and she has another of those being-and-nothingness moments that makes her shiver. Time to go home, to the caravan to have a cup of coffee and some toast and marmalade. She turns and strides back towards Faith-next-the-Sea but she's only gone a few paces when she sees something that makes her change direction. It's a dead seagull, left by the retreating tide, she supposes, white, grey and seemingly untouched, lying on its back, one wing out, one wing folded, its head tipped to the side as if it was sleeping. It looks pure and beautiful, she thinks, and reaches into her bag for her camera, very calm and composed.

She takes a photograph, inspired by the seagull's transcendent stillness, the unblemished smooth whiteness of its breast feathers. There's a play called *The Seagull* she remembers. Who wrote it? She wanders homeward, up the beach towards her caravan, urging her brain to come up with the author. That's right, Chekhov, Anton Chekhov. Perhaps it's a sign, she thinks, a symbol that she shouldn't give up her acting career. Just because her first film has been such a disaster doesn't mean she should pack it all in. No, she is destined to be an actress, she's sure – but if the cinema won't have her there is always the theatre. The theatre, she thinks, the West End, Shaftesbury Avenue . . . *The Seagull* by Anton Chekhov, starring Bethany Mellmoth . . . She walks up the beach towards Faith-next-the-Sea, pondering this exciting alternative future for herself, her stride lengthening with new enthusiasm, then she finds herself skipping – actually skipping along the sand – something she hasn't done since she was a child.

## Four . . .

Bethany is in a quandary – and she doesn't like quandaries. It's 20 December. Five days to go. The fact that this is a Christmas quandary makes it no more bearable. In truth she thinks that this fact makes it more unbearable. Her mother and father – nearly two-decades divorced – both demand her presence on Christmas Day. The quandary will be resolved – Bethany is good at resolving things – but she hasn't quite figured out how – yet.

Her father – Zane Mellmoth – texted her from his home in California. 'Coming to London. Must see you Christmas Day lunch. Big surprise. Lots to celebrate.' Bethany had felt the first prescient pang of worry: all her life, all her twenty-two years, she had eaten a Christmas Day lunch with her mother. She was four years old when her father left home and she has no memories of a Christmas lunch with him ever – although, logically, she assumes she must have had four. She telephones her mother, Alannah.

'Mum – what do you say to us having a supper this year, this Christmas?'

'Our having,' her mother corrects her grammar. 'Gerund.' Then adds, 'You must be joking. Don't. You know how important it is to me – our Christmas lunch.'

Bethany does. Zane Mellmoth walked out on his wife sometime between breakfast and lunch on Christmas Day. Alannah and Bethany had a lunch alone. Four-year-old Bethany and her mother. It is a sacramental, immoveable feast for Alannah Mellmoth that has nothing to do with the notional birth of one so-called Jesus Christ in Bethlehem millennia ago. For Alannah Mellmoth, Christmas lunch with her daughter is symbolic proof of her ability to survive and flourish without that sad pathetic bastard she once called her husband.

As if – Bethany says to herself, indulging in some justifiable self-pity – as if my life isn't complicated enough. Emotionally, the last year has been difficult. Sholto leaving her like that, so suddenly – spontaneously and without any warning – to go travelling in Namibia and Laos. Professionally, also, the picture is just as bleak. After dropping out of her literature course early in the year her various subsequent jobs as shop assistant, novelist and film extra all ended either prematurely or unhappily with nothing really achieved. What she needs is a quiet Christmas at home, nice food and telly, time to chill and regather her thoughts, make new plans for the coming year, see where her destiny lies, set new goals, dream fresh dreams . . .

Bethany has a new motto, a mantra that she chants to herself to ward off the demon procrastination. DO IT NOW! She waits until her mother goes out to the gym and calls her father in Los Angeles where he is a Professor of Psychogeography at a small private university called Brandiwine University California. She apologizes for waking him up: she's forgotten about the time difference.

'Dad,' she says, 'I can't do Christmas lunch. How about supper?'

'We won't be in London at suppertime,' her father says. 'We're driving to Devon after lunch to see Grandma. Why don't you come?'

Bethany says she can't.

'It has to be lunch, honey,' her father says. 'We're only in London for twenty-four hours.' Only when she hangs up does she realize he kept saying 'we'.

Do it now, do it now, Bethany says to herself when her mother arrives home from her work. However, she waits until her mother is on her third glass of wine before she breaks the news that her ex-husband will be in London on Christmas Day.

'So that's why you don't want to have lunch with me,' Alannah says, nodding grimly.

Bethany explains that Zane is only in the city for twenty-four hours, that he's going to see his mother in Devon.

'I don't want to have lunch with him, particularly,' Bethany says, 'but I would like to see him. I haven't seen him for two years.'

Alannah stares at her in that direct way she has, as if she's checking my face for tiny blemishes, Bethany thinks – it's most disconcerting.

'All right,' she says. 'Maybe a Christmas dinner would be nice. I know, I'll get a capon.'

'What's a capon?' Bethany asks, hugely relieved.

'A castrated cock,' Alannah says. 'It'll be ideally symbolic.'


On Christmas Eve, Bethany rides the lift in the Fedora Palace Grand to the penthouse floor. Her father is staying in the Alcazar suite. They hug and Zane Mellmoth kisses his daughter's face many times. His hair is much greyer, Bethany thinks, realizing that her father is now over fifty. But he looks thinner, fitter and his hair is cut in a short neat crew-cut like that playwright, what's his name? Bethany is annoyed she can't remember.

'Come and look at the view,' Zane says and leads her to the floor-to-ceiling window. She looks down the silver river towards Tower Bridge and at the glittering night-time city spread in front of her.

'Wow,' she says, 'this suite must cost a fort –'

'I'm here with Chi-Chi,' her father interrupts quietly.

Bethany is aware that Chi-Chi is her father's girlfriend but that's about all she knows about her.

'Great,' Bethany says, 'I'm really looking forward to meet –'

'We're going to get married. In Bali, on New Year's Eve.'

'Amazing, how romant –'

'She's pregnant. You're going to have a little brother.'

At this moment a tall thin Chinese girl comes in from a bedroom, dressed in black.

'This is Chi-Chi. Chi-Chi, this is my daughter, Bethany. Didn't I tell you she was gorgeous?'

Chi-Chi hugs Bethany and Bethany feels the small hard convexity of Chi-Chi's pregnant belly press against her.

'I love your hair,' Chi-Chi says. Her accent is American. 'It's so cool. So long and thick. God, I'd pay a small fortune to have hair like that.'

As Zane Mellmoth pours champagne at the suite's small cocktail bar Bethany takes the opportunity to look Chi-Chi over as she sits on the white leather sofa, texting, her legs folded underneath her, her back rigid, held like a dancer. She's very beautiful, Bethany realizes, and wonders how old she is. She goes and sits beside her.

'How did you and Dad meet?' Bethany asks.

Chi-Chi stops texting and frowns, as if she can't remember for a moment. 'My Achilles tendon snapped,' she says. 'I was a dancer.'

'Ballet?' Bethany asks.

'Contemporary. So I figured I'd go back to school while I recovered.'

Zane comes over with the champagne glasses.

'I took this guy's class,' she says, pouting a kiss at Zane. 'He was teaching from *Novaville*, it just blew me away.'

*Novaville* is Zane Mellmoth's only published book – and the basis of his academic reputation, Bethany knows – a psycho-geographic, situationist analysis of the modern city as if it were a newly discovered planet. Bethany has tried to read it many times.

'I saw this stunning creature with her left leg in a huge

plaster cast sitting in the front row. Quite threw me off my stride,' Zane says, taking Chi-Chi's phoneless hand.

'No pun intended,' Bethany says.

'Ha-ha, clever clogs,' Zane says.

'No champagne for me,' Chi-Chi says. 'I left my water in the bedroom.'

She places her phone on the arm of the sofa, unfolds herself, and strides across the room in that splay-footed, buttock-clenched way dancers walk, Bethany notes. Zane takes the unwanted glass of champagne back to the bar and, as his back is turned, Bethany picks up Chi-Chi's mobile and quickly reads the text she was about to send. She knows one shouldn't do this, just as one shouldn't read a person's diary or letter, but it's a temptation that no one can resist.

The text reads: 'Missing U xxxxx'. Bethany puts the phone down.


'How old is she?' Alannah asks. She and Bethany are standing in the kitchen on Christmas morning. Alannah is preparing the capon for roasting.

'It's hard to tell,' Bethany says, breezily. 'You know that smooth-skinned Chinese look, almost ageless in some strange –'

'Or rather: how *young* is she?' Alannah interrupts, rephrasing her question with a sneer.

Bethany says Chi-Chi was taking Zane's course at Brandi-wine University.

'How disgusting,' Alannah says, ripping the heart and liver from the capon's body cavity. 'One of his students. Same old sad story. Leopards and spots.'

'Part-time mature students,' Bethany corrects her. 'She was recovering from an injury, she's a dancer, really.'

'Even more disgusting,' Alannah says, 'a lap dancer, I assume.'

'She seems very nice,' Bethany says, loyally, deciding not to tell her mother that Chi-Chi is pregnant. She offers to peel the potatoes instead before she goes over to the Fedora Palace Grand for her Christmas lunch.

Chi-Chi opens the door, gives a small shrill cry of pleasure and hugs Bethany.

'Happy Christmas,' Bethany says, handing Chi-Chi the present she's brought her.

It's a first English edition of *Novaville* with a photograph of the snarlingly handsome, long-haired Zane Mellmoth on the back, when he was a history lecturer at East Battersea Polytechnic in the 1980s.

'Where's Dad?' Bethany asks, going to the window to survey the grey silent city below her, looking down on a police car speeding noiselessly along the Embankment, blue lights winking.

'He's in the gym,' Chi-Chi says. 'Want something to drink?'

Bethany asks for a vodka and cranberry juice. Unthinkingly, she asks Chi-Chi if she can smoke.

'I quit,' Chi-Chi says and taps her belly, 'and little Arnie wouldn't like it.'

She hands Bethany her drink. 'What star sign are you?'

'Ah . . . I'm Pisces,' Bethany says.

'Cool,' says Chi-Chi, picking up her phone and checking for messages. She looks up.

'We're going to get along. I'm a Taurus.'

'The fish and the bull,' Bethany says, suddenly given pause by a worrying thought.

'How old are you, Chi-Chi?' she asks. 'If you don't mind me asking. My asking.'

'I'm twenty-two,' Chi-Chi says, putting down her phone on the bar. 'Where is that Zane? Gym-bunny. I'm gonna go get him.' She pauses at the door. 'Room service should be here any minute to set up the table.'

Bethany goes to the bar and tops up her drink with a gurgle of vodka. Taurus, she thinks. Sholto was a Taurus and his birthday was in May. Bethany's birthday is 7 March . . . She and Chi-Chi are both twenty-two. Which can only mean that Chi-Chi is younger.

Bethany paces round the room munching on peanuts trying to stem her craving for a cigarette and trying to come to terms with the fact that she will soon have a stepmother who is younger than her.

'Don't forget you'll also have a half-brother called Arnie,' she says to herself. Arnie Mellmoth . . .

Chi-Chi's phone begins to ring – that *Dial M for Murder* ringtone – from the bar. Bethany goes over to the bar and looks at it. She picks it up and is about to say: 'Hello, Chi-Chi's phone', when an American man's voice starts talking without introduction.

'Chi-Chi babe don't speak don't speak it's six in the morning and guess where I am – naked in my hot tub drinking wine. Guess what I'm doing? I can't wait for you to come home. Talk dirty to me baby talk dirty –'

'Hello?' Bethany says. 'Who is this?'

Click. The phone goes dead.

Bethany places it carefully back on the bar.

The suite door opens and in come her father and Chi-Chi.

'No sign of room service?' Chi-Chi asks.

'This capon is delicious,' Bethany says to her mother. 'We should have castrated cock more often.'

She's glad she's hungry as she found herself unable to eat much in the Fedora Palace Grand. Her father had ordered the full 'Christmas turkey with all the trimmings' lunch, Chi-Chi chose a *salade niçoise* and Bethany, for some reason, distractedly ordered a selection of sushi and sashimi. Then the thought of eating raw fish had turned her stomach. She was feeling nauseous enough anyway after overhearing that brief monologue from the naked man in the hot tub.

She asked if she might step outside for a cigarette and her father told her to use the balcony off the bedroom. Bethany stood there, high up on the tallest edge of the Fedora Palace Grand, drawing deeply on her cigarette, now feeling both vertiginous and nauseous. When she came back in, her father and Chi-Chi were kissing.

They exchanged presents. Chi-Chi and her father gave her a black cashmere sweater. Chi-Chi was entranced with her copy of *Novaville* – 'My God, look at Mr Too-Cool-for-School! Look at your hair, dude!'

She turned to Bethany, smiling: 'I see where you get your looks.'

Bethany smiled back, queasily. Bethany gave her father an old copy of *The Anatomy of Melancholy* by Robert Burton that she had found in an antiquarian bookseller's when she was looking for Yves Hill.

Chi-Chi flicked through it. 'This seems kind of cool,' she said.

'It's not quite what you think,' Bethany said. 'I just love the title.'

When she leaves, her father says he'll ride down to the lobby with her.

In the lift Bethany says: 'Dad, how can you afford all this?'

Zane smiles. 'I just sold the game rights to *Novaville*,' he says. 'And NBC renewed my contract.'

Bethany has forgotten her father has another life as a TV pundit on all things urban.

'Life is pretty good at the moment,' he continues. 'What with Chi-Chi, et cetera.'

'You never told me she was younger than me,' Bethany says.

'Age is just a number,' Zane says, taking her hand and kissing her knuckles. 'It's not an issue. Chi-Chi may be only twenty-two but she's far wiser than me. I learn from *her*.'

Bethany decides to drop the subject.

As they stand in the chill afternoon air, waiting for a taxi, the sky darkening as the winter night rushes on, Zane asks: 'Have you told Alannah about me and Chi-Chi?'

'Not really,' Bethany says, carefully.

'She should know. She'd want me to be happy.'

Bethany says she'll tell her everything after Christmas.

'How is she?' Zane asks. 'I'm upset she won't talk to me.'

'She's great,' Bethany says, 'you know Mum.'

She decides not to tell him about Alannah's flourishing business as a conference organizer, or her appalling choice in men. Alasdair, Trevor, Jean-Pierre, Jason, Severiano, Kwame, Nigel and Sergei had all entered Alannah Mellmoth's life for a while and then abruptly exited. So many things not said.

'She's doing well,' Bethany says, loyally.

Do it now.

While they are stacking the dishwasher Bethany says to her mother, 'Mum – we need to talk.'

'Let's tidy everything up, first,' Alannah says, pragmatically.

Later they sit down with their glasses of wine and both light cigarettes.

'Fire away,' Alannah says.

'Dad's going to marry his girlfriend,' Bethany says.

'Good luck to her.'

'She's younger than me,' Bethany adds.

Her mother makes a face as if she's just smelt the world's worst smell.

'She's pregnant,' Bethany goes on.

'That's repulsive.'

Bethany takes a sip of her wine.

'And I think she's having an affair.'

'Fantastic!' her mother exults. 'Brilliant!' Then she looks shrewdly at her. 'How do you know?'

Bethany explains about the phone call and the naked man in the tub asking for dirty talk.

Alannah takes this all in, nodding assent: 'Pretty conclusive evidence, I would say.'

Then Bethany asks her: 'What should I do?'

'Do nothing,' Alannah says immediately. 'Nothing. It's none of your business. What if you hadn't picked up her phone? Pretend it never happened.'

'Maybe the child's not his,' Bethany says. 'He's got a right to know, surely.'

'It just keeps getting better and better,' Alannah says. 'If you tell him I'll never forgive you.'


Bethany lies in bed wondering what to do. What to do with her life and what to do about her father. She can hear her mother pottering around in the kitchen above her head and it pains her to realize that she is back at home again with her mother. Back in South Kensington, living in her old basement bedroom.

Her life is regressing, she feels: one step forward, two steps back. There is a new year coming – everything has to change, she has to reclaim her independence. She forces herself to think about Zane and Chi-Chi. She loves her father – and that love is unaffected by the clarity with which she sees him – but it seems to her, at the very least, unfair that she should say nothing given that she is all too aware of the existence of the naked man in the hot tub. If Zane knew about it also, Bethany reasons, then at least he would have the opportunity to talk things over with Chi-Chi and hear her side of the story, before they plighted their troth in Bali and little Arnie was born.

She sits up and reaches for her phone. She feels certain and unequivocal about what she's about to do and at the same time odd and strangely shaky, as if she is crossing some invisible boundary in her life. Maybe this is what she needs – maybe this is the first new step forward. No going back. It is her choice and therefore her responsibility. Do it now. She brings up her grand-mother's number on her phone. She calls and her father answers. She asks about the long drive to Devon. Send my love to Granny, she says. They talk about how good it was to be with each other at Christmas, finally, and agree it was a great lunch.

Then Bethany asks him: 'Dad, are you alone?'

'Well, I'm alone in the hall,' he says. 'Why?'

'I've got something to tell you,' Bethany says, sitting up, straightening her spine like a dancer. 'It's about Chi-Chi . . .'

## *Five . . .*

Bethany stands outside the No Parking Gallery in Dalston waiting for the owner and the gallerist, Howard Christopher, to open the door for her. He is always there, no matter how early she arrives, and sometimes she wonders if he lives in his office – though she knows full well he has a large house and large family (issue of two wives) in Victoria Park.

'Coming, Bethany, darling,' she can hear his deep voice calling from the back, somewhere. He is a friend of her mother – and it was this friendship that secured Bethany the job as a gallerina in No Parking. Her mother shaping her destiny, once again. The gallery is named after a prominent 'No Parking' sign set on the kerb outside its front door. Thinking about names, Bethany realizes that Howard Christopher's name is in fact two Christian names. Funny that, she thinks, not having a proper surname.

Bethany goes down to Howard's basement office with his morning jug of fresh orange juice. They chat about the day's business – one exhibition leaving, preparing for another being installed – as Howard opens his fridge to take out the vodka bottle. He tops up his glass of orange juice with an inch or so of vodka. He waves the bottle at Bethany but she declines. Howard takes out a ready-rolled spliff from a cigarette case and lights up.

'Very excited about the new show,' he says. He looks at her, shrewdly: 'You all right, lovely baby?'

Bethany says she's fine, thanks.

In fact Bethany is troubled this morning by something she read in a newspaper on her short but arduous bus journey to Dalston from Stoke Newington. The average lifespan of a human being, she had read, is around 1,000 months. This is entirely reasonable, she understands, and logical, but it has made her ill at ease. It doesn't seem nearly enough – somehow much worse than knowing one might live to be eighty or more. Eighty years seems improbably long. One thousand months appears almost terrifyingly brief. She does a quick calculation – she has already used up 274 months and what has she achieved in her life? Nothing.

Rod Hurt, the sculptor, supervises the deposition of his show. Bethany stands by his side with a clipboard as they go through the various works.

'Bin it,' Hurt says, 'bin it, bin it. Keep the wood. Bin it, bin it.'

Hurt's show was called *Missing*. And what was missing was the artwork itself: there was a presentation of the raw material – a symbolic block of wood, a chunk of marble, pile of clay, sack of plaster, planks of driftwood, seashore pebbles and so forth. Hurt had made a sculpture from similar materials and had then destroyed it. So set beside the granite rock was a pile of granite chips, by the tree trunk a mound of wood shavings, a cone of ash by the driftwood, iron girder transformed to crushed steel ingot, and so forth.

Bethany had said to him at the show's opening that she kept trying to imagine what was in between. 'Exactly, that's the point,' Hurt said. 'And what you imagined was probably better than what I did.'

Seeing the wanton and carefree dismantling of Hurt's show has increased Bethany's angst. And it is 'angst', she realizes – genuine angst, not the blues or PMT or simply feeling fed up. She is going through a minor but compelling crisis of an ontological sort. The message of Hurt's absent artworks plus the knowledge that she has only around 700-odd months left of life on this planet has shaken her up, somewhat. She will be twenty-three soon and all she has to show for these years, these months, is a series of truncated false starts. Leaving college and abandoning her degree; failing to get into drama school; the novel she started and set aside, unfinished; her short unhappy experience as a film extra – she could go on and on. Nothing seemed to click, or fit. Everything she dreamed of appeared to stall, or she was distracted, or else other people messed it up.

And look at her now – now she was a VARP – a 'Vaguely Art-Related Person'.

\*

The VARP acronym was something else she'd read about and it made her unhappy. She had thought that becoming a gallerina might open doors, might help her with her photography project and the book she was planning to accompany it, but now she wondered if it was just another dead end. Still, at least the next show in No Parking was by a photographer, Fernando Benn, not that she'd heard of him. Perhaps this might be the opportunity she was waiting for.

On the walk from the bus stop after her day's 'work' Bethany passes a derelict garage. In the middle of its forecourt a plant seems to be growing out of concrete.

She takes her camera out and photographs it. It's a small vigorous buddleia that has somehow managed to root itself, grow and flourish in a minute fissure. Bethany's photography project, and its eventual book, is a series of images of plants growing out of rocks – or bricks, or paving stones. It's going to be called *Suffering from Optimism* and this shot of the buddleia in its patch of oil-stained garage forecourt might be perfect for the cover. She has many photos of buddleias – she marvels at how they seem to grow in impossible unnourished places – on roof edges, in dry gutters, in the grouting of brick walls. In fact the buddleia is probably her favourite flower.

Fernando Benn's show at No Parking is called '*WAR*'/*WAR*. It consists of a series of huge photographs, six feet by six, of famous war photographs – all classic shots, almost all familiar to Bethany. Fernando Benn has cut them out of books, pinned them on his studio wall, photographed them so that they are framed by the background and blown them up.

Benn is standing in the middle of the gallery idly supervising the hang. He's a man in his forties wearing a leather jacket, jeans and red cowboy boots. He hasn't shaved for a few days.

'Great, fantastic,' he says. 'No, no, leave it there. It's fine.'

Bethany asks him if she can get him a coffee or a water.

'I'll have one of Howard's vodka and oranges,' Benn says. When Bethany hands him his drink she senses him looking her up and down.

'You're new,' he says. 'You weren't at No Parking for my last show. What's your racket, darling?'

Bethany says she's interested in photography.

'Photography is dead,' Benn says with a cough-laugh. 'Who was it who said that? Now we're in the digital age photography has lost its veracity because it can be manipulated so easily – yeah? The photographic image has lost its power.'

'But you're a photographer,' Bethany says, unreflectingly, reasonably. 'How can you say that?'

'I'm not a photographer,' Benn says, a little wearily, 'I'm an artist who chooses to work in lens-based media.' He gestures at his photos. 'These are digital pictures of photos shot on film. It's the only way they can achieve any power, any veracity.'

Benn favours the glottal stop in his conversation. Veraci'y. He smiles at her.

'Like a cannibal eating the brain of his enemy to make him stronger. Yeah?'

When Bethany arrives home that night, at the house in Stoke Newington where she lives with her boyfriend Kasimierz, she is still thinking about Fernando Benn's assertion and wondering therefore if her own project is rendered meaningless. Should she abandon *Suffering from Optimism*? Another dead end?

She goes into the kitchen and lets out a little shriek of surprise and alarm. Ten swarthy men wearing jeans and T-shirts are sitting round the kitchen table eating food out of cartons.

One man stands up and speaks to her – smilingly, amiably – in a language she doesn't understand or recognize.

She gives him a wave, turns and goes upstairs to her and Kasimierz's bedroom and locks the door.

When Kasimierz comes home late that night he explains. It's a new venture, he says, and it's going to make him a lot of money. He has bought twenty two-year-old Ford Mondeos at a car auction for £1,000 each. The men downstairs are his new drivers. With his drivers and his cars he is now in a position to bid for all the London borough contracts.

'Council work,' he tells her. 'Now I can undercutting all English mini-cab firms by fifty per cent – sixty per cent, even. No competition.'

Bethany asks a few more questions.

Yes, Kasimierz says, the men will be living here in the basement. 'They have TV, they have food, they have bed and roof. They very happy. I paying them £3 per hour – four times what they do in their country.'

Kasimierz kisses her as if he senses her anxieties. 'They will work eighty hours a week. You never see them.'

He outlines the future as he sees it: first twenty cars, then forty, then 200 – every London borough will be coming to him.

'You must meet Chaz,' Kasimierz says.

'Who's Chaz?'

'He is my Englishman. You must have an English for meetings and phone.'

In No Parking Bethany sits at her small desk looking at Fernando Benn's photos of photos of men at war thinking of Kasimierz. This is what drew her to Kasimierz, she realizes, it wasn't simply his rangy frame, his energy, his almost disturbingly pale pale-blue eyes. He achieved things. He made events conform to his wishes. He had ambitions and he realized them.

She picks up the phone and calls him. She says her mother is unwell and she has to go home and look after her for a few days.

'I text you, Bethany,' Kasimierz says. 'Take care.'

Bethany hands in her notice the day *'WAR'/WAR* is due to open. Howard seems barely to register the news.

'Fine, fine – give my love to your mother.'

As she's about to leave the room he calls her back.

'It's nothing to do with that dirty bugger Neville, is it?' he asks. 'Neville hasn't jumped on you or anything, has he? Made a pass?'

'Who's Neville?' Bethany asks.

'Neville Benn. Sorry, Fernando – I keep forgetting.'

'No, no,' Bethany says, nothing to do with Neville.

To celebrate her joblessness Bethany goes to a bar before catching a Tube to South Kensington where her mother lives. Her mother is pleased but also irritated to have her back at home again, Bethany can tell.

Kasimierz has texted her a couple of times to ask if she's missing him. It's early evening and the bar is quiet. Bethany looks at the list of cocktails and orders one called a Crack of Doom – it has many powerful alcoholic ingredients, some with names she doesn't recognize. She wants to smoke a cigarette and think about her plan and is annoyed she can't.

She has found a website called fli-leaf.com where photographic books can be made. Fli-leaf.com supplies a format, you provide images and text and pay them £120. Two weeks later you receive a bound hardback book with glossy pages. Further books can be ordered at £30 each. *Suffering from Optimism* will be born at last, at last she –

Her thoughts are interrupted by the sight of the barman throwing a bottle to the ceiling and catching it behind his back. He balances the cocktail shaker on his knee and pours in liquor from a full arm's length away. He jams the cap on the shaker and spins it on a fingertip, then he juggles four shot glasses, snatches one and sets it in front of her, catches the other three at the same time and finally serves her the drink – it's a fizzing dark purple, with a dense orange froth.

'Wait, I have to set it on fire,' the barman says. 'Just kidding. It's a cool drink. Don't get many requests for it.'

He has a Scottish accent. He's a small stocky young guy, with a broad, open face. He has a thin stripe of beard running down his chin from his lower lip. He is clearly incredibly fit and muscled. Bethany is usually drawn to tall skinny guys but there's something about this person . . .

'That was amazing,' she says. 'How did you learn to do that stuff?'

'I used to be a juggler,' he says. 'But there's no money in juggling. So I became a mixologist. All these tricks are very easy. Beginner's juggling – but it looks good in a bar.'

He smiles at her, Bethany can tell he likes her.

'I'm Bethany,' she says.

'I'm Hunter,' he says.

'Is that your first name or your surname,' Bethany asks, 'or your vocation?'

'Hunter Doig,' he says, smiling. 'Hunter's a first name in Scotland.'

Bethany sips her Crack of Doom – it's very strong.

Hunter leans his muscled forearms on the bar. 'So, Bethany,' Hunter says, 'what do you do?'

Bethany pauses a moment, sets her drink down.

'I'm a photographer,' she says.

## Six . . .

Bethany steps forward and takes a bow.

'Big round of applause for my lovely assistant, Bethany!' Hunter Doig cries.

A few people clap dutifully but they are more interested in Hunter in his top hat, balancing on his unicycle, managing to keep it upright without moving.

Bethany picks up the Indian clubs and hands them to him one after the other, trying to keep the smile fixed on her face as she thinks to herself – is this as low as I've ever been? Have I hit the bottom now – at age twenty-three – and now the only way is up?

She hopes so, she thinks, as she turns and goes to fetch the oranges.

Hunter Doig's best trick is to juggle six oranges simultaneously. Bethany now knows that even for a competent juggler five balls in the air is a challenge – the fact that Hunter can do six while riding on an immobile unicycle puts him in a different juggling league.

The Indian clubs hit the cobbled paving of the Covent Garden piazza with a dull clatter as Hunter lets them fall. The crowd whistles and cheers.

'Bethany – the oranges!' Hunter calls and Bethany steps forward in her silly Pierrot costume with the plunging neckline and throws the orange artlessly over Hunter's head. Laughter.

She runs around and picks it up. She was never good at throwing and Hunter milks her ineptitude for a lot of random hilarity before the finale of his act.

*

It is amazing, Bethany thinks, to see the near-blur of six oranges passing through Hunter's whirring hands and circling in a tall oval in front of his fiercely concentrating face. He can only keep it going for a few seconds and as he tires he heads the oranges into the crowd until he's just left with two, and then one.

'This is still juggling, you know,' Hunter yells. 'Juggling with one orange,' throwing it with one hand up into the air and catching it with the other. 'Try it at home.'

More laughter.

Bethany feels the dread mount in her like vomit in her throat as she knows what's coming next. Hunter flings the last orange into the crowd and takes off his top hat to genuine, admiring applause. Then he spin-throws the top hat, like a strange kind of Frisbee, to Bethany and of course she drops it.

Yes, whoop, laugh and boo at the inept assistant, Bethany thinks to herself, keeping her smile in place and hoping she isn't blushing too much. She always blushes as she moves amongst the people collecting their donations, the coins and occasional notes falling into the dark sweaty crown of the topper.

I'm really no more than a kind of beggar, Bethany realizes, as she collects the money – I can go no lower than this.

Bethany has told her various friends that Hunter is her new boyfriend (after Sholto, after Kasimierz) and that she has 'moved in with him'.

This is true, she supposes, but the reality is that she has moved in with Hunter and his brother, Calder. They share a large ground-floor front room in a house in Stockwell. She unlocks the door of the room and dumps the unicycle and the bag of juggling gear on the floor. Hunter has gone to an audition. Bethany vaguely resents having to cart everything back to Stockwell from Covent Garden but Hunter has given her £40 – her share of the day's take – so she reckons it would have been graceless to have refused.

She's still feeling obscurely down so she goes to the house's communal bathroom on the first floor and, locking herself in, indulges in a brief cry. What is it about life, she wonders, that makes it so hard for it to turn out the way you want it to? Always surprises, always things coming at you out of the blue. She wants a life with no surprises, she tells herself, at least for a month or so.

She sits on the toilet seat, dries her eyes and gives herself a talking to. Don't be such a wimp, she admonishes herself. You're a photographer, she says, you have self-published a book of photographs. Art isn't easy. Many artists struggle and have to do other jobs before they are recognized. She looks at herself in the mirror, drags her fingers through her hair, releasing it, making it big and full, pouts, puts on some lipstick.

She points her finger at the mirror: You're not only talented, girl, you're fucking beautiful as well, she says to her reflection.

Coming down the stairs she can hear the TV is on in the room. Hunter must be back, she thinks, and goes in feeling better, wanting to hold Hunter's stocky muscled body to her, wanting to go to the pub and spend some of her money on powerful alcoholic drinks.

But it isn't Hunter, it's Calder, sitting slumped in front of the TV. Calder is in the street-theatre business, also. He's a living statue. His speciality is 'Man in a Hurry', standing frozen for minutes as an urgently striding man, his face a white mask of make-up, his long thick hair lacquered like stone, streaming in unmoving horizontal curls off the back of his head, his stiffened tie whipped around his neck, his stiffened jacket fronts folded back as if he's walking into a fresh breeze, as he stands there trapped for ever in mid-pace, a rolled-up clutched newspaper in one hand as if he's rushing, late for a train. It's a very effective living statue – so different from the boring, immobile grey or gold simulated public statuary that is the norm.

Calder makes a lot of money playing 'Man in a Hurry' and Bethany admires the mental discipline that he has to summon up to hold that pose, minutes and minutes on end, that petrified dash going nowhere.

Story of her life, she thinks.

'Hi, Calder,' Bethany says.

He grunts, eyes on the news. He's still in his full 'Man in a Hurry' get-up. Stiff hair streaming back from his head, white face, tie whipped around his neck. He seems reluctant to change from this persona and clean himself up – he'll sit around for hours like this – a fact that annoys Bethany, she has to admit.

Bethany isn't sure if Calder welcomes her presence here in the room he used to share with only his brother. He has put a kind of hospital screen around his bed. When she and Hunter make love – as quietly as possible – Hunter assures her Calder wouldn't mind, anyway, even if he could hear what was going on. Which he can't.

Bethany makes a cup of tea. They don't have a kitchen in the room but there is a kettle, a toaster and an electric ring on top of a scarred chest of drawers that allows them to make snacks. Most of the time they eat out or bring home takeaways. Bethany pours in the milk (having thoroughly sniffed the carton first) and stirs her mug of tea, sensing an extraordinary lassitude spread through her.

'Bethany?' She jumps – Calder has silently appeared by the scarred chest of drawers with his white face and horizontal hair, his stiff tie around his throat. It's as if he's standing in the face of a gale, a hurricane.

'Hey, Calder,' Bethany says. 'Gave me a shock there, mate.'

'Sorry,' he says, touching his stiff hair and tie. He turns away, showing the frozen billows of his jacket. Then he turns back as if he's about to say something – but he doesn't.

'Fancy a cup of tea?' Bethany asks.

'No, thanks,' he says.

Bethany picks up her mug, sips her tea and holds it to her chest.

'So, how was your day, Calder?' she asks.

Calder thinks, his face utterly deadpan.

'I love you, Bethany,' he says, softly, his voice cracking.

'I love you,' he repeats as Hunter comes in the door.

## Seven . . .

Bethany sits under the awning of the Kafé Klee and looks at the traffic snailing by on the Fulham Road. Where are all these people going on 2 January, she asks herself? Her friend Moxy appears with two double-shot cappuccinos and sits down. Moxy offers her a cigarette (Bethany accepts) and they both light up in the style of the Sean Young character in Ridley Scott's *Blade Runner*. They both agree, Bethany and Moxy, that no one has ever lit a cigarette in a cooler way than Rachael, Sean Young's character, and this is a judgement based on long analysis of smoking scenes in key cult movies. Bethany, as it happens, thinks she is better at replicating Rachael than Moxy.

They exhale, blowing smoke strongly out of the sides of

their mouths, and sit for a while sipping their coffee. Bethany likes the Klee, not simply because of the half-dozen reproductions of the master's work inside, but also because it is cheap and you can smoke comfortably on the pavement under the awning thanks to the glowing orange heaters bolted on to the wall above their heads. She and Moxy are trying to come up with a list of achievable New Year resolutions, and are stuck on the subject of sex.

Moxy claims she had no sex during this last year, something Bethany finds a little shocking, given that she, Bethany, had enjoyed so relatively much – though on reflection perhaps the word 'enjoy' is wrong. Still, clearly she had many more sexual connections with men in the year than Moxy. This is also somewhat surprising as Bethany thinks Moxy is a very attractive girl in a slightly feral, grubby way. Bethany indulges in a short, clandestine thought experiment – imagining if she were a man confronted by Moxy. Slim, vivid (the rusty-maroon hair contrasting with the pale face), fashionable, intelligent (Moxy dropped out of her Fine Arts degree at Edinburgh after a year), confident and edgy. What's not to like?

Being ruthless, Bethany decides that, if she were a man, she would be somewhat put off by Moxy's nose stud. It's on the large side, a stylized silver multi-petalled flower, but the tarnished grey petals are surrounded by a pink areola of inflamed skin, as if the tissues of Moxy's left nostril are reacting angrily to this piercing, as if cleanliness, basic hygiene, had not been part of the process. Bethany knows that Moxy had this flower inserted in her nose over a year ago, in Goa, on her twenty-first birthday but it has never truly settled, its hot pink ring forever visible. Moxy says she feels no pain, the flower can be removed and easily replaced with no unseemly oozings but, all the same, there it is in the middle of her face and it gives off its own little aura of sepsis, of incipient purulence.

So, Bethany says, keen to move her mind on, 'What's your New Year resolution, then?'

'I've just got to have a shag,' Moxy says, flatly. 'Simple as that. That's all I want. Once that happens everything else can move forward.'

Bethany remonstrates – surely there must be other important ambitions? But Moxy won't hear of anything more high-minded.

'It's all very well for you,' Moxy says, with an edge of bitterness to her voice. 'You lived with three men in the last year. Nympho.'

This hurts, but it's true, Bethany realizes. She tells Moxy everything – well, almost everything – so Moxy knows about Sholto and then Kasimierz and then Hunter (but she doesn't know about Hunter's brother, Calder). Suddenly Bethany wonders if there's something wrong with her: she's only twenty-three but she lived with these three young men pretty much one after the other, all interestingly alluring and strangely sexy guys in their own special way, under different roofs. With each one the same routines and rituals applied: they slept together in the same bed, they shopped together, ate together, went out together, did rudimentary housework together, paid bills together, each had a set of keys to the front door of their habitation – but one by one these relationships were unilaterally ended. Just for a moment, a few weeks, a month or three, some sort of stasis of contentment was reached. And then it went wrong and Bethany declared it was over.

'Any news of Sholto?' Moxy asks. Sholto was Moxy's friend and she had introduced him to Bethany.

'Deafening silence,' Bethany says. 'For all I know he's in

Alaska with an Inuit wife.' She smiles. 'Yeah, to hell with Sholto.'

They sit for a while, smoking. Then Bethany asks Moxy if she'd like to hear her New Year resolutions. Moxy sighs and says, get on with it.

'One,' Bethany says, 'move out of my mother's house. I can't live there any longer.'

Moxy says that's also one of her New Year resolutions – after getting laid.

'Two,' Bethany continues, 'experience a period of deliberate celibacy – no men.'

'You bitch,' Moxy says.

'Only in order to, three, kick-start my acting career again,' Bethany explains.

'I thought you were going to be a photographer,' Moxy says.

'I'll still be a photographer,' Bethany says, 'I can act and take photographs. Like that actress, what's her name, the one who was in the Woody Allen films.'

'Penelope Cruz,' Moxy suggests.

'No, the older one – Diane something.'

Moxy doesn't know who she's talking about.

'And, four (a) and (b) get an agent and start going to auditions.'

Bethany feels a sudden surge of optimism notionally laying out her future in this way. It immediately seems very possible. Move out of her mother's house, get an agent, go to auditions, be offered a part in a play/sitcom/TV drama/ movie/commercial and begin to realize her dreams of acting on stage or screen – she's not fussy. In fact she's annoyed that she can't be going to meetings with her agent and deciding what auditions she'll do and what she'll ignore. London is closed, she knows, England is on hold, Great Britain is immobile while its enforced, enervating seasonal holiday plays out, interminably.

Of course, there is still the problem of money . . . Resolution five: find a short-term, interesting, well-paid, part-time job.

Sunil comes out from the café and Moxy asks for the bill.

'On me, ladies,' he says. 'Happy New Year.'

Bethany likes his Liverpudlian accent.

Moxy says she has to go as she's 'on air' at midday. She reads the news, weather and travel reports on a small digital radio station called Radio Lube. It doesn't pay well but it is the media, at least, Moxy says. Her dream is to be a TV presenter, or one of the guest presenters, of a TV show. Children, Reality, Quiz – she doesn't care. She also works part-time as a website designer – she says she's paid but Bethany doesn't believe her as she's also still living at home, with her parents in Wandsworth. Moxy hugs her goodbye, they promise to text each other, to meet up for a drink. Bethany watches her walk away – a pretty girl on the Fulham Road – surely the men should be queuing up? . . .

Sunil comes out again and sits down at her table. He has lank long hair and wire-rimmed specs that fail to disguise his good looks.

'You got a second, Bethany?' he asks.

Bethany says she has – she likes Sunil.

Sunil starts talking about his band, the music he makes. 'We got a couple of tracks on our website,' he says, writing down the address.

'What's it like?' Bethany asks.

'Very electronic,' Sunil says, 'but not dance/hip hop, you know. More electro-folk-modern-classic.'

'Oh yeah,' Bethany says, 'like chamber-pop.'

'No,' Sunil says. 'Nothing like chamber-pop. Listen to it, you'll see.'

'I'll *hear*,' Bethany says.

Sunil looks blank for a moment. 'Yeah, you'll see what we do.'

Bethany stands. 'Great,' she says, 'thanks for the coffee. You should talk to Moxy if you want some work done on your website.'

'What kind of name is Moxy?' Sunil asks.

'Her real name is Araminta,' Bethany says. 'Araminta Trinder – but she didn't like the way it nearly rhymed so she changed it. See you.'

She heads off but Sunil calls her back. He looks nervous all of a sudden, tucking his long hair behind his ears.

'Can you sing, Bethany?' he asks.

Bethany says, immediately, without thinking, 'Yes, course I can. Why?'

'We need a singer,' Sunil says. 'Somebody cool and beautiful, like you.'

Bethany narrows her eyes and stares at him forcefully, sceptically.

'Hey. Are you joking me?' At moments like these she knows she resembles her mother a bit. That *look*.

'I'm dead serious,' Sunil says. 'Come down to the studio – meet Sven. I've told him all about you. Give it a try. Nothing to lose.'

'Maybe I will,' Bethany says. 'I'll listen to your music – see if I like it.'

'It's very electro,' Sunil says, almost plaintively. 'But we feel we need a voice.'

Bethany walks along the Fulham Road heading for her mother's house in Hollywood Road. We need a voice, Sunil said. Bethany sings out loud in a husky low jazzy monotone – 'I have a voice, a voice that can sing almost anything, do-bee-dad-dad-da-boo, yeah, yeah, I can sing for you, baby, any time of day, yeah . . .' It sounds pretty good, she thinks. She's never thought of a singing career. Why not? Maybe Sunil and Sven are talented. Maybe their electro-folk-modern-classic sound could catch on.

Bethany pictures herself on one of those late-night television music shows. What would she wear? She would be very still, she thought, as she sung, holding herself immobile, concentrating on the song and its lyrics. She would write the lyrics, definitely. Sunil and Sven could add their music once she'd written the words.

She turns left into Hollywood Road and for an absurd moment thinks she sees Sholto across the road from her mother's house. She laughs to herself: get a life, girl. Then she realizes – it *is* Sholto.

'Fucking Sholto,' she says, out loud. Then, anger building in her like a mushroom cloud, she yells, 'SHOLTO!'

Sholto looks round and takes off, running up Hollywood towards Cathcart Road. Bethany is after him immediately, thankful that she's wearing flats, and quickly begins to gain on him – a fact made all the easier because Sholto is carrying two rucksacks, one slung over each shoulder. He skids into Cathcart and then begins to slow. Bethany catches him and pushes him against a wall, tears of pure rage in her eyes, wanting to strike him.

'Don't hit me,' Sholto pleads, in between huge gulps of air.

They stand facing each other for a while. Bethany feels herself beginning to calm down. She steps back – Sholto looks different. He's wearing black, top to bottom: black Converse sneakers, tight black jeans, black leather blouson over a black hooded sweatshirt, black scarf. Even his two rucksacks are black. He looks different, somehow. Then Bethany realizes it's his hair. The wild tufts and waves have gone. His hair seems blonder, also, and it's swept forward over his forehead and on to his cheeks even, like a kind of hair-helmet, as if his hair is embracing his head. Bethany's not sure if she likes it that much.

'How was Namibia?' she asks, her voice reedy with cynicism. 'Or should I say Alaska?'

'I've been living in Amsterdam,' Sholto says.

'Oh, great,' Bethany says. 'Brilliant – so far away. Why Amsterdam?'

Bethany senses rather than sees the tears well in Sholto. He pinches his temples fiercely and shuts his eyes. She can see his knuckles whiten as if he's trying to force his eyes together in his head to form one Cyclopian eye.

'I'm sorry to get so emotional,' Sholto says in a small croaky voice, 'but I think I'm gay.'

That evening after supper Bethany asks her mother if she knows many gay men.

'Almost every man I know is gay,' her mother says, and starts to list them: Nico, Luis, Terry, Fela, Toshiro, Clive . . .

'Is Clive gay?' Bethany asks. 'I thought he had a wife and two kids.'

'So did Oscar Wilde, darling,' says Alannah, thinking. 'Well, he's certainly bi. Whatever. In fact I thought your father was gay for a while after he left – but I was clearly wrong about that.' Alannah looks at Bethany shrewdly. 'Why do you want to know?'

'I'm just curious,' Bethany says and then, as casually as she can manage, asks, 'Have you ever had an affair with a gay man?'

'No,' Alannah says with a sigh. 'Sometimes I wish I were gay: life might be simpler, but unfortunately I'm attracted to the opposite sex and that happens to be male. Hetero man for me.' She looks at Bethany again. 'Do you think you're gay?' she asks.

'No,' Bethany says. 'Sholto does.'

\*

Bethany meets Sholto in the Kafé Klee. She decides she really does not like his new Amsterdam hairstyle. He seems more relaxed, more like his old laconic self.

'I've found a flat,' he says with some pride. 'Kentish Town: two bedrooms, sitting room, kitchen and bathroom.'

Bethany asks how he can afford it. The last job she was aware that Sholto held down for more than a week or so was replacing and watering plants in office blocks, working for his brother.

Sholto shows her – under the table – a big wad of money, blocks of euros with rubber bands round them.

Bethany does a quick count. 'That's nearly 8,000 euros,' she says. 'You're not selling drugs, are you?'

'Giel gave it to me,' Sholto says. 'He told me to find a flat. Had to put down £2,000 as a deposit.'

'Who's Giel?' Bethany asks quietly, suspecting the answer.

'He's my friend from Amsterdam,' Sholto says.

'Your lover,' Bethany says.

'Sort of,' says Sholto. 'It's complicated.'

'How did you meet this Giel?' she asks.

Sholto tells her: he was at Heathrow, that day he'd left her, trying to figure out how to get to Namibia. He started a conversation with this guy – an older guy, late thirties. He said he lived in Amsterdam, suggested that Sholto check out Amsterdam for a few days before he flew on to Africa – there were plenty of cheap flights from Schiphol. Sholto shrugs.

'I can't really explain why,' he says, 'but I went to Amsterdam with him and never left.' He frowns for a moment, then smiles. 'Do you want to see the flat? You can choose your room.'

Bethany says she'll think about it, somewhat astonished at Sholto's nerve. Does he think this is normal? First he leaves her, just like that, walks out of their flat and their life together to go 'travelling'. Then he doesn't make contact with her for months, and then he turns up outside her mother's house, tells her he's gay and asks her to move into his new flat with him. Bethany steps outside for a smoke.

Sunil joins her. 'Did you check out the website?' he asks.

'Yeah,' Bethany lies spontaneously. 'I see what you mean about needing a voice.'

'Exactly,' Sunil says, with enthusiasm and relief. 'You've got to come down to the studio.'

'Where's the studio?'

'It's in Sven's flat, in Streatham. We've got everything we need there.'

Bethany exhales. It's only 4 January and the year is speeding up.

'What's the name of your band?' she asks.

'Xenon,' Sunil says.

'Why Xenon?'

'Because it sounds like a sort of cool distant planet,' Sunil says.

'Actually, Xenon is an inert gas,' Bethany tells him, gently.

'Oh. Right.'

'We've got to get a new name, Sunil, I can't be in a band named after an inert gas.'

'You think of a name, Bethany,' he says. 'I know it'll be great.'

Bethany walks round the flat in Kentish Town. It's ground floor and the kitchen is quite new. She'll need to repaint her bedroom, of course, but it's not bad. Also there's a little tufty patch of back garden with an ancient apple tree – which is pleasing, as she's never really had a garden of her own.

'What do you think?' Sholto asks.

'It's pretty good,' says Bethany.

'I've paid two months' rent in advance,' he says, 'so, everything's cool, you know.'

Everything's not remotely cool, Bethany knows, and she's about to say – what's the deal with Giel? – when there's the sound of a key in a lock and a skinny young woman comes in wearing a red leather coat and a red beanie. Sholto gives her a kiss.

'Hi,' he says. 'Noémie, this is Bethany.'

Bethany raises a hand and says hi.

'*Bonjour*,' Noémie says. 'Excuse me, one moment.' She whips off her beanie cap to reveal cropped spiky blonde hair. She's so thin and frail she makes Bethany feel like a giantess. She darts into the bathroom.

'Who's Noémie?' Bethany asks.

'She's from Brussels.'

'Who's Noémie?' Bethany repeats, patiently.

Sholto runs his hands through his neat Amsterdam hairstyle, disarranging it.

'She's Giel's wife,' Sholto says. 'She's staying here for a couple of weeks.'

On the bus back to Fulham, Bethany goes through the pros and cons. Sholto said that he and Bethany would share the big bedroom. As long as Noémie was staying there would be nothing to pay. Then she'd go and the flat would return to them. On further questioning, Sholto admitted that Giel might be popping over from time to time. He and Noémie were looking for premises to start a club.

'I miss you, Bethany,' Sholto had said, 'I feel I need to spend time with you, make up,' adding that he'd told Giel all about her.

A 'club', Bethany thinks. Maybe they'll play electronic music. Maybe she and Sunil and Sven could do a gig there . . .

She looks out at the wet streets, her stop coming up. The rain has gone and the sky is brightening, promising some sunshine. Maybe Sholto is right: it's a stroke of luck – moreover it solves all immediate problems and confirms several of her New Year resolutions. She and Sholto could share a bed, no problem, but that hair would have to go.

Suddenly she freezes – she has it. An inspiration. The Promise of Sunshine. She likes that. Sounds good. She steps off the bus and walks up Hollywood Road. Her mother will pretend to be upset but will secretly be delighted she's leaving home again. Yes, it might work out, everything: Sholto back, the new flat, her resolutions already on the way to being achieved.

She hears applause in her ears, shouts of acclaim, whoops, whistles . . . Ladies and gentlemen – finally they're here, what you've been waiting for, big hand, please welcome Bethany Mellmoth and the Promise of Sunshine!

### *Eight . . .*

Bethany sits patiently on the Tube train that is stuck in a tunnel somewhere between Knightsbridge and South Kensington. She's unperturbed; she's calm – because this is normal, this is life. This situation conforms to her new understanding of the world and the human predicament. Life, she now knows, is a malfunctioning system. Failure, breakdown, dysfunction – this is the norm. As soon as you acknowledge this fact then everything becomes easier. 'Things Go Wrong' – this is the essential feature of our world. It applies to washing machines, motor cars, computers, staplers, central heating, ballcocks, the Internet, stock markets, incredibly expensive fighter aircraft, printers, toasters, nuclear power stations, kettles, cameras, fountain pens – and, of course, human relationships of all kinds. Things Go Wrong.

This will be her new dictum, her private mantra – she'll write it on a piece of card and stick it above her desk . . . She senses irritation, panic, frustration building amongst the other passengers in her carriage. They see this enforced wait in a tunnel beneath London as abnormal, wrong, anger-inducing. Big mistake – a train that runs smoothly and arrives on time is the exception to the implacable rule. Once you understand that then life's irritations and inconveniences change their nature – it's like complaining about the weather. What's the point? You get the weather you get. Look at me, Bethany thinks, look how at ease I am. And, she notices, someone *is* looking at her – a young guy diagonally opposite with short, dark cropped hair and a pointed Robin Hood beard. He's attractive, handsome in an unobtrusive, unshowy way, Bethany sees instantly, but there's something wrong with his good looks, something not quite right. Maybe it's the short hair, she thinks, as if it's growing back after a brain operation. Or, she thinks again, it's as if he's a soldier and has grown the beard to demilitarize himself, somehow.

She looks down at her book, slightly irritated that their eyes had met and that therefore he knows she knows he was looking at her. She turns a page. *Metamorphosis and Other Stories* by Franz Kafka. She hears the guy clear his throat in the way that a throat-clear can be a signal, like a 'shhh' or a 'tsss'. It says: look at me. Unreflectingly, she looks up.

He is holding up the book he is reading. *The Trial* by Franz Kafka.

The train starts with a lurch.

Bethany walks up the Fulham Road towards her mother's house, her rucksack heavy on her back and her carrier bags bumping annoyingly against the side of her knees. There is no humiliation in coming back to live at home, she says to herself, reasonably – that's what 'home' is for: a place you can come back to when required, no questions asked. Perhaps it's a little awkward that she left home a mere five days ago, she admits, but that's life – certainly that's life as a dysfunctioning machine, as she now understands it. When she called her mother to say she was coming back there was little welcome in her voice.

'What's wrong?' Bethany said.

'I've met someone,' her mother said. 'It's a bit inconvenient having you in your room, just at this stage, if you see what I mean.'

'I won't be there long,' Bethany reassured her. 'It's just a blip.'

'Five mistakes', Bethany writes in her diary.

1. Meeting Sholto.
2. Getting upset when he left me to go travelling.
3. Missing him while he was away, thinking I was still in love with him.
4. Not telling him to fuck off when he came back.
5. Not believing him when he said he was gay.
6. Agreeing to share a flat with him and his gay lover Giel.
7. Not moving out when Giel's wife came to stay.

Bethany crosses out the 'five' and writes 'seven' in its place.

Bethany goes down to the Kafé Klee and asks for Sunil. Sunil quit, she's told. Had a row with the manager and walked out. Do you know where he lives, Bethany asks? No one knows where he lives. So much for Sunil asking her to sing in his band. She checks her mobile but she doesn't seem to have Sunil's number. Shit. She buys a cappuccino and sits down.

Her mother has asked her to stay out of the house until at least 2 a.m. Her new friend, Demerson, is coming for dinner. Bethany is to come home late and go straight to her room as quietly as possible.

'Hi.' She looks up. The guy from the Tube who was reading Kafka is standing there. She knows this is not a coincidence. He asks if he can join her and she says yes, after a second's pause.

'You followed me from the Tube, yesterday, didn't you?' she accuses him.

'I was going the same way as you,' he replies.

'Then you stalked my house and followed me here,' Bethany says.

'I saw you walking in the street and followed you here,' he says. 'You had this aura about you. You've broken up with your boyfriend, haven't you?'

'How can you tell?' she asks, unreflectingly.

'Because of this aura around you. I can sense someone with an aura.'

'Aura you just a twat?' Bethany says, sharply.

'That's good,' he says. 'That's funny, I can use that.'

'Use it to improve your chat-up lines,' she suggests. 'Feel free, be my guest.'

'I'll use it in my act,' he says.

She knows he wants her to ask him what his act is but she decides not to, for the moment.

'So you read Kafka, as well,' she says.

'Kafka is the most-read author on the Underground,' he says. 'It's a well-known fact.'

She looks at him quizzically – this could almost be true. She's getting used to his beard: normally she doesn't like young men with full beards. A bit of stubble – a few days without shaving, fine. But this is a proper beard, trimmed, grown to a sharp point on his chin like a figure in an Elizabethan miniature, she suddenly thinks.

'I'm Bethany,' she says, offering her hand.

He looks at her in surprise and hesitates to take it.

'I had a shower this morning,' she says. 'Clean as a whistle.'

He makes a conscious effort and shakes her hand.

'I'm . . .' He hesitates again. 'I'm Aldous.'

'You don't seem that sure,' Bethany says.

'I have a few names I go by,' he says. 'It's important to make the right choice at the first introduction. It shapes everything.'

'What are your other names?' Bethany asks.

'Shel,' Aldous says. 'Sometimes Sheldon Stone. Sometimes just Stone.'

'Aldous Stone, then.'

'No, actually, Aldous Peploe.'

Bethany Peploe, she says to herself – don't like it. She does this unconsciously when she meets guys she's attracted to. It's a tic, a habit she can't rid herself of, always projecting forward into some unimaginable future, fast-forwarding.

'Why are you frowning like that?' Aldous asks.

'Sorry, nothing,' Bethany says. 'Why do you have other names?'

'They're my stage names,' he says.

'Ah, your "act", of course,' she says. 'I hope to hell you're not a conjurer.'

'I'm a stand-up comic,' he says.

At eleven o'clock that night Bethany is waiting in a small queue outside a comedy club in Dalston called the Quota System. There's a poster with names of the comics who are appearing but she can't see Sheldon Stone on the list. Then she sees there's an open-mic session as well and, wearily, she realizes that when Aldous said he was a stand-up comic what he really meant to say was that he *would like to be* a stand-up comic.

Still, she has to stay out late so she might as well try to have a laugh. Her phone bings. She sees it's Sholto.

'Hi, Bethany –' he begins.

'I shouldn't speak to you again,' she says.

'Bethany, please,' Sholto begs. 'How was I to know she would do that?'

'You knew – you set me up.'

'Well, I know they have this weird sexual thing going but I never believed she'd do that.'

'They can do what they like,' Bethany said harshly, 'I'm paying rent, I'm their lodger not a sex slave.' She lowers her voice as she senses the queue's growing interest in her conversation.

'Hold on a second,' she says, and lights a cigarette, turning to the wall.

'Giel wasn't in,' Sholto says. 'Maybe Noémie wanted some company.'

'Noémie was naked, for God's sake,' Bethany says.

She and Sholto had been lying in bed, half asleep, when the door opened and, before she could properly respond, a naked woman, Noémie, had slid into bed beside her and started kissing her and then Sholto.

'You pimped me out,' Bethany says harshly.

'I swear,' Sholto says, his voice cracking, 'I'd never do that to you – I love you.'

'Oh well, what's done is done,' Bethany says, suddenly tranquil, as she's just reminded herself of her new philosophy. Things Go Wrong. Malfunction, disorder, chaos – the natural state of things. To expect that a middle-aged Belgian woman would *not* want to have spontaneous threesome sex in the middle of the night is the mistake she's making.

'It's not your fault,' she says to Sholto, appeasingly. 'It's *life's* fault.'

'What're you talking about?' he says. 'I don't understand.'

'I have to go,' she says, 'I'm meeting someone.'

Salt in the wound.


Shel Stone's act was not bad, actually, Bethany thinks to herself, standing in the bar, waiting for Aldous to appear. It showed promise, anyway. He was the last one on for the open-mic session and the three comics before him were hopeless so expectations were low and the crowd's attention was waning, the hum of conversation growing. 'Please welcome Shel Stone!' the MC said and left the stage. The lights went off and a spot shone on the microphone on its stand. No one appeared. Five seconds. Ten. Then some sort of loud banging about occurred in the wings. Muffled grunts and curses. Then Shel Stone burst on stage and fell heavily to the ground. The spot found him and he staggered to his feet. He was wearing a tight black suit and a white shirt with a thin black tie. 'Bastard fucking bastard!' he bellowed in a thick Scottish accent at someone in the wings. Then he jolted, as if he suddenly realized where he was and had spotted the audience for the first time. He dusted himself down and stepped up to the microphone, thumbing away a trickle of blood from the corner of his lip. He stared out into the audience and smiled slowly. The place was quiet. 'HULLOOOO GLASGOWW-WWW!' he shouted, throwing his arms wide. The audience said nothing – then the catcalls and jeers began.

'Sorry, sorry,' Shel Stone said, his accent cockney all of a sudden. 'Lost me bearings.' He turned to the wings and pointed. 'I'll sort you out later, you BASTARD!' The audience were completely with him now. He straightened his tie and smiled at them.

'I don't do this all the time, you know. This is like me hobby. I got the day job . . .' Smile. 'Guess what I do.' There were a lot of ribald suggestions. Shel quietened the crowd.

'I'm a sperm donor,' he said.

Boos, hisses. It didn't get much better.

Bethany sees Aldous slip out of the stage door and look for her in the bar. He's back in his usual clothes – a zip-up jumper and cargo pants – and no one in the bar seems to recognize him as Shel Stone.

'You were great,' she says.

'No I wasn't,' he says. 'I want your honest opinion.'

'Okay. Let me buy you a drink,' Bethany says. 'You find a table.'

'It started quite well,' Bethany says, 'but I'm afraid wanking jokes are so pathetic. Sad. Didn't you see? Only the men thought it was funny.'

'Yeah, I know,' Aldous says, 'it's pathetic, you're right.'

'It's not original,' Bethany goes on. 'I think you stole it from a film, anyway.'

'Everybody steals everything,' Aldous says, defensively. 'It's the comic ethos.'

Bethany, mollifying, analyses further.

'The beginning was such a shock, you see. You shook us up. We all went quiet – nobody knew what was going to happen. It was kind of dangerous. Funny and dangerous. That's the way to go, I reckon. Your accents were good.'

'Yeah . . .' Aldous says to himself, nodding. 'See what you mean. Keep it surreal, yeah. Don't let them relax. I've got to be more surreal.'

'Kafkaesque,' Bethany says. Aldous chuckles, drains his drink and tries to kiss her.

'What's he like?' Moxy asks, lighting her roll-up.

'He's cute,' Bethany says. 'He's got a beard –'

'Yech,' Moxy says.

'– and he thinks he's going bald so he cuts his hair really short.'

'How old is he?'

'Haven't asked yet,' Bethany says. 'Twenty-seven, twenty-eight. He tried to kiss me but I wouldn't let him.'

'Not like you,' Moxy says.

'Bitch.' Bethany smiles at her and tells her about Sholto and Noémie – having leapt out of that frying pan she had no desire to be burned again for a while.

'So what're you going to do?' Moxy asks. 'You can't stay at home.'

'Try and get in to drama school,' Bethany says.

'You tried that before,' Moxy says, 'and you didn't get in.'

'Ah, but I've been in a film since then,' Bethany says.

'An extra in an unreleased film,' Moxy says, 'very impressive. Oh, yeah.'

'It'll be different this time around,' Bethany says. 'I've changed.'

Aldous and Bethany sit in a sushi bar on the Dawes Road near Aldous's small flat.

'I'm having a bit of trouble rewriting my act,' Aldous says, dabbing wasabi on to a rectangle of tuna. 'The Quota are going to try me out on the bill – five minutes – and I've only got material for two.'

'You've only got material for thirty seconds,' Bethany says. 'Let's be honest.'

He looks at her. 'I'm going to need your help, Bethany.'

'I'm very busy,' Bethany says, 'I'm applying for drama school – you know, interviews, learning lines.'

'I'm manic depressive,' Aldous says, 'I can't do this on my own.'

'You mean bipolar,' Bethany corrects him.

'I prefer manic depressive,' Aldous says. 'I get periods of mania and then I get depressed. What's the North Pole and the South Pole got to do with it?'

'You're right,' Bethany says, 'the poles are rather similar.'

'There's something there,' Aldous says, pointing his chopsticks at her. 'I don't go white to white – pole to pole. I go blazing red to pitch black.' He pauses. 'There's a gag there. See? Told you I needed you.'

Bethany goes back with Aldous to his flat.

'I'm not sleeping with you,' she warns, 'not staying the night.'

'We're going to work,' Aldous says, a little wanly, disappointed. 'Yes. Come up with a new act.'

The flat is small and incredibly neat – a bedroom, painted black with a black blind, a kitchenette and a bathroom with a shower. The sitting room contains a sofa, a TV, and a desk beneath some shelves filled with books.

'Very spartan,' Bethany observes, prowling around – she's curious about dwelling places, perhaps because she's had so many herself in the last year or so. They tell you a lot about the occupants.

Aldous makes her a cup of coffee and sits at the desk facing her on the sofa.

'How do we start?' he asks.

'Open a newspaper,' Bethany says, 'see what grabs your attention – instantly, no thinking about it.'

He fishes in the wastepaper basket and takes out a *Standard* and begins to flick through.

'Right,' he says, after a minute. 'Here's something – makes me fume. Pets aren't called "pets" any more, they're called "companions". How bloody stupid.'

'There you are,' Bethany says, 'instant material. Take a pet on stage, introduce it as your "companion".'

'I can't take a dog or a cat on stage,' Aldous complains.

'I'm not talking about mammals,' Bethany says. 'We need something more surreal. Remember?'

Bethany experiences a simultaneous thrill of pride and anxiety when she sees the name 'Shel Stone' on the poster of comics appearing at the Quota System. Then, in the auditorium at the back, she feels strangely anxious again, even a bit sick, as if she were going on stage, not Aldous.

She watches unsmilingly and silently, with apprehension, as the audience laugh. Shel starts with his usual banging and drunken fall on stage and says, 'Hello Brisbane,' in a good Australian accent and launches into an Australian anecdote before the yells and the boos quieten him. He asks them to guess his day job. More obscene suggestions.

'I'm a cage-fighter,' Shel says to incredulous heckling, and from the wings a small hamster cage is thrown on stage that he then proceeds to stamp flat with maximum force and aggression.

'I'm against animals being imprisoned,' he bellows. 'So I fight cages whenever I see them.'

Then he reminds everyone that pets aren't called pets any more, no, they're called *companions*.

'I've brought my companion on stage,' he says. 'He's an ant, called Archie.' He reaches into his pocket and holds out a finger that 'Archie' is perched upon. 'He does backflips,' Shel says and puts Archie on the ground. 'Go on, boy, backflip, back-flip.' After ten seconds more cajoling ('He was a bit hung-over this morning') Archie still won't do a backflip. So Shel stamps on him. 'Sod it. Plenty more where he came from.'

Bethany relaxes – this is all her stuff and it has worked well. Surreality, that is Shel's schtick.

Then Shel goes off-message. 'Hands down all you guys who watch Internet porn,' he says. 'See, ladies, it's universal.' Then he goes into a riff about the 'pornification of everyday life' and Bethany senses half his audience leaving him, the room going quiet.

Bethany has applied to twenty-four drama schools in the London area. In the space of three days she has had eleven rejections – then she had an acceptance from the English National Institute of Drama. The address was in Hampstead, no interview required ('because of your impressive film-acting experience'); fees £3,000 a term plus VAT.

Bethany weighs this up shrewdly. There is the problem of the fees; there is the problem of chicanery. Still it is an offer, she thinks: if I can't go to RADA or LAMDA then at least I can go to ENID. She accepts the place offered. What she needs, she realizes, is some stability in her life – however half-baked or half-cocked or half-assed ENID is, she calcu-lates, she might be able to make it work for her.

Coming home late from Aldous's flat – she is sleeping with him but not spending the night – Bethany is frightened by the shadowy figure of a man trying to open the front door of her mother's house.

'I'm calling the police!' she shouts.

'No, no. Please,' the man says with a heavy accent. 'I living here.'

A light goes on in the porch and Bethany sees he has a set of keys in his hand.

'I am Demerson,' he says. 'I living with Alannah.'

Bethany introduces herself and they shake hands. Demerson is a thickset young guy, handsome with astonishingly white teeth, but with strangely old-fashioned-looking curly long hair – almost as if it has been permed. He looks a bit like a footballer from the 1970s.

Alannah finally opens the door and lets them both in. Bethany thinks it's time she moved out again.

Shel's new act is going down well at the Quota System. He does variations of the Archie the Ant gag. He invites an audience member up on stage to stroke Archie. Then he or she stands on him. 'You killed him! You killed Archie!' Tears, recriminations, abuse.

He and Bethany work on new material. Bethany comes up with another runner about how crap children's jokes are. Shel, she has to admit, does a fine free-associating job deconstructing them. 'When are your shoes like the sun? When is a door not a door? No, you little prat – your shoes do not look like the sun when they shine. They look like clean fucking shoes!'

Bethany goes up to Hampstead to inspect ENID and is surprised to find a bona-fide acting school with classrooms and a small but professionally well-equipped theatre. All the other students she meets there seem to be foreign, however. Her mother says she'll pay for the first term and Demerson finds her a job dog-walking at £20 an hour, as many hours as she wants.

Bethany is suspicious – this is not normal: everything seems to be going well and this is not how the world works – no. Life is a dysfunctioning system, she knows: failure, breakdown, disappointment, frustration – where are you hiding?

Aldous is offered a gig at a comedy festival at the Soho Theatre. A TV company has asked him to audition. Bethany is due to start at ENID in a week and when Aldous suggests she move in with him it seems the natural thing to do. They are lying in bed when he asks her. She says she'll go back to her mother's and fetch a few things – see how it works for a week or so, she says. Nothing hard and fast, you understand – a test. Aldous slips out of bed to open a bottle of wine to do honour to their potential cohabitation.

'You're incredibly thin, Aldous,' Bethany says. 'I'm thin but you're thinner than me. You're not a male anorexic, are you?'

Aldous thinks about this, strums his ribs with a thumb. 'Just not very interested in food,' he says. 'Like drink, though.'

He opens the wine and they celebrate.

Aldous gives her a spare set of keys, symbol of the fluidity of their new arrangement.

'Come and go,' he says. 'Be capricious.'

Bethany returns home to pick up a few clothes, books and her make-up. A rucksack's worth of commitment, she says to herself, climbing back up the stairs to Aldous's flat. She's about to ring the bell but instead decides to use her new keys and lets herself in.

Music is playing in the sitting room but there's no sign of Aldous. She hears the loo flush and heads for the bathroom – she can set her face cream out, her stuff, claim her space. Then she stops. Aldous clearly hasn't heard her come in and for some reason is talking to himself, it seems.

Bethany leans forward, ear to the door and hears what he's saying.

'Come on Archie,' he says. 'Time for your bath, there's a good boy. Hop in. We'll lather you up, get you all nice and clean. Bethany's coming to stay. Don't want to be a dirty little ant-mucker, do we?'

Bethany stands there for a second, thinking. Then she turns and lets herself quietly out of the flat.

Things go wrong.

## Nine . . .

Bethany is running into Victoria station trying not to look too distraught but probably failing, she thinks. She glances back, wondering if somehow Demerson has managed to follow her but she can see no one in the thinning crowd of the hurrying commuters. Her eyes flick to the departure board looking for destinations. Trains that are about to depart for distant destinations. She sees: Hastings. Leaving in three minutes. Battle of Hastings. War. 1066. Arrow in the eye. That's for me. Buy a ticket on the train. She runs to the platform.

*She had come home, heavy-hearted, to prepare for her mother's hen party. Why would a woman of fifty-three want to have a hen party, given that her first marriage had turned out to be a grievous and miserable train wreck? She rang the doorbell and Demerson answered. 'Hey, Bethany,' he said. 'You mama she out.'*

On the train Bethany pays for her single to Hastings, end of the line. £32 – fuck. She has £4 and some change left. And no mobile phone. How could she have run out without her phone? How was she going to function – to live? Never mind, she says to herself, you're safe, that's the main thing.

Demerson can't follow you. He could never know you caught a train to Hastings.

*Bethany went to her room and looked at her dresses hanging in the cupboard. She picked out the red one – the Coco Fennell – and laid it on her bed. Now she had her own flat she really should clear her stuff out – especially given that Demerson would be living here in future, in the 'family home'. She quite liked Demerson – he was friendly, jolly – but she wished her mother wasn't marrying him. However, she told herself firmly, it wasn't her life – it was her mother's. She had her own road to travel and the nest had to be left once and for all – she was twenty-four years old, for God's sake. She had to stop coming back home. Maybe this marriage was a blessing of sorts – it would drive her away – make her truly independent, finally. She took her clothes off and tried on the red dress. Looked good. Bloody zip. How were you meant to – . Demerson came into the room without knocking. 'No worry, Bethany, I zip you. Very beautiful dress. Sexy.'*

After Hayward's Heath, heading south-east, the names become strange, as if she's entering a foreign country. This train seems to stop at every station, she thinks. Plumpton, Lewes, Polegate, Pevensey and Westham, Cooden Beach, Collington. It's as if I've fallen down a rabbit hole and entered this bizarre toytown England, she says to herself. Diddley-dum, diddley-dum. She rests her forehead on the cold window and looks out at the late afternoon landscape. Trying not to cry.

*Demerson zipped her up and before she could say 'thank you' he was feeling her breasts, reaching round from behind, pulling her against him. 'I real like you, Bethany,' he mumbled in her ear, and kissed her neck. Bethany thought: this is my soon-to-be stepfather. 'You beautiful, ver' hot, Bethany,' he said, nuzzling into her hair as she struggled, shouting his name, saying, 'Fuck off, Demerson!'*

The train stops again, seemingly having gone only another 200 yards since the last station. She sees the sign, mistily, through her tears: BEXHILL-ON-SEA. She thinks at once – I'm getting off here. This is the place for me. She feels safe, all of a sudden.

*In her struggling, Bethany managed to free her right arm and, reflexively, swung her elbow round and thwacked Demerson on the side of his face. He went down in a sudden slump, as if he'd been felled by a gunshot, shouting, cursing loudly in his Brazilian Portuguese. She stepped back. He was on his hands and knees, shaking his head. Her elbow was aching – she must have connected with his temple, she thought, in a momentary flash of rationality. Knockout blow. She watched him keel over, then right himself. He tried to stand but she was out of the room, slamming the door behind her. At the bottom of the stairs she realized she had left her handbag, her mobile and her wallet in her room. She flung open the drawer in the hall table where her mother left money for the cleaning lady. She grabbed some notes, some coins. Hauled her coat on, hearing her door open and Demerson emerge. He was shouting down the stairs, 'I get you, Bethany! I find you!' Then she was gone. Out of the door, down Hollywood Road, running for the Tube station at Fulham Broadway. Not looking back.*

Bethany leaves the station at Bexhill-on-Sea and walks down Eversley Road, instinctively heading for the coast, the sea. She passes a phone box and remembers what has happened. Her mother and her friends are meeting in a karaoke bar in Putney. Drinks, nibbles, songs. She steps into the phone box, dials her mother's mobile and shells in a precious pound coin.

'This is Alannah Mellmoth. Please leave a message after the tone.'

She thinks fast. 'Really, really, sorry Mum, I can't make it tonight . . .' She improvises. 'Sholto's ill. I have to take him to hospital. I'll call later. Love you.'

Beep-beep-beep. Sholto will do whatever she tells him, back her to the hilt.

She hangs up. Now's not the time to tell her mother about her future husband.

*As she raced to Fulham Broadway she kept thinking she could hear running steps behind her. Could Demerson have followed her so quickly? Surely not. She paused and looked back – and thought she saw him! She ran into the station and went to the very end of the platform. No sign. A train came and she waited until the very last moment, ducking in between the sliding doors as they closed. No – he must have missed her.*

Bethany stands at the end of Albany Road and looks at the De La Warr Pavilion in some amazement. What is this extraordinary building doing on this modest seafront? Like an art-deco spaceship that has landed – like that film, what's it called? *Alien*? No. Yes, *Alien*, the first one. She goes inside and finds the ladies' lavatory off the lobby. In a stall she sits down on the toilet and allows tears to flow, silently, her shoulders shaking. She calms herself. She's safe – she doesn't need to do anything. Don't think, girl, don't think, she says to herself. Just let life flow by you for an hour or so.

She checks her money. £3.77. She's hungry. She mooches around the lobby for a while and goes into the shop, pretending to look at the postcards and the merchandise. She picks up a free brochure: *The Official Guide to Bexhill-on-Sea. The*

*Birthplace of British Motor Racing*. She slips it in her pocket and wanders out on to the promenade.

Bethany walks up the West Parade, the shingle beach and calm grey sea on her left, the light in the sky beginning to fade as evening comes on. She imagines her mother in the karaoke bar – she'll be first up, singing '(I Can't Get No) Satisfaction'. Bethany smiles, despite herself: her mother thinks she's got a great voice – which she hasn't – and she always claims that Bethany has inherited her talent as a singer. When Bethany once told her she was going to join a band as its singer she saw the clear green jealousy shine in her mother's eyes. She tries to stop thinking about her mother. How is she going to tell her about Demerson? What's the best strategy in this situation? 'Mum, by the way, your future husband tried to fuck me.' Bethany feels her anger mount. She rubs her bruised elbow. She hopes Demerson's head is very sore, throbbing, bruised – maybe she's blackened his eye. Good.

She reaches into her pocket, unthinkingly looking for her pack of cigarettes. Not there. In her handbag in her room. She needs a cigarette – very badly.

The Sovereign Light Café, it says. A small wooden boxy caff on the Parade with a few aluminium chairs and tables outside. Bethany wanders around and peers inside. Wainscotted wooden walls painted a creamy primrose yellow with purple blinds, two or three customers hunched over their cuppas. She shivers – it's getting dark and the windows of the Sovereign Light Café glow with unearthly warm light in the advancing gloom.

*Demerson never looked at her in that sidelong way – that way men look at you when they think you don't know what they're thinking but you do. There was nothing in his manner towards her that would have made her suspicious or uneasy in his company. A stocky, quite good-looking Brazilian man who had a window-cleaning business – which was how her mother had met him. He and his team cleaned the windows of the office block where her office was. Bethany had thought it was just another fling – her mother was attracted to foreign men – but she was wrong, it was more serious this time. Any nationality would do for her mother – she wasn't fussy – as long as the man wasn't English. She'd had a Greek boyfriend, a Ghanaian boyfriend, a Croatian boyfriend, two Spanish boyfriends. Bethany imagined it was her subconscious way of getting back at Zane – or of eroding her memories of him with all these foreign men, so different.*

Bethany does another turn around the Sovereign Light Café, thinking. Maybe that's the answer – she should call her father, see what he suggests. But her father is in Los Angeles and she has no mobile phone and £3.77 in her pocket. She stops by a blackboard and looks at the list of sandwiches on offer. Ham Mustard Tom. Egg Mayo. Brie Cranberry. Cheese. Crab Sticks Mayo. White or Wholemeal Bread. She feels the saliva squirt in her mouth and goes inside.

There's a young guy wiping down the serving area.

'We're closing,' he says, without looking at her.

Rude, Bethany thinks. 'Cup of tea to go and a Kit-Kat,' she says.

Now he looks at her and she can see his interest suddenly quickens. She realizes she must appear somewhat exotic in her black coat and her red dress here on the West Parade at Bexhill-on-Sea. He's dark, this guy – lean, almost gaunt – and he looks very tired, his eyes shadowed. He hasn't shaved for a few days. He serves her the tea and hands her the Kit-Kat with a new friendly smile. She pays him. Now she has less than £2.

'Closing time, gents,' he says to the locals. He has a slight burr to his voice. *Toime*. He's wearing chef's checked trousers and clogs with his sweatshirt.

That's the look, she analyses, that exhausted chef's look. Too many drugs, she thinks, as she walks past him, saying, 'Night. Bye.'

Bethany sips her hot tea from its Styrofoam cup and walks round the Sovereign Light Café. The young guy pulls down the blinds and the lights go off. At the back there's a busted aluminium chair by a wheelie bin. Bethany sits on the chair – rocky, but it holds. She folds the collar of her coat up and eats her Kit-Kat. She almost feels normal – out of the sea breeze the late spring air is mild. She takes a big gulp of hot tea, wanting the throat-burn, the chest-glow. She would kill for a smoke, she thinks. She looks out to sea and, at the dark line where the water meets the sky at the horizon, she sees a powerful light flash – miles away.

The back door opens and the chef comes out. He looks at her.

'What're you doing there?' he says, locking the door behind him. He's wearing a parka with a fur hood, jeans and trainers, changed out of his chef gear, carrying a plastic bag that no doubt contains his clogs and checked trousers.

'No law against sitting in a chair, is there?' Bethany says, with some aggression.

He shrugs and rummages in his pocket, taking out a pack of ten cigarettes.

'Can I have one?' Bethany asks. 'Please. I'd be really grateful.'

He lights her cigarette and then his own.

'Where you from?' he says.

Bethany decides to tell him. 'I've run away from London,' she says. 'A man attacked me – and I'm sort of hiding out.'

The chef looks at her closely. 'I hate London,' he says, simply, as if that covers every possible eventuality, as if that explains everything. He leans against the café wall. 'Yeah. Worked there for a while,' he smiles at her. 'Not my cup of tea, darling. I do like to be beside the seaside, I do.' The smile makes him look different for a moment, all the weariness gone. He has white, even teeth – Bethany notes: she likes that in a man.

'This your café?' Bethany asks.

'Nah – just on for the day,' he says. 'Someone called in sick. I'm with an agency. Job here – job there. Suits me.' He frowns as if he's thinking of something. 'Wouldn't mind owning one of these caffs, though,' he says. 'Make a fortune in the summer. Laze around all winter. Good life.'

Bethany thinks: he's right – your life would be very simple. Here on the front at Bexhill-on-Sea, working hard half the year, travelling the other, doing the things you wanted to do knowing you would be coming back, money to be earned, security . . .

'What's your name?' she asks.

'Carl,' he says.

'Carl what?'

He looks at her, suspiciously.

'Why do you want to know?'

Bethany stubs out her cigarette under her shoe.

'I like to know people's full names,' she says. 'It differentiates them.'

'Carl Trueman,' he says, with a little cough.

Bethany Trueman, Bethany thinks and is immediately angry with herself – she has to stop doing this, it's ridiculous.

'Bethany Mellmoth,' she says.

Carl Trueman holds his hand out and they shake hands – she finds this formal gesture oddly reassuring.

'Well, I got to be going,' he says. 'Got an early shift. Cheers.' He walks two steps then spins round. 'You going to stay here all night?'

'Maybe,' Bethany says.

He shrugs off his parka and hands it to her. 'You'll need this, then.'

Bethany stands there surprised.

'Two fags left in the pack. Bring the parka to me in the morning. Seafront Brasserie on the De La Warr Parade.' He points. 'About a mile down there. I'll make you some breakfast.'

Bethany doesn't know what to say as she takes his parka.

'Have you got a phone?' she asks. 'I just need to send one text.'

He hands her his phone and she texts her mother: DONT MARRY DEMERSON. DANGEROUS. I WILL EXPLAIN. BETHANY XXX. She hands Carl his phone back.

'See you tomorrow,' she says. 'Thanks.'

He walks away. 'Keep warm, Bethany,' he says, over his shoulder. As he walks away Bethany sees the light flash out at sea.

'What's that flash out on the horizon?' she calls after him.

'That's the Sovereign Light,' he says. 'Massive lighthouse platform. That's how the café got its name.'

Bethany is surprisingly warm in Carl Trueman's parka with the hood up. She wedges the chair against the wheelie bin so she can rest her head against it and hugs her knees to her body. The fur fringe of the hood frames the dark patch of sea and sky that contains the Sovereign Light and she counts its steady flashes, stopping after a hundred, trying to remember the name of that book where there was a light – a green light, she recalls – that has some heavy symbolism attached to it. Hope – symbol of hope. Perhaps the Sovereign Light could be her symbol of hope, she thinks idly, deciding to stay awake until dawn, reaching into the pocket to fish out one of Carl's remaining two cigarettes. Then she might look as tired as he does.

Bethany wakes at dawn to the sound of a dog yapping. She stirs, stiff, and realizes one hand has gone to sleep. She massages the blood back into it, stands and runs on the spot for a while. She needs a pee very badly.

There's a man on the beach with a small dog and a metal detector, waving it slowly over the pebbles, to and fro.

'Morning!' he shouts at her.

'Morning,' she calls back, unreflectingly, as if it's the most natural thing in the world to spend the night sleeping on an aluminium chair in a borrowed parka outside a café on the West Parade in Bexhill-on-Sea.

Yes, she thinks, and heads off east, down the promenade, in the direction of the Seafront Brasserie where Carl will be serving up the first of the day's breakfasts. She would kill for some bacon and eggs. Carl Trueman. Well named, she thinks – like the Sovereign Light Café.

She walks on, more briskly now, the silver sea on her right, the first rays of the morning sun striking the perfect hemispherical curves of the De La Warr Pavilion's glassed-in staircase, setting star-spangles and flare-dazzles dancing in her eyes, and for some reason she feels oddly sure that all will be fine now – now that she's here in Bexhill-on-Sea, Birthplace of British Motor Racing, heading for a breakfast to be served by her new friend Carl Trueman – and that all her problems will be solved, one way or another, eventually.

## *Ten . . .*

Bethany Mellmoth sits behind the reception desk in the No Parking Gallery in Dalston, East London, on 20 December, feeling a little sorry for herself. It wasn't her fault that her drama school had gone suddenly bankrupt, but to have had to become a gallerina once more was a major disappointment – it was never in her plans and, moreover, the current show is both depressing her and driving her quietly insane, she thinks. The show is called *The Times of Sand*. Throughout the capacious gallery space are various sizes of neat sand cones – one must be half a tonne, another could be held in two cupped hands – and embedded in each cone of sand is a timepiece of some kind. An hourglass, a kitchen-wall clock, a metronome, a carriage clock, a ladies' watch in the smallest cone, a grandfather clock, a sundial, a winking green LED timer . . . Moreover, an amplified *tick-tock*, *tick-tock* is being played through the gallery's PA system. It's not so much the irritant of the noise that bothers her, as the reminder that – also – her life is slipping away in those audible seconds. That's what depresses her, she realizes. Two years ago she was working in No Parking. And here she is, back behind the desk as if nothing had happened, as if no life had intervened in the meantime.

Bethany picks up her laptop and goes downstairs to the storeroom where there's a small desk. There's a buzzer on the front door that will alert her if anyone wants to come in. *The Times of Sand* with its remorseless ticking reminds her that she's only written three pages of her novel, *2084*. It's an overt homage to George Orwell but not even the month she spent on the Isle of Jura seeking inspiration made her write any faster.

She opens her laptop and changes the name of the central character from Churchill to Jones. This seems like progress and she begins to feel better. Her phone gives a little shrill ping. It's a text from her father in Los Angeles, she sees, entitled SPOOKY. Oh God, she thinks, what now? No, it's not SPOOKY, it's SP100KY. It's a reservation number. He's booked her on a flight to Los Angeles. He wants her to come and stay with him for Christmas.

Bethany's mother looks at her in a strange way, her face mildly contorted. A kind of baffled hostility, Bethany thinks, or bitter incredulity. Then Alannah turns abruptly and pours herself three fingers of vodka and squeezes the juice from a wedge of lime into it.

'I won't go if you don't want me to,' Bethany says. 'I just wanted to let you know that he'd asked me.'

Bethany is fully aware that, paradoxically, the bitterness engendered by her parents' divorce has intensified in the many years since it occurred. Time is no healer, at least as far as her mother is concerned.

'How could you want to spend Christmas with that . . . that piece of filth, that scum?' Alannah asks, reasonably, then takes a large swallow of her drink.

'He's my father. I haven't seen him for nearly two years. I feel guilty for what I did. He forgave her, they got married, for God's sake. I never expected he'd divorce Chi-Chi –'

'You did him a massive favour, my sweet. Serves him bloody well right.' She exhales. 'Go if you must. I'll be fine with Ogunmokun. In fact it might be better if you aren't here, come to think of it.'

Ogunmokun is her mother's Nigerian boyfriend. He's a medical student. Bethany really likes him.

'Have you never been to LA?' Howard Christopher asks, astonished. He's drinking from a can of Speyhawk Special Brew.

'No,' Bethany says. 'I'm quite curious, actually.'

'Never been to El Lay. Good Lord. How old are you? Twenty-eight? Twenty-nine?'

'Twenty-four,' Bethany says.

'That's the time to go, darling. When you're young. I can't stand the place.'

'Can I get you a glass?' Bethany asks.

'It's better straight from the tin,' Howard says. 'More kick.'

'I thought I might stay on a bit, you know,' Bethany says. 'Having gone all the way over there.'

'When do we open in the new year?' Howard asks.

'January the fifteenth.'

'Really? I think I'm skiing then . . . You take your time, darling. Your job is safe.' He laughs and glugs Speyhawk, reaching for his cigarettes. 'Last time I was in LA I was arrested for smoking – outside. Terrible place. You'll be back.'

On the plane to Los Angeles, Bethany opens her father's book. *A FALSE ECONOMY: Aspirations, Evasions and Illusions in Everyday Life* by Zane Mellmoth. It's her father's second book, after *Novaville*, and far and away his most successful, having reached number eight on the *New York Times* non-fiction chart. He sent this new one to her almost six months ago when it was published but somehow she can't bring herself to read it. Too close to the bone. She has read the inscription – 'With love! Hang tight! Big Daddy' – and has studied the author's photograph and bio. 'Zane Mellmoth is Professor of Psychogeography at Brandiwine University, California. He lives.' In the author's photograph he looks absurdly handsome – lean, unshaven, short grey hair, a black V-neck T-shirt. He's holding a pencil in his hand – an old-fashioned wooden pencil. It's all deliberate, Bethany realizes, all *knowing* – as if he's somehow living out the very concept of his subtitle. It always gives her something of a shock to realize that her father is well over half a century old.

She puts the book down and picks up her journal.

22 December, en route to LA. A turmoil of emotions is raging in me. Guilt, principally. Why did I ever tell Dad about Chi-Chi's betrayal? What if I'd just kept quiet?

She crosses it out, vigorously. The man beside her has come back from the toilet, changed. He's wearing shorts and flip-flops – ready for the heat, those Californian rays. He has fat hairy legs, Bethany notices. People shouldn't be allowed to fly in shorts, she thinks, it's disgusting. There's still three hours to go and I have to sit here seeing his horrible legs out of the corner of my eye. She puts on her sunglasses and hunches away from him, looking out of the window at the clouds, a line coming into her mind from a novel she's read. We are the first generation to see clouds from both sides, from below and above. Who said that? George Orwell? No. Then she thinks: that's not true. If you climbed a high mountain you could see clouds from above; you could look down on the tops of clouds. Even cavemen, Neanderthals, must have looked down on clouds.

Bethany comes through from customs and immigration at LAX and glances around for her father – where's Zane? He's not there. She closes her eyes – typical – and wanders about for a while, through the throng of limo drivers. She sees a young guy chatting to a couple of chauffeurs. He has a sign under his arm and she can tell it has 'MELLMOTH' written on it. She taps him on the shoulder. He turns. He has brown skin and the whitest teeth, a close soft beard and his longish hair is held up in a knotted bun.

'I'm Mellmoth,' she says, not smiling. Just do your job, mate.

'Hey, Bethany,' he says, shaking her hand. 'Happy holidays. You were out fast. I'm Jagjit. Everyone calls me Jag.'

He takes her suitcase and she walks with Jag into the car park. Jagjit – he must be Indian, she thinks. His accent is pure Californian, however. He's skinny, wearing jeans and a loose white linen shirt. He's quite attractive, Bethany thinks, for a limo driver.

Jag opens the door to a curvy-looking low-slung car and Bethany eases herself in.

'What kind of car is this?' she asks as he settles down beside her.

'It's a Tesla,' he says. 'It's totally electric.' He smiles. 'It's not mine, it's your father's. I'm his driver. Part-time.'

He takes out a card and hands it to her.

JAGFILMCO, she reads. Chief executive: Jagjit Chaturredi.

'Where is my father?' she asks as they pull away from the airport.

'He's mentoring. He asked me to pick you up. We're not far away.'

'Where are we headed?'

'Venice.'

Zane Mellmoth's place in Venice is one street back from the beach. A big clapboard two-storey, split-level house painted pale blue. Jag lets her in, tells her to make herself at home and then leaves, wishing her 'Happy holidays'. Bethany stands in the middle of the wide sitting room – white sofas on stained wood, rug-strewn floors, a stone fireplace, abstract paintings on the walls – and feels absurdly like crying, wishing she'd never come. She wanders upstairs looking for a room that might be hers and passes a terrace where a naked woman is lying sunbathing.

*

'So you and Regina have met,' Zane Mellmoth says, putting his arm around Bethany.

Regina is now clothed. However, after Bethany coughed politely and introduced herself, Regina stayed naked for at least half an hour as they chatted before she pulled on a towelling dressing gown and went to take a shower.

'Oh, yes,' Regina says. 'I now have the whole backstory. You're a dark horse, big boy.'

Her father laughs, visibly enjoying the banter. He releases Bethany and tries to grab Regina, who backs away, her hands raised in a karate pose.

'These hands are lethal weapons,' she says.

'All my secrets are safe with Bethany,' Zane says. 'You devil-woman, you.' They both laugh – like fiends, Bethany thinks.

After supper Bethany goes for a walk with her father along the beach, heading for a bar. Regina doesn't drink, it turns out. And she's also a vegan. Regina is his new girlfriend, he says. We're very close. She has a small chain of deluxe spas called Therapositi. Santa Barbara, Carmel, Pacific Palisades. Hugely successful. At least she's over forty, Bethany thinks, as they sit down and order some wine. Her father tells her more about Regina, how they met, how their relationship is on a new serious plane – marriage might be on the cards: she could be the third Mrs Mellmoth – how she's the cleanest woman he's ever known. Bethany concedes this might be true: Regina is always massaging a gel of some kind into her hands.

'What happened to Chi-Chi, after the divorce, and the baby – Arnie?' Bethany asks, carefully.

'Actually, it was a girl, not a boy. She's coming over for Christmas.'

'Chi-Chi?'

'No. Light.'

'Light?'

'The baby's called Light. She's a girl. I get to see her one weekend a month. Californian law is very . . .' He thinks. 'Draconian, when it comes to divorce.'

'But *she* was cheating on you.'

'I would never have suspected – if you hadn't told me.'

'That's what's troubling me, Dad. You see, I never meant to break up –'

'No. No. Nooooo. No-no-no.' Her father takes her hand, kisses it. 'You did me the biggest favour, pumpkin. You did the right thing. You found out what Chi-Chi was up to. I forgave her – we got married, for Christ's sake. You told me – you had to. Then I found out it had never stopped – the cheating, the affairs. She is one sensational liar, I will give her that. I might still have been with that . . .' He searches for a word. 'Ball-breaking, hate-filled, *basket-case*,' he says with venom, with bitterness. 'You warned me and I didn't listen – but you saved my life, darling.' He smiles, raising his glass. 'Anyway. Everything's great now. Happy holidays.'

Bethany writes in her journal:

Christmas Day. The temperature is 92 degrees. A chef arrived and prepared roast turkey with all the trimmings. We ate outside on the roof terrace. Regina pointed at the Brussels sprouts and said: what are those things? *Eugh*. I kept forgetting to pronounce her name properly. She became quite cross. She said to me, 'Honey, it *doesn't* rhyme with vagina.' Regeeena, Regeeeeeeena. After lunch Jag arrived in the Tesla with a German girl called Beate and the little baby, Light. Beate is in her twenties and on the plump side. She is Light's nanny. Only Beate and Dad are allowed to touch the baby, it turned out. I said to Beate: she's my half-sister, for God's sake. Beate said

I had to get permission from Chi-Chi. Light is nearly two years old. She seems very sweet. A surprisingly quiet, thoughtful child.

On Boxing Day Bethany borrows some running shoes and goes for a run along the beach. She stops after two minutes, thinking she might vomit. I must get fitter, she says to herself. She rolls a cigarette and strolls down to the surf edge for a tranquil smoke. The Pacific Ocean looks grey, like slate, even though the sun is shining and the sky is uninterrupted blue. How many times have I stood on a beach looking at the waves, contemplating my life, Bethany asks herself? The question is rhetorical, she decides.

Feeling a sudden craving for food, she wanders back to the promenade and finds a cool pizza joint called Peet-za-za! She takes her seat, orders a margherita and consults the menu. She looks up to see Regina sitting in a corner with a beer and a pepperoni pizza with fries on the side. Regina glances over and their eyes meet. They both look away. It never happened. The waiter – a girl with a ring in her nose – rollerblades over.

'Hi there, welcome to Peet-za-za! Ready to order? My name is Naiyala-tae. Happy holidays.'

Jag is driving Beate, Light and Bethany back to Chi-Chi's house. It's 27 December. Bethany has hitched a ride as she needs closure on the whole Chi-Chi/Zane Mellmoth divorce issue, and her role in it. If nothing else this will make her trip to LA worthwhile.

Chi-Chi lives in a cantilevered moderne house high on Coldwater Canyon. As they wind up the swerving road – air con at full blast – Bethany spots a life-size Santa sleigh and four model reindeer on a front lawn and then a house bedecked with thousands of winking fairy lights. Oh yes, it's Christmas, she remembers. Of course, the season of good-will. Bethany steps out of the car, feeling a bit sick about meeting Chi-Chi, following Beate and Light into the house. Chi-Chi stands in the hall, waiting. 'Happy holidays!' she cries and greets Bethany like her oldest friend – hugs and kisses – and showers compliments on her: her hair, her skin, her jeans, her necklace, her shoes. Bethany keeps a smile on while noting that Chi-Chi is living in some style for an out-of-work dancer. Chi-Chi allows Bethany to hold Light for a few seconds and kiss her on the forehead then Beate takes her off upstairs for her nap. Jag says he'll wait in the Tesla – he has some calls to make.

Chi-Chi leads Bethany to a terrace and offers her some tea. Bethany says yes, please, thank you, not daring to ask if she can smoke. They drink their tea and finally Bethany summons up the necessary courage.

'Chi-Chi, I want to apologize – I have to apologize.'

'No. Stop. Stop now. You did me the biggest favour, girl. Seriously.' She flicks back her long, incredibly straight black hair. 'I just need to know one thing: how did you figure it out? I mean before you told Zane.'

Bethany flashes back. Christmas in London. Christmas lunch in the Fedora Palace Grand. Chi-Chi pregnant with what turned out to be Light. Bethany swallows.

'You went to get Dad from the gym in the hotel and you left your phone behind. It rang. I picked it up and before I could say "Chi-Chi's phone" this guy started talking. Intimately. Very intimately. Extremely intimately.'

'What did he say?'

'He said he was in a hot tub, thinking about you and that he was actually –'

'Got it. Left you in no doubt.'

'None at all. I had to tell my dad. It was a real moral dilemma. I couldn't stay silent because I knew, you see –'

'Don't blame yourself. He said he'd forgiven me – but then he put a private detective on me when we got back to LA. It was over in two months . . . I just could never figure out how he figured it out.' She frowns. Then smiles brightly. 'Best thing that could have happened.'

'And you have Light.'

'Excuse me?'

'Little Light. My sister. Light Mellmoth.'

'I won't have her use that name. Not Mellmoth. Never.'

On the drive back to Venice with Jag, Bethany is thoughtful. Has she closure? Chi-Chi bears her no ill will. She seems rich and happy. Moreover, Bethany thinks, her father is in a new relationship. Regina is age-appropriate. Bethany keeps forgetting that Chi-Chi, when she was briefly her stepmother, was in fact younger than her. Everything for the best, then. Jag is talking.

'Sorry?'

'I may be coming to London. Next month, maybe. Perhaps we could have a drink.'

Bethany refocusses and says she'd love to meet up with Jag in London. When he drops her at the house they exchange numbers. Bethany takes out his card when he's driven off. Jagjit Chaturredi . . . Bethany Chaturredi . . . She has to stop doing this.

Bethany goes in but the place is empty. There's a note above the fireplace from her father. He and Regina have gone up to Santa Barbara to the Therapositi spa there to 'detox'. Join us or stay on, he invites her. Chill. We'll be back in a week. Happy holidays, Dad. Bethany sighs. Typical. I come all this way. All the same, she's now living in a large comfortable house in Venice, California. There are worse places to be. Maybe she could do some work on *2084*. Hang out with Jag . . .

Bethany writes in her journal:

> 29 December. I find it hard to work here, for some reason. I haven't written a word of *2084* except to change 'Jones' back to 'Churchill'. And I'm bored. I called Dad and he said come up to Santa Barbara but I don't feel like being with him and Regina. I told Dad about my meeting with Chi-Chi, how it went. Cool, he said. Then I remembered – thinking about the surnames in *2084*. What's Chi-Chi's maiden name, I asked? She won't let Light be called Light Mellmoth. I know, Dad said, she's a very bitter woman. So what's her maiden name? T'an, he said. Mandarin Chinese. Tee, apostrophe, ay, en. That's Light's name? I repeated, shocked. It's impossible. What's wrong with it? he said. I'm sorry, I said, you can't let someone go through life being called Light T'an. I think that's when I decided I had to go back to London.

The mood in the Tesla is strange, Bethany thinks, as Jag drives her back to LAX. Something has changed and she wonders if it's because they're going to see each other again. They are no longer 'driver' and 'passenger'. Jag keeps glancing at her and smiling, showing his incredibly white teeth.

He pulls up at the drop-off point and lifts her bag out for her. 'Well . . .' he says. Probably standing just a little too close.

Bethany doesn't know what comes over her but she feels she has to kiss Jag. There has to be something about this trip that she'll cherish. So she puts her arms around him and they kiss. Then they kiss like lovers for a full sixty seconds. Bethany breaks off.

'See you in London,' she says, managing to get the words out.

She turns and walks away.

'Bethany!' Jag calls.

Bethany freezes. Please don't say it, she says to herself as she turns. Please.

Jag waves. 'Happy holidays!'

She waves back, wordless, smiling, then turns away and strides briskly towards the plane that will carry her back to London and her own world and a whole new year beginning.

# PART III

# The Vanishing Game: An Adventure . . .

> It has been my philosophy of life that difficulties
> vanish when faced boldly.

> Isaac Asimov

## Part One: The Girl with the Broken Ankle

It's all about perception, so they tell you. Was I the right
guy in the wrong place? Or was I the wrong guy in the
right place? From my point of view – *my* perception – I was
the wrong guy in the wrong place so it was no surprise
that my troubles multiplied. But this is all with benefit of
hindsight and its 20/20 vision. At the time I thought my
luck had changed. At last, I said to myself, things are going
my way. And I needed a break; I was due a break, or so I
thought.

London. October.

Three days after my flat had been burgled and five days
after my car had been sideswiped by a white van that didn't
stop, my agent, Gervase Somerville, called.

'Alec, darling boy, you've got an audition. An "American"
movie, no less.'

I tried not to let my excitement overwhelm me.

'What's it called?'

'Ah . . .' Rustle of papers. 'Um . . . Yes, *Transfigured Night*.'

'Isn't that a Schoenberg sextet?'

'Quite possibly. Anyway it happens to be the title of this fillum.'

The script was embargoed, he said. I thought this a good sign. And the producers were in final negotiation with an A-list director, he added, they would announce next week.

'Where's the meeting?'

'The Metropole Grande, Mayfair. Ten thirty, Monday morning.'

'Any idea what this film's about?'

'A "dystopian thriller" is all they told me.'

Story of my life, I thought.

'I'll be there.'

Now, I have appeared in many films and I know the industry's cruel and ruthless disappointments as well as anyone but, despite my better judgement, I allowed myself a little frisson of pleasurable anticipation. After all this bad luck – the burglary, the totalled car – here was the world paying me back. I liked dystopian thrillers – I'd already had minor roles in at least two – and I sensed that something about my looks, my track record, word of mouth, had paid dividends this time. I hadn't worked in three – no, five – months and money was running very low and, despite my better judgement, I allowed myself to fantasize that I'd get this role. What do they say? Earn your own luck. I reckoned I'd earned it, all right.

The Metropole Grande was one of those smoked-glass eight-storey blocks just off Park Lane. On entering, you left London and could have been in Singapore or Dubai, Tokyo or Acapulco. Granite, marble, palm trees, chilled lounge-muzak, foreign staff in black, zipped jumpsuits and a curious transnational clientele.

I was shown up to the conference suites on the third floor where a young woman called 'Shirlee', according to her name badge, asked me to wait in an anteroom. Is there a script I could read, I enquired? I'm afraid the script is embargoed at this moment of speaking, she said. I handed over my résumé and she disappeared behind heavy teak doors.

I drank some water from the water-cooler. I looked down at the traffic silently circling Hyde Park Corner. I switched my brain to neutral – it's work: don't be picky, don't be pretentious, I told myself. Be nice to everyone.

Shirlee opened the teak doors and ushered me in. A thick-set man, forties, swarthy, unshaven, in a loose V-neck T-shirt and carefully distressed and torn jeans came round from behind a desk piled high with scripts and shook my hand.

'Hi,' he said, introducing himself. 'Ron Suitcase. There's been a blunder. I'm so sorry.'

'A blunder?'

'I'm expecting a twenty-three-year-old young woman called Alexa Dunbar.'

I felt like falling to the floor. This had happened on three previous occasions.

'I admit,' I said, 'I am not a young woman. But I am a thirty-five-year-old man called Alec Dunbar. Any good?'

'It's so easy for things to go wrong,' Ron Suitcase said with a sad smile. 'One vowel.'

'And one consonant,' I added.

'What? Oh, sure . . . Coffee? Iced tea? Water?'

I sat down and Shirlee brought me a double espresso as we commiserated. Casting agents – you'd think they'd do their bloody homework. Tell me about it. Nightmare. Alec/Alexa Dunbar. I recounted my Alec/Alexa anecdotes – the misdirected (obscene) fan mail; the twenty-five paparazzi waiting outside a restaurant for me to emerge and their collective rage; the phone calls offering me swimwear-modelling work.

'One of you should make a change,' Ron suggested.

'I was there first,' I said. 'Apparently her real name is Agatha Duguid.'

'What can I say?' Ron rose to his feet – the meeting was over. 'If there's a part for you in *Transfigured Night* I'll call your agent. Stay in touch, Alec. Be well. Take great care.'

He handed me his card and I glanced at it: Ronaldo Sudkäsz, Alcazar Films. There was an address on Wilshire Boulevard, Los Angeles. I slipped it into my jacket pocket and we shook hands amiably – for the last time, I assumed.

Shirlee showed me out and handed me back my résumé. I was feeling that leaden sense of failure that we actors experience occasionally: a kind of existential certainty that somewhere early in our lives we had taken the wrong turning.

'How did it go?'

I looked round. A young woman sat there on a sofa, a script open on a coffee table in front of her. She had thick shaggy blonde hair and one of those long lean faces with a nicely prominent jaw. I'm drawn to long lean faces with a nicely prominent jaw.

'A sex confusion,' I said. 'I'm meant to be a twenty-three-year-old woman called Alexa. Alas, I'm not.'

'Didn't they spot it instantly?' she said. 'I did.'

I was intrigued and sat down opposite her, stuffing my résumé into my rucksack.

'You've a script, at least,' I said. 'Good role?'

'I've got pages. I get to speak,' she said. 'That's a plus.'

For some reason I unburdened myself, telling her about the persistently annoying Alec/Alexa confusion, my run of bad luck, how I was stupidly counting on this part in *Transfigured Night* to put everything right and that I was now bracing myself for the next kick in the teeth.

She listened sympathetically, not interrupting. She had green eyes.

'Burgled as well,' she said. 'Did you lose much?'

'Funnily enough they only stole my clothes – my best clothes. Strange selection. Three suits, an old leather jacket that I loved, a pair of new, unworn shoes, swimming trunks, T-shirts. I think they were going to steal my computer – someone had been fiddling with it – but I guess they were spooked and ran off.'

'Yes. What did Shakespeare say? When sorrows come, they come not as single spies –'

'– But in battalions. Yeah. Tell me about it. I'd better go,' I said. 'Thanks for hearing me out. And good luck.'

I stood, gave her my little brave soldier salute, and just as I turned away she said:

'How would you like to earn £1,000 in twenty-four hours?'

I paused and then sat down again.

'That depends,' I said. 'I charge more for a contract killing.'

'I need something hand-delivered, something precious. It has to be in Scotland tomorrow.'

'Can't you courier it?'

'Too fragile.'

'Catch a plane?'

'It would have to go in the hold. That's impossible. It has to be driven north. Hand-delivered, as I said.'

'Why don't you do it yourself?'

She eased her posture and drew her left leg out from under the coffee table. Her ankle and lower leg were encased in a bright blue plastic boot leg-cast.

'I've broken my ankle.'

'Ah. I see,' I said.

We looked at each other. I was definitely attracted to this pretty young blonde woman in the leg cast but I tried not to let that affect my judgement.

'Look, it was just a spontaneous idea,' she said. 'Don't worry. I'll find someone else. Not a problem.'

'Cash?' I said.

'In advance,' she said.

Shirlee appeared at the teak doors.

'Miss Devereaux?'

'I'll be right there,' Miss Devereaux said, standing with some difficulty. I had a name. She smiled at me. 'Nice meeting you,' she said. 'Good luck yourself.'

'I'm in,' I said, quickly. £1,000, twenty-four hours. What the hell – it was better than nothing.

'Do you have a car?' she asked.

'Ah. No. It's off the road.'

'Okay. I can lend you mine.' She glanced at Shirlee then lowered her voice.

'Meet me at the Peace Pagoda in Battersea Park this evening at six o'clock. We'll sort everything out.' I gave her my details – phone, email, etc. – and then she limped into the room for her audition with Ron Suitcase.

The Peace Pagoda was constructed in Battersea Park in 1985. When I first saw it, when I moved to London to go to drama school, I thought it a shocking affront, an act of vandalism to construct an oriental temple in a stretch of landscaped Victorian urban greenery facing the select mansion flats of Chelsea across the River Thames. How had it obtained planning permission? Who had been bribed? But, over the years, I became used to it, and started to rather like it, and now as I stood there looking at it, set in its backdrop of autumnal plane trees, the river at high tide, I thought it was rather wonderfully inappropriate – a symbol of London's easy welcome to the polyglot, multicultural presences drawn to this great sprawling city. Bring it on – we can take it, the city seemed to say. Pagodas? Yeah, no problem.

I leant on the embankment wall looking at a cormorant diving for fish. It was twenty past six and no sign of my actress and her £1,000. Some kind of sick joke, I thought, another young woman messing with my head, another sign of my bad –

'Alec!'

I picked up my rucksack and headed towards Miss Devereaux. It was absurd that I didn't know her first name. She was standing in the car park to the east of the Pagoda, leaning against an old grey sun-bleached, weather-battered Land Rover Defender, long-wheelbase variety. The door on the driver's side was a pale salmon pink. On the door, still legible, was a faded black stencilled code-number. KT-99. Legacy of some trans-Sahara 4x4 rally, I assumed, or something. This motor had had an interesting life, clearly.

We shook hands.

'What's your first name?' I asked. 'By the way.'

'Stella,' she said handing me the keys. 'You're insured to drive it, by the way, also.'

'Good. What am I delivering?'

She opened the rear door and took out a cool box, unclipped the top and lifted out a thick glass flask about nine inches tall. Its lid was sealed with rubber and held down by metal clamps, like a large Kilner jar – airtight. It contained a pint of clear fluid, I calculated.

'This is water from the River Jordan,' Stella Devereaux said. 'My godson is being christened tomorrow in Scotland and this is my gift to him and the family. Holy water. I'd have driven it there myself, but –' She pointed to her plastic leg cast.

'Where in Scotland?'

'The west coast, south of Skye.' She reached in to the front seat and brought out a plastic envelope-file. 'A church, St Mungo's, in a small village called Alcorran.' She showed me maps, addresses, a slip of paper with her telephone number and email address on it. 'You've got everything there. But it's a long drive,' she said. 'You'll need to go all night.'

'I've done it before,' I said, half lying. I'd endured a three-day, non-stop 'drive' across the USA in a film called *Beyond the Edge* (2007) so I vaguely knew what was required to keep you going. 'No worries,' I said, smiling reassuringly at her – she was really rather attractive; such thick, tousled hair . . .

'Did you get the part?' I asked.

'What part?'

'*Transfigured Night*.'

'Oh. They're calling me back,' she said.

'Bravo,' I said. 'When are they shooting?'

'Ah . . . Later this year.'

'We're already in October.'

'Or early next year.'

'Well, your ankle will be fixed, at least.'

'Yeah. Of course.' She smiled and rummaged in her pocket, taking out a crumpled envelope and handing it over. I glanced inside. A wedge of £50 notes, twenty of them. This is all beginning to seem just a little bit weird, I thought. What was really going on? But I stopped thinking – £1,000 in the hand. I was just a delivery boy. What else was I going to do tomorrow?

'You're very trusting,' I said.

'You've a trustworthy face.' She leant forward and kissed me on the cheek. 'Bon voyage, Alec Dunbar.'

She limped off into the dusk, heading for the gate on Chelsea Bridge Road.

I sat in KT-99, familiarizing myself. I'd driven a Land Rover Defender in *Delta Five Niner*, an SAS, behind-enemy-lines film (I played a sergeant) that was never released, not even as a DVD. 'Straight to radio', as we say in the business, but at least I felt at home behind this wide wheel and dashboard. I eased the seat back from Stella's cramped driving position (I'm six feet two) and looked at the many maps of Scotland she had given me.

London to Glasgow, then the A82 up the west side of Loch Lomond. To Arrochar and Loch Fyne and on to Inverary. Then Loch Awe and on up to Oban, Fort William – and there was Alcorran, south of Mallaig, right on the coast across the sound from the southern tip of Skye . . . I should be there by noon, all being well. That gave me eighteen hours, all told. If I made good going I could even have a nap on the way.

I felt strangely excited: this was an adventure, out of the blue. A beautiful woman had offered me this bizarre opportunity – and a lot of money for one day's work. This was what life was all about, I told myself – to be lived to the full, come what may. Happenstance. The roll of the dice. I had £1,000 in my pocket and I was sitting at the wheel of a Land Rover Defender in Battersea Park ready to drive through the night to deliver holy water to a small church on the west coast of Scotland.

Route determined, I searched my rucksack for my iPod. Every type of driving music was available to me. All I needed now was an overdose of caffeine. I started the engine, revved it, flexed my shoulders. Off we jolly well go, I said to myself, and pulled out of the car park, on to Chelsea Bridge Road, crossed the river and headed for Marble Arch and the north.

## Part Two: Headlights in the Mirror

I drove steadily out of London following the A40 to Hanger Lane and then right on to the North Circular and on up to the start of the M1 north. It was dark by now and I was listening to Steve Reich's *The Desert Music*. I found these cool, minimalist ostinatos perfect for long drives. The mesmeric loops kept me awake, paradoxically, as if my brain were searching for a moment when they would break down rather than endlessly repeat themselves. It maintained me at a nice pitch of concentration.

My first stop was at the Watford Gap service station. London was eighty miles or so behind me now and I was well on my way. I strolled into the fluorescent, swarming echo-chamber of the cafeteria and ordered three double espressos and a bottle of Evian. I took them to a table, let the espressos cool and then necked them as if they were cough medicine and washed them down with a gulp of water. I felt I could drive all week.

I sat there looking at my fellow human beings – as they scoffed food and drank sweet liquids, as they laughed and chatted – conscious of the unique nature of my business, here, on the road north to Scotland and feeling somewhat distanced from all this routine banality of driving, of getting from A to B. I often experienced this sensation of slight remove from everyday life and I wondered if it was because of my profession. If you act in movies for a living then sometimes everything you do seems like a scene from a movie – even if you're pouring milk on your cornflakes, having a shave, posting a letter or taking your shirts to a dry-cleaner. It can be fun – this sense of a heightened reality – as if you're lit and made up, that there's a camera turning over somewhere; but it can also be dangerous: real life is different. Real life is never, never as simple as a movie.

I was thinking about this as I motored down the exit road from the service station and saw the small band of hopeful hitch-hikers with their signs: rare beasts in this day and age. There were three young soldiers in their fatigues, a car-delivery man with his special number plate and, most oddly, a girl dressed in white. Not so much a girl, I noticed as I slowed instinctively, passing her, but a young woman in her late twenties. This was what I was trying to express: all of a sudden I felt I was taking part in somebody's film.

She had dark short tousled hair and was wearing a white

denim jacket and grubby white jeans and trainers. She was holding a piece of torn cardboard with 'Scottlan' scrawled on it. Nice touch. Who thought of that? She had a pretty, gaunt, feral face and, somewhat disturbingly, seemed to be staring right at me. She was fourth behind the three soldiers. Could I stop for her? Should I stop for her? No, Dunbar, you fool, I told myself – your agenda is clear. Concentrate.

I pulled on to the motorway and accelerated off into the night, Philip Glass's *Violin Concerto* keeping me company.

North of Manchester on the M6, now, I saw the fuel gauge was dipping below a quarter. Also I had run out of chocolate. I turned into the next service station and filled up. I paid at the counter and bought more chocolate. Sugar, coffee, music – all I required. I felt surprisingly alert and I was making excellent time – no traffic, no roadworks. I'd be in Scotland in an hour or so, at this rate. Perhaps I could stop somewhere for a snooze.

As I was about to climb into KT-99, a five-axle articulated lorry pulled up at the pump with an immense catarrhal wheeze of airbrakes. I looked round and, three seconds later, saw the feral girl in white walk round from the passenger side of the cab. She wandered into the service station shop and I saw her buying cigarettes.

I stood there for a moment – unsettled – taking this in, wondering how the movie had changed so suddenly. Was this significant, this new crossing of paths? Was I meant to play my role now? All the signs seemed to be indicating that an encounter should take place. Scene seventeen. Motorway service station. Night. Action.

I climbed into KT-99, started the engine and drove away from the pumps, parking up in the bay beyond and sauntered back to find the girl.

She was standing outside the door, smoking.

'Hi,' I said, 'can I give you a lift? I'm heading north to Scotland.'

'I not going to Scottlan no more,' she said, calmly. She had an eastern European accent, I thought. Polish? Czech? Russian? She had big dark eyes and a nervous fidgety manner about her. She drew heavily on her cigarette, as if it contained some essential life-enhancing ingredient.

'That's okay,' I said. 'It was just that I saw you before – at Watford Gap – and saw your sign.'

'I want to go Edinburgh,' she said.

'Edinburgh's in Scotland,' I said.

'You go there?'

'No.'

'Where you go?'

'I'm going to Glasgow and then further north.'

'Where north?'

'Far north. Mallaig, Skye.'

She thought for a moment, then dropped her cigarette on the ground and stood on it. 'Is no good for me,' she said. 'I need to go Edinburgh.'

'Yeah, well, whatever. Good luck,' I said and turned away.

'What your name?' she called after me.

'Alec,' I said.

'Thank you, Alec. You nice man.'

Yeah. Cut.


As I drove on, now well past midnight, the traffic thinned and for long periods I seemed to be the only vehicle travelling north. I didn't feel tired at all, enjoying the familiar romance of driving through the night, comfortable with the thrum of the tyres on the roadway, the music in my ears, thinking this wasn't a bad way to earn a grand, cash.

What is it that makes you notice these things? It was just

past Penrith when I became aware of the lights in my rear-view mirror. Two hundred yards or so behind me, never wavering, never falling back, never attempting to overtake. I let ten minutes go by and then signalled and pulled into the hard shoulder. I watched a big black saloon flash by, its red tail lights soon lost to view round a curve in the motorway. You've been in too many crappy movies, mate, I said to myself, as I put KT-99 in gear and pulled into the near lane. Get a life.

But a few minutes later, as I was approaching Carlisle, the lights in my mirror were back, sitting there, keeping their careful distance. All right, I thought, more fun and games being played – people had to stay awake somehow, let's have a bit of a laugh and pretend to follow someone. So I pulled off the motorway at the next exit and headed for Dumfries on the A75. There were many ways to skin a cat and many roads to Scotland – and I didn't want company, that much I was sure of.

## Part Three: Welcome to Scotland

I saw the sign by the roadside, lit by my headlights – 'Welcome to Scotland' – and felt a curious flow of relief course through me. Job done, nearly. I turned off the A75, parked up on a grassy verge and had a pee in a small copse of trees a few yards from the road. It was distinctly colder these few hundred miles north from London. I inhaled and exhaled loudly and ran on the spot for two minutes. No fatigue at all, I was pleased to note – onwards.

I swept through Glasgow in the small hours, heading west out of the city, and had reached Loch Lomond as the sun began to rise. I found a deserted campsite, parked up, and wandered down to the edge of the loch as the darkness leached out of the air and a watery, hazy sun began to fall across the hills. The water was as still and flat as heavy glass and the place possessed a primeval beauty because I couldn't see any sign of our human presence anywhere. Across the loch, on the east side, the steep hills plunged abruptly into the burnished sheet-metal of the water's surface, their reflections as fixed as a still photograph. I breathed deeply, arched my back, and went through a few t'ai chi exercises I remembered from that Samurai movie I'd been in for a couple of days. What was it called? Oh yes, *Banzai Dawn*. The less said about that one, the better.

I was about three hours or so from Oban, I calculated, then on north towards Fort William and the A830 to Mallaig and the village of Alcorran on the coast across from the island of Eigg and the Sound of Sleat, the stretch of water separating the mainland from the Isle of Skye. I'd arrive with some hours to spare, I reckoned, so I could stop somewhere for a proper breakfast – lots of unhealthy saturated fats required. I sat down on a rock and listened to the birds begin their early-morning chirping. What was bothering me? . . .

The following car, of course. Coincidence? Malign fun? And something about the wild girl in white was troubling me, also. I had left her at Watford Gap standing hitch-hiking to 'Scottlan'. Three hours later she steps out of an articulated lorry just as I was filling up. That was fast . . . Hold on a second, Dunbar, I said to myself: did you actually see her get out of the lorry? No. She just appeared from behind it. I was jumping to too swift conclusions: for her to arrive at the service station at the same time as me she wouldn't have been travelling in an articulated lorry. I told myself to forget it – in a few hours I would have delivered my River Jordan water to St Mungo's Church and would be heading back to London on a train. I took one last look at the bonnie banks of Loch Lomond and strolled back to KT-99.

I stopped for a proper fry-up, heart-attack-on-a-plate break-fast at a roadside café in Inverary, a small town on Loch Fyne. Eggs, bacon, sausages, baked beans, fried bread, black pudding and all washed down with a couple of mugs of scalding black coffee, heavily sugared. I was feeling tired by now – that tiredness you feel at the end of a long night-shoot – an ache in the joints, a sensation of fine grains of sand aggravating your eyeballs, an uncontrollable urge to yawn, the body craving oxygen, saying stop, stop, don't do this to me any more.

I paid my bill at the counter. I was about two and a half hours from my destination, I thought: so I'd be there well before midday. I walked out into the car park thinking that maybe I should find a hotel in Mallaig or Fort William, have a break, get some sleep – when would I be back on the west coast of Scotland again? *Il faut profiter*, as my ex-wife, Séverine, used to remark (she was French – *is* French, I should say. A French actress. Tricky).

I slipped the key into the front-door lock of KT-99 and was about to turn it when I saw the big black saloon turn into the car park behind the café. I went rigid. It swung by me and through the window of the front passenger seat I saw the pale feral face of the girl in white staring out at me, impassively, one palm spread on the glass pane. Then with a throaty roar of its powerful engine the car swerved round, pulled away and disappeared off down the road to Oban.

Yeah. Got it. Scrub the coincidence explanation. Ditto the 'malign fun' notion. Something was going on here and I wasn't happy about it.

I opened the rear door and unfastened the lid of the cool box, lifting out the heavy glass flask. I stared at its limpid contents as if some answer might be found there. River Jordan water for a christening in a small church near a remote village . . . That was beginning to sound like a fairy tale.

However, the sooner I reached the church the sooner I'd be out of this particular conundrum.

I put the flask away and unfolded one of the ordnance survey maps Stella Devereaux had given me: two and a half inches to one mile, every rutted track and landscape feature of any tiny notable significance delineated. I didn't need to take the main Oban–Fort William–Mallaig road to reach St Mungo's – I was driving a Land Rover Defender, for heaven's sake, so let's go cross-country.

Ah yes, Stella Devereaux, I thought: maybe she could throw some light on my unexpected and unwelcome companions. I took out my mobile phone – showing a weak signal that would probably weaken as I drove into the Scottish wilderness – now was the time to phone her. I punched out her number. It rang and rang – no voicemail. Right.

I took the first single-lane road as I left Inverary and drove on through increasingly rugged and hilly countryside. There were great tracks of industrially planted pine forest on these lower slopes of the hills and a whole network of dirt roadways that connected them. As the day went on I bumped along rutted lanes, forded small rushing streams and manoeuvred myself northwards, pausing every now and then to consult the map. Such precise, loving detail, I thought – it was a thing of beauty.

Two hours later I found myself in a remote glen. Small lochans gleamed like silver monocles amongst the tawny bracken and the heather and I could see on the highest mountains the first icing-sugar dusting of autumn snowfall. I looked back, looked ahead. There was a glen in front of me and an ascending array of small hills behind. Beyond them were big craggy mountains. Sunlight drenched the pewter clouds of a weather front moving in from the west. I was the only motor vehicle within the vast horizon that bounded me.

I drove on down a track, heading for a junction that would put me back on the road north, the A82 to Fort William, passing a row of shooting butts as I circled what was a vast heather grouse moor. A lot of these muddy roads were for hunters as well, I realized. Grouse had been shot on these hillsides for well over a hundred years, and deer stalked, these crisscrossing tracks webbing the contours and undulations of this wild country had their own history.

I allowed myself a small indulgent moment of smugness as I forded a shallow brown river and accelerated up the bank and on to the first metalled road I'd encountered in over two hours. And here was a signpost – A82 Fort William. I was going to be an hour later than planned but one thing was for sure – I'd be without company.

Turning on to the road I saw the narrow waters of Loch Linnhe appear on my left. Across on the far side were the promontories of Ardgour and Moidart – Moidart where Alcorran was to be found. Nearly there. The day was breezy, the sky full of moving clouds – running shadows on the loch and luminous flashes of sunshine. I fitted my headphones into my ears and John Adams's *Short Ride in a Fast Machine* set the heart beating in time to its mesmerizing rhythms. And, just as I began to speed up, I glanced in my rear mirror and there it was – a hundred yards behind me – the black saloon.

My new feeling – smugness long gone – was alarm with a dressing of fear and a sprinkling of utter bafflement. What to do now? I remembered, all of a sudden, what I'd done myself in a rather good and underrated low-budget thriller called *Incandescence* where my character, who was in a car and was being followed, did exactly the opposite of what a man who is being followed was expected to do.

Unfortunately in the movie I was then shot and killed but

the ploy seemed to me an admirable one – particularly in these circumstances.

I put my foot on the accelerator and sped away, though the saloon was soon safely at its usual distance. I was looking for a long stretch of straight road and after a couple of minutes I found it. Again I sped up and again I managed to put a few hundred yards between us for a moment. Then I braked and pulled off the road, stopping KT-99 on the grassy verge and flinging the door open.

I stepped on to the road and waited. Here came the black saloon hurtling towards me. I held my hand up and stupidly shouted 'Stop!' It didn't stop – it accelerated and came straight on at me. In the film *Incandescence* the pursuing car had stopped, turned and drove away – but here on the Fort William road it obviously wasn't going to. Plan B, Dunbar.

I hurled myself out of its way as it barrelled past and sped off into the distance. I dusted myself down. My throat was dry. No – this was no joke, I hadn't signed up for this. I uttered a few colourful expletives and called Stella Devereaux again. Number unobtainable.

Of course.

The phone.

That was how, despite my glen-crossing, stream-fording, hill-climbing evasion, they had picked me up so easily. I closed my eyes and exhaled. It was all coming back to me. There was a pilot I had shot in the US three years ago, what was it called? Oh yes, *The Undead, Dying* (it wasn't picked up). Not my character but the character I was trying to kill thought all he had to do was switch his phone off and he couldn't be followed, couldn't be triangulated. Not so, sucker.

I opened my phone and removed the battery. It's the

battery – they can always pinpoint you from the signal the battery gives out. So, here I was, phoneless. And I realized they would know – whoever was in the black saloon – that I had removed the battery, also. Time to make myself scarce. I took the first right turn off the Fort William road and drove as fast as I could. After ten minutes and three more random turns at junctions I stopped. There was a sunken farm with its steading a quarter of a mile away. The day was growing less kindly, big grey continents of clouds massing out to the west. I opened the cool box and took out the flask. I prised off the metal clamps and lifted the lid. I sniffed, nothing. I dipped a finger in the fluid, tasted it. Watery. I put the lid back on and sat there for a while, thinking.

Something was wrong. Perhaps something was seriously wrong. Should I go to the police? . . . But nothing had really happened. What could I reasonably complain about? It seemed to me that all I had to do was earn my £1,000 and leave the problem, whatever it was, for somebody else – no doubt in my mind that this would be Miss Stella Devereaux, or whatever her real name was – to sort out herself. Various scenarios suggested themselves to me – some kind of family feud being the most likely, with the girl in white being some insane, aggrieved sister, or something – but I realized all speculation was fruitless. I was going to deliver this flask with whatever it contained to St Mungo's Church in Alcorran and then, sayonara. However, after my acrobatics on the Fort William road I intended to do this with due caution, not to say exceptional, ridiculous caution. I looked at the map and calculated roughly where I was. I needed a town with shops. Fort William was a few miles away and, one thing I knew now, I couldn't be followed any more. I started KT-99, turned her round and headed off. It was time I equipped myself.

## Part Four: The Church of Death

In fact I didn't head on to Fort William. A moment's further thought made me retrace my steps and go back down the coast road to Oban – it seemed altogether more unexpected and therefore safer. I hadn't made my initial rendezvous so I had ceased to worry about time any more. If my employer gave me an unobtainable number then what could she expect? – I might have had a puncture or a breakdown or an accident. Of course, I realized that I couldn't be called myself, any more, now my phone was shut down. Still, there were other routes and methods of getting in touch – Stella Devereaux had all my information and contact numbers and there was always social media.

Oban is a small resort town and important ferry port to the Hebrides and the Western isles, once rather pretty but now showing some of the signs of twenty-first-century tourism fatigue. Its heyday probably began in the 1890s and terminated in the 1960s. However, one advantage of twenty-first-century tourism was that there was always an Internet café to be found, somewhere. I asked a few passers-by and was directed to Oor Wullie's Webcaff on Shore Street by the railway station.

I paid my money, bought a cappuccino and a cheese and tomato sandwich from the small snack counter and took a seat at a computer and logged on, wondering if there would be a perplexed message from Stella.

There was no message from Stella but a lot of posts from me . . .

I sat in a fog of incredulity reading about the holiday I was enjoying in Honduras, looking at photographs of myself, wearing the clothes that had been stolen from my flat the week before – my leather jacket, my Hawaiian baggie swimming trunks, my frayed panama hat. As Photoshop jobs went it was first class. My friends were envious and raucously abusive. I read on: 'This place is amazing!' I had posted. 'I think I may never come back. Enjoy winter, losers!'

For a moment I was tempted to replace my battery in my phone and make some calls but along with my incredulity came a colder awareness. This spontaneous invitation to drive to Scotland had been long in the planning and meticulous in its execution. Clearly, I had been targeted, duly investigated, set up and selected. The burglary, the partial destruction of my car, the invitation to the *Transfigured Night* audition, Stella Devereaux's broken ankle . . . What seemed random events, part of the here and now of an ordinary urban life, were in fact beads carefully slipped on to a string. But what about the girl in white and the black saloon? Where did that fit? Were they trying to frighten me in some way? . . .

The police, I thought again. But what could I complain about? An Internet prank? I suspected I had a little time on my side. Whatever was in the glass flask was key and now I had disappeared – vanished, temporarily – I could perhaps swing the power-pendulum my way. Of course, I reasoned, I could drop the flask in a roadside waste bin, abandon KT-99 and return to London and my life. But that cold awareness I was experiencing, that chill creeping round my kidneys, made me think that, even if I did that, I wouldn't be safe for long. While I had the flask, I was valuable, I reasoned; as soon as I didn't – I was expendable.

I had a feeling that all the answers lay in St Mungo's Church in Alcorran. Time to check it out.

I sent Stella an email.

'Breakdown. Running twenty-four hours late. See you tomorrow. Sorry! A.'

Before I left the café I also searched online for a sports shop in Oban – camping, mountaineering, cliff-climbing – that kind of emporium. I found it – Great Outdoors, a retail unit in an industrial estate on the outskirts of town on the Fort William road. I spent an hour there, filling my trolley with everything I'd need.

When I made *Exit Wound* (2008) for Gregson David Defoe he had insisted that all the young actors spend two weeks in a boot camp run by ex-Royal Marines. We all hated it but we learnt a great deal, however reluctantly, and I think I can say I've never been as fit as that again in my life. I also became a bit of an outerwear fetishist as a result, I confess, with a finicky knowledge of fabric types, warmth-to-weight ratios, breathability quotients, types of walking boots, fleeces, thermal underwear, headgear and all the rest of the paraphernalia that the rugged, self-sufficient outdoorsman requires, with a pedantry and brand knowledge that would rival the most ardent fashionista.

I bought wisely in the store and took my booty to the checkout desk where it was rung up and my credit cards were duly refused, one after the other. Again, I felt the muscle-stiffening weight of dread drape itself around my shoulders. Credit card refused – someone would be watching: they would know where I was.

I used a wad of Stella Devereaux's cash to pay and flung everything in the back of KT-99. I took out the ordnance survey map and searched for a place where I could hole up for the night. I'd scope out the church in the morning – see what was what. Now I had a plan, I felt better. There was always the option of cut-and-run, with whatever dangers that involved, but I had a feeling that once the flask with its 'holy water' was out of my hands the way ahead would appear obvious.

Night was drawing in as I drove KT-99 up a steep dirt track

heading for the summit of a mid-sized mountain on the Moidart peninsula called Clachan Mor. I'd chosen it because it seemed equipped, as far as I could tell, with more of its share of cliff faces and corries, rock buttresses, shale slopes and moraines. And sure enough, halfway up I saw a mass of huge boulders, the size of haystacks, detritus from some ancient glacier, with a Defender-sized gap at one end. I backed in and made camp.

I managed to semi-cover KT-99 with the olive-green tarp that I'd bought, holding it in place with rocks. I unrolled my length of foam rubber and sleeping bag in the rear between the bench seats and then I cooked myself some supper on my camping gas stove, sliced square sausage and baked beans followed by a bar of chocolate and strong tea.

I'd also bought heavy-lugged walking shoes, thick socks, waterproof trousers, a thigh-length olive-green polyamide jacket with hood, a compass, a weighty long-handled LED torch and powerful binoculars. I was going to hike to St Mungo's with my holy water, observe it for as long as necessary and then make my appointed rendezvous at midday, all being well, twenty-four hours later than planned. I hoped that would be an end to this bizarre adventure but a warning voice in my ear – Gregson David Defoe's, in fact – told me that 'hope is for wimps'. One step at a time, I said, pleased to think at the least that for those chasing me, whoever they were, I would have vanished again. I was snug and secure in my cleft between the rocks on Clachan Mor. I had eaten well and I had a roof over my head.

I slept well, also, but woke abruptly at first light. I boiled some water on my stove, made some tea and had a shave. The unsought-for thought came into my head that in the British Army in the First World War no soldier was allowed to go unshaved for a day, even in front-line trenches. I happen to know this because I was in an overly sentimental First World War movie called *Pack Up Your Troubles*. My symbolic act of shaving was a preparation for my going over the top, into no man's land.

I set off, rucksack on my back with the flask of holy water inside, compass and map in hand. It was a straightforward piece of orienteering to make my way across the face of Clachan Mor and over a hog-backed ridge to a glen called Coire Creag. There I would pick up a stream of some size, called Eas Braglen, according to the map, that flowed west from a very small lochan, and following that would lead me downhill towards the minor road to the village of Alcorran. As I strode across the mountain's west face, hood up, through the knee-deep heather, the fresh wind stinging my cheeks with a fine drizzle, I felt that all I needed in my hand was a C8 carbine and this could have been an out-take from *The Upside-Down War* (2011), one of my favourite films, where I played a member of a special-forces unit in Kosovo. I was a young lieutenant – I died early on in the film: my speciality.

But here I was, instead, hiking through the rugged landscape of the west of Scotland on another mission entirely. But the memory of the film made me think – a weapon . . . Perhaps I should have bought a knife, at least . . . Too late now.

Alcorran was a small, classic Scottish village on the Moidart peninsula, huddled in the lee of some low hills that protected it from the Atlantic gales. There was a narrow high street flanked by low cottagey houses – whitewashed, small-windowed with heavy lintels painted black – with a few shops, a hotel and a church with a clock tower at the end. This church wasn't St Mungo's – St Mungo's was a different denomination, some dissenting branch of the Free Church of Scotland, and was two miles out of town on a rocky promontory looking out over the sound towards Skye.

I paused outside the Tallen Brae Hotel. It was just after eleven o'clock and the bar was open. I pushed open the door. Tartan carpet, painted taupe wainscoting, rows of mounted antlers below the ceiling line and a small stone bar with a massive array of whiskies behind it. An old man sat in a corner with his Scotch and half-pint chaser staring into infinity. I was the second customer of the day. I shucked off my rucksack and jacket, hung them up, and took a seat at the bar.

A young woman was serving. Her hair was vermilion, her eyes black with kohl, and she had three rings in her bottom lip. Her maroon, cap-sleeved T-shirt revealed that one arm, the right, was heavily tattooed to the wrist – a full sleeve. Work had begun on the left.

'Hiya,' she said brightly, with a wide smile. 'What can I do for you, this lovely day?'

I had a powerful urge for some Dutch courage before I made my way to St Mungo's and asked her what whisky she'd recommend from the eighty or so she had on display behind the bar.

'You've got to try the Glen Fleshan,' she said. 'Distillery's two miles from here. Double wood. Peaty, of course, but with notes of clove, dried fruits and green apple. Some people claim to taste crème brûlée, but I can't. Light, though, for a malt from hereabouts. A good whisky to start the day with.'

I ordered a double Glen Fleshan and asked her how to get to St Mungo's Church. She told me: down the high street, turn left and take the B-road to Ardsault. You'll see the sign to St Mungo's about a mile yonder.

'Thank you,' I said. 'This is a delicious whisky. What's your name, if you don't mind my asking?'

'It's Stella,' she said. 'What's yours? I think I know your face from somewhere. Are you on telly?'

I lay up in some wind-battered gorse bushes on the rocks above the small beach by St Mungo's, studying the church through my binoculars. It looked more like an isolated village hall than a church: a basic, solid, whitewashed, pebble-dashed rectangle with a steeply pitched slate roof and a small bell set in a wooden belfry on the end of the ridge of the gable end. It had been built about a hundred yards from the sea and in winter must have to take a fair battering from the Atlantic gales.

How many Stellas was I going to meet on this journey, I wondered? – not beguiled or amused by the coincidence. I rather wished I was back in the bar of the Tallen Brae Hotel benefiting from Stella number two's astonishing whisky expertise but I knew that closure was more important, and I was pleased to see that a mid-range silver people-carrier was parked outside the small porch at the front of the church. Maybe Stella number one was inside waiting for me. I looked at my watch: 12.45. I'd deliberately made her wait. There was nobody else around and the church looked in some disrepair, now I could see it clearly, its congregation dismayed, perhaps, by the bleakness and exposure of its setting. A church for a particularly implacable, humourless and demanding God, I thought to myself, as I stood up and walked towards it, trying to ignore the palpable increase in my pulse rate.

The front door was an inch ajar. I had a final look round and pushed it open, slowly, and stepped in. Inside, there was a powerful smell of dust and mould, almost astringent, a place that hadn't been aired in weeks. The simple room with its high-beamed ceiling was austere in the extreme and very cold, colder than outside. Two rows of sturdy wooden pews flanked an aisle that led to a heavy oak table with a brass crucifix in the middle. The small windows were clear glass. No organ, no pulpit, no images of any kind, just an ebony lectern set to one side. I stood in the vestibule looking around, hugely disappointed that there was no one waiting for me. Where the hell was Stella? There was a closed door to one side behind the altar table.

'Hello?' I called out. 'Stella? It's Alec Dunbar.'

Silence.

'Hello!' Louder.

Nothing. I swore to myself. Maybe the car outside wasn't Stella's. Maybe the people who owned the car were simply hikers out walking somewhere, ramblers who'd parked up and headed off to Ardnamurchan Point, say. So I made my decision. I was going to place the flask of holy water on the altar table beside the crucifix and leave, get the hell out of there. I'd earned my grand and it was time to bring this sinister farce to an end.

I strode down the aisle and stopped abruptly. From my angle I could now see, in the gap between the first and second left-hand pew from the front, a leg, supine.

A leg in a blue plastic leg cast.

I took a couple of paces. Stella Devereaux, lying there, inert, on her back. Dead, to all intents and purposes. Something made me turn. In the gap between the second and the third pew on the right was another still body. A man, prone.

I closed my eyes. I was in shock and some more primitive self inside me had taken over, ruthlessly shutting down emotions and feelings. I knew I shouldn't do this but it was impossible to resist. I reached forward, grabbed the shoulder of the man's jacket and heaved him over a bit, just enough so I could see his face. I let him roll back, gently.

Ron Suitcase – aka Ronaldo Sudkäsz. The producer.

I could hear a shrill keening noise in my ears and realized it was just a sudden symptom of my baffled panic.

Control yourself, Dunbar. Gather yourself. One more check. I leant over Stella Devereaux. She was definitely dead – she was as still and cold as the dummy plastic bodies they use now to simulate dead bodies in movies. Not a breath and not a sign of any fatal cause. Her eyes were closed, her expression neutral. Fully clothed, nothing disarranged. She might have been taking a nap but no one was ever that still, even in the deepest sleep. I decided not to examine Sudkász. I left the church and closed the door behind me.

The car was a rental, locked, nothing inside that gave anything away.

Paradoxically, once I was outside and the trembling in my body began to diminish, I felt a strange wave of relief wash through me. Something was over – I wasn't on my own any more. Now I could justifiably call the police.

## Part Five: Night on Clachan Mor

Stella (the barmaid) poured me my second Glen Fleshan, all agog at my news. I had just called the police in Mallaig and reported the discovery of two dead bodies in St Mungo's Church, Alcorran. I told them I was at the hotel and would be waiting for them in the bar.

'Were they dead?' she asked, full of appalled curiosity.

'Well, I think so. I don't know. I didn't hang around. Deeply comatose, at best. Not moving, not a flicker of life that I could see.'

'It's a funny wee church that. Maybe two or three services a year. Some priest comes up from Glasgow.' She shivered. 'Don't know why they keep it open.'

'Well, I was just walking past, saw the door slightly open –'

Two uniformed policemen came into the bar. I introduced myself and we sat down at a table. One was a young guy, good-looking, I thought, a sergeant. He introduced himself as Sergeant Callum Strang. The other, an older man, had the flushed cheeks and the dead, puffy eyes of a functioning dipsomaniac. He kept glancing at the bar and its ranked bottles, I noticed.

I retold my story to Sergeant Strang. I was on a hiking holiday, I said – walking past the church, saw the door open, the car outside, went in. Two dead bodies.

'You didn't touch them?'

'No.'

'How did you know they were dead?'

'They looked dead. Extremely.'

'Let's check it out,' Strang said and stood up.

We drove in their police car back to the church. The people-carrier had gone, I saw at once. Strang pulled on a pair of blue latex gloves and pushed the door open. We walked in.

The church was empty. No Stella Devereaux, no Ronaldo Sudkäsz.

'They were here,' I said, pointing out where they had been lying. 'She was there, face up. He was there, face down.'

'You said you were sure that they were dead.'

'I'm not a doctor but they looked dead to me.'

I was trying to remain calm but a cacophony of jabbering counter-explanations was ringing in my ears as I tried to guess what might have happened. I remembered once, filming in the Bahamas, I had guilelessly swum out beyond the coastal shelf of the island where we were shooting and the water had turned from the palest sun-shafted blue to fathomless black, or so it seemed, as some sort of oceanic trench opened up beneath me. It had been a most uncomfortable feeling and I was feeling it again now.

Callum Strang was looking at me intently, shrewdly – I sensed he was aware of my unease.

'Did you know these people?'

'What? No. How could I have? I was walking past – I just popped my head round the door.' I lied as convincingly as possible. Sometimes I was glad to be an actor.

'Sure you hadn't had a dram too many?' the older cop said.

'I assume that's some kind of a joke,' I said stiffly, offended.

Callum Strang handed me his card.

'It looks to me like a sick prank,' he said. 'You know – scare the life out of a visiting churchgoer. Did you take the number of the car?'

'Ah, no. I didn't,' I said. Stupid idiot. 'I was in a bit of a state of shock.'

'Totally understandable, sir.'

Strang paced around, thinking. 'Probably their vehicle. Let me know if you run across them again, or spot the car. We'll give them an official warning. Get them into the police station, you know. Shake them up.'

'Right. I will.'

'Where are you staying?' Strang asked.

'I'm camping – up on Clachan Mor.'

'Have you a phone?'

'I did – but I dropped it in a stream yesterday. Stupidly,' I improvised. 'It's not working. I've ordered a replacement.'

'We'll have to rely on you to get in touch, then,' he said with a hint of a smile. Strang was no fool – I'd better not forget that.

They took me back to the hotel and then drove off. I bought a bottle of Glen Fleshan from Stella and set off back to my mountain hideout before the light began to go.

It was slower going, heading uphill, following the rushing shallow river back up to its source, and my mind was full of baleful and depressing thoughts. There was no doubt, as far as I was concerned, that the two bodies I had seen were dead bodies. Though I have to confess I've never actually seen a dead body before – a real dead body. In the films I've made I've wandered over battlefields littered with dead bodies; I've stood in rooms swimming with stage blood and plastic body parts after some gangland massacre but I've never actually seen a real corpse. How many of us have? Death is hidden away from us in our century – it's become something secret that happens in hospitals or morgues. We only see it on a screen – filtered, lit, factitious.

In any event, I was under no illusions: Stella Devereaux and Ronaldo Sudkäsz were no more. So who had killed them? The only candidates I could think of were the girl in white and whoever had been driving the car. Had I somehow led them to Stella and Ronaldo? Was that why I had been followed so assiduously from London? And why had they been killed? And who had removed the evidence so swiftly and effectively? What high stakes were being played for here?

I plodded on up Coire Creag as the answerless questions multiplied, hearing the bottle of Glen Fleshan clinking against the glass flask in the rucksack on my back. Whatever was in the flask held the clue, I realized, deleting all my previous speculations about family feuds and sibling rivalry.

As I was crossing the ridge that led up to Clachan Mor, in the roseate gloaming of a Scottish evening, I heard the sound of a helicopter approaching, flying low – that inimitable pulsing chop of the blades. Something told me to take cover so I squirmed down into the springy heather and pulled my hood up. A small black helicopter – an Enstrom Falcon, I thought – swept over the north side of the glen and swooped down the river, veered round and clattered off over the next line of hills. Forestry Commission? Mountain rescue? Electricity board? Or someone looking for me? I imagined the police radio network was being listened to intently. Strang would have routinely called in to the station in Mallaig to inform them that the report of two dead bodies was negative and that he was heading back to base from Alcorran . . .

I was home at my cleft in the rocks before night fell, extra pleased that I'd rigged the tarp over KT-99 now there was a helicopter flying around. I wanted deep camouflage, needed time to think, to contemplate what I might do next and I felt secure hidden up here on the mountain, realizing, with a certain pang, that nobody in the entire world knew where I was – and then, with another sharper pang, realizing further that my entire circle of friends and acquaintances, my scattered family, my ex-wife, my Facebook prodders and Twitter followers thought I was larking it up on holiday in Honduras.

In a dark and somewhat self-pitying mood – why had this happened to me? What had I done to deserve being in this hideous predicament? – I cooked up my usual supper of square sausage and baked beans, washed down with liberal draughts of Glen Fleshan. Ambrosial feast, I thought, and my sombre mood began to improve and mellow as I began to analyse what had happened to me and sense some sort of plan of action emerging.

Stella and Ron had something, something important, contained in the glass flask and that 'something', evidently, other people wanted badly for themselves. It must be precious, I reasoned, because they had taken special care to line up a patsy, a fall guy, who was going to transport this 'something' to a remote part of Scotland for them. But why me? What research had led them to Alec Dunbar as the perfect, unquestioning mule? Then to burgle my flat, steal my clothes, penetrate my computer and immobilize my poor car – all achieved before the fake audition for the fake film where the casual offer of earning £1,000 for a simple drive to Scotland is mooted . . . What if I'd said no thanks? . . . Maybe there was another actor waiting, and another – until somebody bit.

In any event, I had taken the bait and was soon off and running with the glass flask and its contents. Enter the girl in white and the black saloon. Who the hell were they? Why were they chasing me? Why the hitch-hiking charade? Why the encounter in the filling station? What if, by chance, I'd actually given the feral girl a lift to 'Scottlan'? I saw the line of unanswered questions stretching on to the crack of doom. Maybe the feral girl and her unseen driver were checking me out. Maybe they thought I was working with Stella and Ronaldo, in cahoots, somehow, a member of the gang . . . The spiralling ramifications of this scam or scheme were completely beyond my comprehension. Or maybe, it came to me, they thought I was some kind of diversion meant to lure them away from London while the real action took place in their absence – which was why they came so close, why they tried to spook me . . .

I stopped, had another sip of Glen Fleshan, trying to clear my head of its overload of conspiracy theories, burgeoning exponentially. And then there must have been some kind of encounter in St Mungo's Church. Some kind of fatal encounter, to be more precise. How were Stella and Ronaldo killed? I was pretty sure I was not meant to find them dead, so had the killers been surprised by the people-carrier pulling up outside and had made a quick escape? Innocent hikers, as I'd surmised, parking up beside the church to go on a coastal walk. And then I'd appeared. And while I was calling the police in Alcorran the killers had returned and the bodies were whisked away . . .

I forced myself to stop thinking. Time for some sleep, I realized, fatigue suddenly overwhelming me like a drug.

Drug. Yes, drug . . . An idea was taking shape. I was recalling a film I'd made, early in my career, *Beautiful Lie, Ugly Truth* (2002). My only memorable line in it was 'Knowledge is power' – but it had been enough to get me noticed because of the manner in which I'd acquired that knowledge (before I was killed). Perhaps the same trick might work here and now. I still had a good portion left of the £1,000 that Stella had given me – this ruse required a certain disbursement of funds – but it might just give me the leverage I was clearly going to need if I was going to extricate myself from this particularly noxious can of worms.

I locked all the doors of KT-99 from the inside and slid into my sleeping bag. Under the tarp the darkness was absolute and reassuring. I had a final slug of Glen Fleshan and settled down to sleep. Knowledge was power, yes, but action was consoling: at least I was going to do something, not just be buffeted around by these people and these forces I didn't understand, flipped here and there like a steel marble in a pin-ball machine. No, I was going to change the game, I was going to bring my own intelligence to bear on the whole sordid . . .

I woke up an hour later with a lurch, my heart thudding, timpanically. Funny how your unconscious mind still remains on watch while you sleep. There had been a noise, an unusual noise – no night-bird calling, no sudden rain-patter or wind-rush. A pebble-fall, something stepping nearby.

I groped for my big metal LED torch. With three fat D-batteries inside this thing could not only send its 750-lumen beam some 200 yards, it could also do duty as a lethal club. I wasn't going to switch it on just yet, though. I pulled on my boots and quietly opened KT-99's rear door, jolting at the coldness of the night air that rushed in. I stepped out. *Rattle*. That was the sound I'd heard. Something had slid on the scree beyond my rock enclave – someone circling round. I moved away from the Defender, back to the huge boulders, and stepped out into the darkness, my eyes wide, trying to see but seeing nothing. Of all my senses my ears were going to be most useful. And my nose. I could smell something – like gasoline, something rank. I strained to hear. Breaths. Someone panting, someone who'd climbed as high as I'd driven. My hearing seemed to zone in on some presence in the dark, a few yards away. Something living, as if I could feel the hot blood pulsing in it. I pointed the torch.

Click.

Two eyes glowed.

Then I saw the branched twin trees of ten-point antlers. A huge bloody great big stag stood there, blinded and affronted by my blazing white torch beam. It gave some sort of hoarse throat-tearing bark, not like a dog, more like a sea creature, and was gone, veering round and galloping off into the night, the sound of boulders and shale slipping as it careered across the moraine.

I stood there, swaying, a shivering, shriven homunculus, driven back to my inarticulate Stone Age self as a result of this encounter with a looming stag in the impenetrable night. So big! Like a house, and its glowing eyes and branched antlers making it seem like some mythic night-figure haunting the dark.

I calmed down after a few seconds and went meekly back to KT-99 for a consoling dram of Glen Fleshan. My hands were trembling as I settled down again in my sleeping bag, the acrid smell of the deer still in my nostrils. That was enough excitement for one night, I thought.

## *Part Six: Knowledge is Power*

In *Beautiful Lie, Ugly Truth* my character had to bluff his way
into a gentlemen's club in Pall Mall. I remember standing
chatting to the director (forgotten his name) saying, is this
really plausible? They have people on the door in these estab-
lishment clubs; club servants who know every member from
birth, you can't just walk in off the street.

Wrong, the director said (Guy Start, that was his name).
Everybody in that world wears a uniform; everybody in that
world has a certain ordained attitude. Don the uniform,
mimic the attitude and then all you need is a plausible reason
for being admitted. Doors will open. It made a kind of sense –
and, now I remember, Guy was obsessive about what we
wore, how we reproduced that uniform: our haircuts, signet
rings, choice of tie, of shoe, how much dandruff on the shoulders, one vent or two in your jacket (or 'coat', as Guy called
it – he was a bit of a toff himself ), but the point was well made,
all the same. The right clothes, the right bravura and a con-
vincing reason – ensure these factors are correct and access
was possible almost anywhere.

I took out the glass flask from the cool box and decanted
some of the fluid into a thoroughly washed-out cola bottle
and drove into Mallaig. I found the shop I was looking for just
off the high street: Fraser Niven, Gentleman's Outfitters. I
bought a dark charcoal grey suit, a white shirt, a banded tie
and a pair of black lace-up shoes. Before I left the shop, thus
suitably attired, my old clothes in a carrier bag, I asked directions from Mr Niven, the gentleman's outfitter himself, to the
nearest secondary school.

Fraser Niven was a small portly bald man with a diffident
air but he was happy to answer my question and listed three

of the secondary schools that the town of Mallaig and environs boasted.

Of the three proffered I instinctively chose the private school a few miles out of town, set in its own estate – my 'attitude' might have more purchase there, I calculated, and there would be more social pretensions swilling around than in a state school. Ardenthill College, the place was called, co-educational, 400 boys and girls from thirteen to eighteen years old, fees £25,000 a year, plus extras.

Ardenthill was clearly an old stately home sold off and transformed into a school. I drove past twin lodges through open gates up through parkland towards a rather ugly red-sandstone, over-decorated, but very Victorian Gothic Revival castle. Battlements, turrets, flying buttresses, tracery windows, gingerbread trim – nothing had been left out of the Gothic inventory. The castle was surrounded by newer, duller buildings – a cafeteria, classrooms, sickbay, drama centre and so on and, dotted here and there amongst the landscaped park, I could see other boarding houses and playing fields.

Ardenthill was a mid-level private school no doubt struggling to survive in the current economic climate, despite the exorbitant fees charged to the class-conscious, socially aspirational parents who were sacrificing themselves to send their offspring there. It had a less than well-tended aspect on closer inspection. Rusting scaffolding on the west wing. Unmown lawns in front of the chapel. Peeling paintwork on the cast-iron guttering – its discreet shabbiness telling you that, alas, corners were having to be cut, expenses being spared. Perfect.

I parked KT-99 outside the main entrance and strode in, telling the first member of staff I encountered that I had an appointment with the headmaster. I was shown up a wide, sweeping staircase to the headmaster's office on the second floor where his secretary could find no record of the appointment I had made with Mr Feveral, she was extremely sorry to say, and indeed the headmaster was away at a Scottish Public Schools conference in Perth and wouldn't be back until tomorrow. I've come all the way from Edinburgh, I said to the secretary, in my coldest, most patrician English accent – this is inexcusable. I want to enrol both my children, Ben and Annabel, in this school and you can't even manage to keep a simple appointment.

She was abjectly apologetic. I calmed down, and a new appointment was made for the following week. I was well inside the citadel now, all doors would be open for me. Could I take a stroll around in the meantime, I asked? Gain some sense of the school and its amenities? My son, Ben, loves chemistry. We're very proud of our science block here at Ardenthill, the secretary said, and showed me how to reach it, a short walk back down the drive and turn left.

The science block was a featureless glass and concrete building. Boys and girls were streaming out at the end of class. One of the girls – rather pretty in the school uniform of a Fair Isle sweater and navy corduroy skirt – showed me into the chemistry wing.

I walked up scuffed linoleum stairs, scenting the familiar astringent odours of chemistry labs the world over. Tears prickled at the corners of my eyes as I peered into a classroom – wooden benches, high stools, sinks, ranked bottles with multicoloured fluid inside.

'Can I help you?'

I turned. A young woman stood there in a white coat. She had long dark hair pulled back in a ponytail and was wearing heavy-rimmed spectacles. In her mid-twenties, I guessed. A chemistry teacher? Yes, it turned out. I explained I was a prospective parent. She showed me into another, grander lab – pointed out pieces of equipment that were clearly meant to be impressive. Centrifuges, distillation towers, powerful microwave ovens and the like. She mentioned terms such as vacuum filtration, separatory funnels, titration, condensers and I nodded as if I knew what she was talking about, duly impressed.

I stopped her and introduced myself. We shook hands. She said her name was Isla MacNab. She had a soft Highland accent and, as she removed her heavy spectacles and slipped them in a pocket of her white coat, I realized – in the time honoured way – that she was really rather beautiful with an innocent, unselfconscious style. Wasted as a chemistry teacher in an undistinguished private school, I thought, spontaneously. She was one of those women who didn't really know how attractive she was, I surmised. And then wondered if this was a male fantasy . . . Is there such a person as an attractive woman who is unaware of her attractiveness? No matter, Isla MacNab was between chemistry lessons and she could tell me everything I needed.

We sat down. I asked her if she would do me a favour. I was aware of her staring at me rather more intently than was normal. She had the whitest skin and blue-grey eyes. Not a trace of make-up. A small perfect nose – the kind of nose you would buy in a nose shop. Perfectly straight, flared nostrils. Her lips were –

'What can I do for you, Mr Dunbar?'

I took out my bottle of River Jordan water.

'Somebody told me this was water but I don't think it is. Is there any way you could analyse it for me?' I smiled as engagingly as I could. 'In about ten minutes.'

She looked at her watch, then at me for a moment, shrewdly, reminding me of Callum Strang's pointed assessment of me.

Was it something they did up here on the west coast of Scotland? Look at people askance . . .

'I could try,' she said. 'Maybe. What exactly –'

'I'll pay you,' I said quickly. Then added, 'For your time and expertise.'

'That's a plus,' she said and picked up a test tube. 'Anyway, I've got a spare hour now, before the fifth form.'

She poured some of the fluid into it, shook it and sniffed it.

'If it's not water,' she said, 'then it's probably a salt of some kind in solution. Pretty basic stuff. You need a precipitate.'

'Right.'

'You lower the solubility by adding a reagent – so it falls out of solution.'

'I see. Yes.'

'Ethanol, for example.'

'Indeed.'

She fetched a rack of clean test tubes and poured some of the fluid into four of them. Then she went in search of other bottles and with a pipette added a few drops from them to each test tube. Immediately the third test tube clouded with some sort of chalky precipitate.

'Bingo,' she said.

She took the test tube to a centrifuge and within seconds, it seemed, returned with a watch glass containing a fine layer of crystals, like crushed rock salt. I reached to dip my finger in it to taste it but she grabbed my wrist firmly.

'Not a good idea.'

'Good thinking,' I said.

She looked at me disapprovingly and said, with some sternness, 'That would have been an extremely foolish thing to do, Mr Dunbar. What if you'd tasted it and dropped down dead in ten seconds? That would've rather messed up my day.'

I felt my blush spread from my cheeks to my neck.

'Sorry,' I said. 'Just an instinct.'

She took some kind of tiny spoon implement and dipped it in the crystals. Then she lit a Bunsen burner and held the crystals in the flame. The orange burnt blue and green in a quick flare of colour.

'Could it be a drug?' she said. 'A pharmaceutical drug? That would be my guess. If you hide a new drug in solution it's a very effective disguise.' She smiled. 'I used to work for a drug company. Before I became a chemistry teacher.'

A drug. Yes, things were beginning to make sense, suddenly. I had failed to get a part in a film called *Artificial Fire* but had read the script with interest, if only because it revealed how many billions of dollars could be made from a successful drug. Super-drugs, they were called. Every major drug company in the world was searching for that mother lode. A global marketplace. Erectile dysfunction, antidepressants, a cure for Alzheimer's. Billions and billions of dollars as long as the licence was granted. In this film, *Artificial Fire*, a whistle-blower in a huge multinational drug company had tried to alert a journalist to the fact that –

'Will that be all, Mr Dunbar?'

'Thank you, Miss MacNab. You have no idea how helpful you have been.'

I took out my wallet and laid two £50 notes on the laboratory bench.

'My contribution to the staff Christmas party. I'm incredibly grateful.'

I smiled at her. She had that shrewd look on her face again, contemplating me. She really was incredibly attractive in that kind of pure, unselfconscious way . . .

'Lovely to meet you,' I said. 'I'll be sure to tell the headmaster how kind you've been.'

She picked up the £50 notes.

'Were you in *Die Standing*, by any chance?' she asked. 'Are you *that* Alec Dunbar?'

'What? Ah, yes, I was. I am.'

'Good movie. Shame you got killed.'

I drove back to Mallaig, thinking hard. It was not so much a precise plan that was forming in my head – more a general course of action that was emerging. The details could come later once my motivation was clear. If the mountain won't come to Mohammed, Mohammed must go to the mountain, was that the expression? It seemed to me it was time to make my presence known and felt, I thought, one way or another.

In Mallaig high street I found a general store. I bought a roll of gaffer tape, a pair of pliers, a packet of firelighters, five wire coat hangers, an oven tray and a simple wind-up kitchen timer. Down on the dockside I found a ship chandler's and bought the other key ingredient I needed.

I drove around a bit, taking care I wasn't being followed, and then headed back to Clachan Mor and my cleft between the huge rocks. I backed KT-99 in and secured the tarpaulin.

I cooked myself a supper of pork sausages and fried potatoes, washed down with what remained of the Glen Fleshan. This would be my last night on the mountain, I calculated. If everything went to plan, tomorrow would see some kind of reckoning – and with a bit of luck this baffling, annoying, potentially dangerous, vanishing game would be over.

## Part Seven: The Trap

I spent the morning preparing myself. I cut my wire coat hangers into the requisite lengths and bent them into shape with the pliers. Then I studied my ordnance survey map with due concentration looking for the ideal location for my emerging plan. I wanted somewhere not too far from Mallaig, a twenty-minute swift drive would do, and I needed a sea cliff and a nearby forest. After ten minutes or so I had narrowed the possibilities down to two and eventually settled for the one closer to Mallaig. Timing was key, if this plan was going to work, a few extra minutes in my favour could be a life-saving dividend.

I hauled down the tarp covering KT-99, bundled it away and packed up my camp. I didn't think I would ever forget my two nights on Clachan Mor. I climbed into the front seat and replaced the battery in my phone. I called my agent. Where've you been, dear fellow? Gervase said, piqued. They want to see you for *Fatal Assignment III*. I'll be back in London tomorrow, I said, with more confidence than I was actually experiencing.

The problem that faced me was that having called the police to a double-murder that promptly vanished, and that they assumed was a malign prank, it would be hard to persuade them of my continuing reasons for feeling menaced. Everything I was wholly convinced of would seem like paranoid fantasy to a disinterested listener. The water wasn't water – it held some sort of powder in solution. But if I took the flask to a police station what would or could they do? It wasn't lethal, it wasn't poisonous – what charges could be pressed, what protection could I be offered? No, the key aspect of my little ruse was that I had to manufacture some real culpability – only that way would I be able to make my case to anyone prepared to listen.

I left the battery in the phone and drove off down the mountain, sure that I would now be registering on the surveillance screens. Target activated. I didn't feel excited – I felt faintly sick. But for some reason I found my mind turning to my very first film, *Giorni di Mal* (2001), directed by the late great Ruben Mavrocordato. He had cast me straight out of drama school – I think he thought I was the new Terence Stamp or David Hemmings or Peter O'Toole. He had perverse faith in me and my talent, bless him, and made me dye my hair platinum blond and I only wore black throughout the movie. We shot the film in the toe of Italy in August and I wandered through this rocky, burnt-out southern Italian landscape, in merciless heat, carrying a sawn-off shotgun looking for someone. There were encounters on the way – a priest (of course), a blind tinker, a lost child – the most interesting being with a young prostitute (played by the incandescent Fioralba Tizzi – Mrs Mavrocordato, as it happened).

I was completely bewildered, the script changed daily, and I remember taking Ruben aside two weeks into the shoot and politely enquiring why was I armed and who, exactly, was I looking for? Why you asking me these stupid questions, Alec? Ruben said, patiently, kindly – you know the answer inside. He tapped my forehead with a finger. Of course, I said, chastened, of course I do. We completed the movie after five weeks; it just fizzled out after my torrid affair with the Fioralba Tizzi character – Ruben called an abrupt halt one day, he seemed to have lost interest – and I didn't even shoot anyone. We won a prize at the Karlovy Vary film festival. The career boost I was expecting never quite materialized.

As I drove down from Clachan Mor I felt a similar conflicting stress of emotions to those I'd experienced during *Giorni di Mal*: I knew what I was doing, or was about to do, but I didn't know *why* I was doing it. Perhaps whatever I was about to provoke would provide some answers. I think this crucial uncertainty was responsible for my nausea.

I headed for a small heavily wooded promontory just south of Mallaig. Half an hour later I was driving through mature

pine forest on a dirt track. Up ahead at the fringe of the plan-
tation I could see the refulgent light of the ocean beyond. I
pulled up, cut the motor, stepped out and walked into the pines
looking for a small clearing. The trees were closely planted
and it was difficult, scratchy going. It was a cool, breezy day,
thankfully, not much sun showing between the hurrying
clouds. I came across an outcrop of rocks – angled slabs of
granite where no trees or shrubs could gain purchase – and I
decided to look no further. This would have to do. I slipped
off my rucksack and unpacked it.

First I set up the gas stove. Beside it I placed the roasting
pan and filled it with white blocks of firelighters. Then I took
my bent pieces of wire coat hanger and, pushing them into
the fissures of the rock outcrop, managed to suspend three
of the distress flares that I'd bought in the ship chandler's
above the roasting pan, fixed in my rudimentary wire armatures. I had bought half a dozen of these flares. If I'd had a
neat bit of turf I could have fixed the lot of them over the pan,
but three was all I could manage now.

I looked at my watch. Hurry up, Dunbar, they'll be coming
after you.

Now came the tricky bit. I found some thin slabs of shale
and gaffer-taped them together to form a kind of rocky stand
by the gas stove. Then I gaffer-taped the kitchen timer to the
flat rock on the top, the timer's face upwards. Tearing off
thinner strips of tape I managed to fix securely a ten-inch
wand of wire coat hanger to the finger-grip on the timer face.
I twisted the clockwork dial back and reset it to twenty minutes. It began to tick and, as the mainspring unwound and the
timer face revolved as the seconds elapsed, so did the wire
wand attached to it.

I eased the gas stove back an inch or so, positioning it carefully, and then lit it, setting a pebble under its base, to make it

unsteady and therefore relatively easy to tip over once it was nudged. As the clock ticked down on the timer, the wire wand would approach the gas stove. It would touch the uneasily balanced stove, the clockwork pressure would increase, the stove and its lit burner would fall into the roasting pan and set fire to the firelighters. The fierce, near-immediate blaze that ensued would ignite the wire-suspended distress flares. Whoosh! Whoosh! Whoosh! At least that was the plan. Heath Robinson would have been proud of me.

I was sweating. This device had been used as a primitive time bomb in my last film, *Die Standing*, though not by me. I had been killed in the vast explosion it had caused – all of which explained how I knew how to construct it. I looked at the slowly revolving timer. I had fifteen minutes left. I made my last, vital phone call. Voicemail. Leave a message. I swore vilely, profanely. I prayed to the gods of luck and left the message and pushed my way back through the pine forest to the track, jumped into KT-99 and drove out on to the promontory.

I turned the Land Rover 180 degrees so it was facing the track and then, very carefully, door open, leaning out, I backed it inch by inch up to the turf margin of the cliff face. The rear tyres were a foot from the drop. I peered down. Sixty, seventy feet to the surging waves on the rocks below.

I looked across the sound to the islands of Rum, Eigg and Muck and beyond them to the Cuillin hills of Skye. A brief flash of sunshine appeared and for a moment the scene was typically, heart-rendingly beautiful – blue mountains on the islands, scudding clouds, hammered silver-foil sea, the wash of waves and the cry of gulls. I felt sick again.

I took the flask of River Jordan water out of its cool box and climbed up on to the roof of KT-99. I sat down at the rear, my back to the sea and the beetling cliff, and waited.

They came far too early. Two minutes later I heard the sound of the engine and there was still around ten minutes to go on my timer in the woods, I realized. I swore again and stood up on the roof, flask cradled in my arms.

Slowly, bumping over the ruts in the track as it emerged from the pine forest, the big black saloon edged forward and stopped. It sat there for a moment, squat and still, engine running. I could imagine the occupants in some perplexity, wondering what was going on as they looked at a man on the roof of a Land Rover, backed up perilously close to the edge of a high cliff over the sea.

I glanced round and inched backwards and held out the flask over the drop. I heard pulsing wave-surge below me – I didn't look down. They would get the message.

The engine was switched off in the car. Both doors opened. A woman stepped out – and then a man. The man had an automatic pistol in his hand.

'Don't be a fool, Mr Dunbar,' the woman called in an eastern European accent. 'Just give us flask and you will be free to go.'

## Part Eight: The Edge of the Cliff

The woman and the man slowly approached. Now I could see that the woman was, in fact, the feral girl in white, though she didn't look feral any more. The hair was smooth and glossy, she was wearing black designer jeans tucked into black boots and wore a soft mushroom-coloured leather jacket. She looked corporate and sternly pretty but still with the generic eastern European accent.

The man, thin and limber, wiry hair gelled back into corrugated waves, wearing jeans and a blouson jacket, was carrying a big Desert Eagle .50 AE, one of the most powerful handguns in the world. I knew a lot about guns – I'd used and been killed by many specific brands during my career in action movies. A Desert Eagle .50 had slotted me in *Entry Wound*, it so happened. I hoped this wasn't a bad omen.

'Give us flask. Don't be stupid, Mr Dunbar,' the woman repeated. 'We'll leave you alone.'

'Oh, yeah, sure,' I said. 'Just stop right there.' They were about ten feet away. 'I know exactly what's going on,' I said, bluffing somewhat.

Gratifyingly, they both stopped advancing on me and stood there. The man held his Desert Eagle down. The woman, the feral girl turned corporate maven, took half a step forward.

'You are innocent party,' she said. 'We have nothing against you, no grievance. You didn't know what you were getting into.'

'I know it's a drug,' I said. 'Some new pharmaceutical product, worth a dozen kings' ransoms. My bet is that Stella and Ronaldo used to work with you, at whatever Big Pharma company you represent. They stole this drug and were going to sell it to someone else. But you were on their trail trying to get it back.'

'I don't know any Stella or Ronaldo,' the woman said, not very convincingly, as if caught out by my analysis. She put on a pair of sunglasses – the sun was lowering in the west. More and more this scene was resembling some fraught denouement to a future film I might make. Or might not. I had to keep a grip on reality. One shot from the Desert Eagle could blow my arm off. My arm that was now beginning to ache, holding out the flask. I lowered it.

'You are right in one thing,' the woman said. 'The fluid in that flask was stolen. We were hired to recover it. We weren't sure what role you were playing. Which is why I subterfuge you at gas station.' She allowed herself a smile. 'Now I know you have nothing to do with the theft. So – let's be sensible, Mr Dunbar. Hand it over. We leave. You leave. End of story.'

'What happened to Stella and Ronaldo?'

'I don't know who they are.'

'I found their dead bodies in a church. An hour later they had gone.'

'You're talking in mystery and riddles, Mr Dunbar.'

'Have you buried them somewhere?'

She continued with her denials. I continued with my questions, conscious of my kitchen timer ticking away in the forest.

Then the man with the gun said something to her in a low voice and she shook her head slightly.

'Listen. How about this for a scenario,' I said. 'It's just struck me that the fluid in this jar is all that's left of this pharmaceutical goldmine, whatever it is. Stella and Ronaldo not only stole it, they eradicated all trace of its previous life – that's why it's so precious.'

'You have been in too many bad movies,' the woman said, allowing a little contempt to creep into her voice.

'I couldn't agree more,' I said. 'But you've no idea what an education bad movies provide when it comes to understanding the ways of the world.'

I smiled at her and held my arm out again, dangling the flask over the cliff edge. I thought Wiry-Hair was losing patience and just wanted to blow me away.

'How about *this* movie?' I went on. 'Stella Devereaux has stolen the drug. She knows you're on her heels so she takes elaborate pains to find the perfect patsy to transport her precious cargo to a place of greater safety. That patsy was me. I was meant to meet her in St Mungo's Church in Alcorran – but you got to her and her partner first. Killed them. What was it – injection? Gas? There was a funny smell in that building.'

'You are fantasist,' the woman said. 'Just give us flask before we lose all patience.' She nodded at Wiry-Hair, who raised the Desert Eagle and pointed it at me. I shuffled backwards to the very edge of KT-99's roof. I conjured up an image of my makeshift rescue device in the pine forest. The wire wand attached to the timer making contact with the teetering gas stove. Tick, tick, tick. The stove tumbles, the firelighters burst into flame under the wire armatures holding the distress flares. How long before the licking flames detonate the propellant in the flares and –

BANG! Silence. Then – BANG! BANG!

The woman and the man looked round in pleasing incredulity as three cherry-red distress flares rose hundreds of feet in the air behind them, launched from the fastness of the pine forest.

Wiry-Hair swore foully in a language I didn't understand and swivelled his gun back at me.

'Don't be stupid, mate,' I said. 'Now the police know exactly where you are.'

On cue – sometimes life works like that: life works like a movie – distant police sirens sounded from within the forest. My voicemail message had been picked up – swiftly, obviously – and now seeing the flares the police had switched their sirens on. The flares were now dropping slowly, fizzling out, trailing their puce contrails. Here, they were saying, here be villains.

The woman had lost her composure, I could see.

'Give me flask!' she said in a shrill, strangled voice.

'You know what?' I said. 'I don't like you people. You've been very tiresome. So I don't think I will.'

As casually as I could, I tossed the flask over my shoulder, over the cliff. We could all hear the crash of shattered glass as it hit the rocks below and, at the same moment, two police cars roared out of the pine forest, blue lights flashing, sirens wailing, and lurched to a stop.

Sergeant Callum Strang stepped out of the first car. Three other policemen followed. I noticed that the Desert Eagle had abruptly disappeared, back in its shoulder holster. Now was the time for my master stroke.

'Sergeant Strang,' I called. 'Very good to see you.'

'I got your message,' Strang said, taking in the other two. 'You said it was very urgent.'

I was in full acting mode now: being cool when in fact I was in a state of trembling shock, so closely run had events been.

I jumped down off the roof of the Defender and pointed at the woman and Wiry-Hair.

'These were the two playing dead in the church.'

'Really?' Strang said.

'I don't know who is this man,' the woman said, insistently. 'We were just admiring view when he arrive with his Land Rover. He's being most objectionable.'

'I recommend a thorough search of this gentleman,' I said, pointing at Wiry-Hair. 'You might find it interesting.'

Strang turned to the woman.

'I think it might be best if you accompanied us to the station in Mallaig, madam,' Strang said, all official politesse. 'Please follow this car.'

The woman protested, huffed and puffed, but she and Wiry-Hair were shepherded into their car. Strang turned to me.

'What's going on, Mr Dunbar?'

'I would put an officer in the car with them, Sergeant,' I advised.

'Why?'

'I think he may be armed.'

'Right . . .' He turned. 'Malky,' he shouted. 'You go with them.'

One of his constables climbed into the back of the saloon.

'I'll repeat my question. What's going on, Mr Dunbar?'

'I don't know. I recognized these two in a ship chandler's in Mallaig. They were buying flares. And I followed them.'

'What about those flares? Why would they let them off?'

'Another of their pranks? Perhaps. Lure out the fire brigade. I don't know.'

Strang didn't really believe a word I was saying but he knew the tip of an iceberg when he saw one. He asked me to give him my address and contact numbers. I did with great pleasure – a new worry was creeping up on me and I wanted as much proximity to the police as I could muster. The more they knew the better.

'Got your phone back?' Strang asked.

'Ah, yes. It dried out.'

'Returning to London?'

'Not immediately. I've a friend in Mallaig I want to see,' I said, thinking of Isla MacNab and how I owed her a proper thank you.

'Good,' Strang said. 'I'll let you know what our search of the gentleman unearths. I'll call you later.'

'Have a good look in their car, as well,' I suggested. 'I've a feeling they're not quite who they'll claim to be.'

Strang gave me that look again – shrewd, askance – shook my hand and we made our farewells. I was thinking. They'll find the gun. They'll find all their GPS tracking paraphernalia – and goodness knows what else. They would be detained in Mallaig a good few days at the very least answering charges for possession of a deadly weapon. Carrying a gun – let alone a Desert Eagle .50 – in Great Britain was a serious offence. There might even be terrorist issues – Special Branch, MI5.

And who knows, maybe Stella's and Ronaldo's bodies would be discovered, though I doubted that – there were too many remote, deep lochans in this part of the world. Still, I reckoned I had some time on my side but I couldn't ignore the little keening note of worry. Who were they working for? Would they forget about me or come seeking retribution? Surely I was small fry, not worth bothering about, causing more trouble for them – a tiny random player in this global pursuit of billions? . . . I held on to that thought. It consoled me. And what to do about KT-99, I asked myself, as I climbed into the front seat? Was she mine now? Or should I turn her in as evidence? I'd think about that tomorrow, I told myself, happy to procrastinate, looking for the number of Ardenthill College on my phone. Isla would know a good restaurant and I hadn't seen a wedding ring on her finger.

I saw Strang's car bump across the grass towards me, his window winding down and his hand beckoning me over. Oh God, no. What now? I stepped out, throat tight, pocketing my phone.

'Were you in *Die Standing*, by any chance?' Strang asked.

'I was,' I said, disguising my relief. 'I was indeed.'

'Thought it was you,' Strang said with a smile. 'Good movie.'

He drove away into the pine forest, following the saloon, and I climbed back into KT-99 and called Ardenthill, asking to be put through to the science block. I was safe, I considered, as safe as I could reasonably expect to be, given the circumstances. But for how long?

Yes, I said, I'll wait, no problem.

Then another unwelcome idea infiltrated itself into my crowded brain. Maybe Stella, Ronaldo, Feral and Wiry-Hair were all working together. Maybe it was their collective plan – they had stolen the drug together but some dishonour amongst conspirators had meant that two of them had been eliminated. It made more sense somehow – explained how I was followed so easily, how Stella and Ronaldo were killed in St Mungo's with no apparent struggle. Maybe I was the one meant to be identified as the thief, the fall guy. The man on the run, heading north to Scotland with the crucial flask. Maybe I was the one meant to be caught and served up – but I'd made it all go wrong for them . . .

I didn't understand much, but I knew that I had been the unwitting part of an elaborate conspiracy of some sort – an innocent passing asteroid drawn into the gravitational pull of a larger malevolent planet. I was to be used in some way in a plan concerning the theft of a prototype pharmaceutical drug and its resale. That was all I could possibly allege with any kind of confidence; I could have no idea of the full ramifications of this scam – what was at stake or how much money was involved. The fact that I had managed to extricate myself was the crucial achievement.

No, I thought: stop thinking, Dunbar, it'll drive you insane. In this instance ignorance really is bliss. You'll never know what was really going on. Ever. Just be glad you're parked here on this promontory on the west coast of Scotland watching the sun set over the Atlantic Ocean and your enemies are secure in Mallaig police station.

I sat still, waiting, my phone to my ear.

Then Isla MacNab came on the line and I relaxed.

'Hello?'

'Hi. It's Alec Dunbar here.'

One day at a time.

**READ ON FOR AN EXTRACT FROM
WILLIAM BOYD'S NEW NOVEL,
*LOVE IS BLIND* . . .**

# *Prologue*

Port Blair
Andaman Islands
Indian Empire

11 March 1906

Dear Amelia,

There was an attempt to escape from the jail last night and a small riot ensued. Most unusual. Three of the prisoners were killed but a number managed to flee. Consequently we have a twenty-four-hour curfew imposed on the town so here I am in my house at luncheon writing this long-overdue missive.

All is well, my leg is much better (Dr Klein is very pleased, he says, though I'm walking with a stick – very elegant) and the new tribe we've found is slowly becoming accommodating. Colonel Ticknell, the British superintendent here, is most helpful. 'Your every need, Miss Arbogast, is mine. Please don't hesitate, the merest trifle, etc., etc.' And I don't hesitate (you know me). Transport, bearers, diplomatic postal facilities – even a firearm – have been supplied. I think Col Ticknell has a soft spot for me and he imagines diligent concern will win my heart. No harm in thinking, I suppose. You will call me a calculating minx, but needs must out here.

And, *mirabile dictu*, the advertisement I placed in the local newspaper and that I personally affixed to the wall in the post office has been answered. I have a new assistant – finally!

A policeman is knocking on the door. The curfew is over, I suspect. I will write again, later.

In the meantime, with my love as always, your sister,

Page

PS. By the way my new assistant is a tall young Scotchman, about thirty-five years old, called Brodie Moncur.

# PART I

# EDINBURGH
## 1894

### 1

Brodie Moncur stood in the main window of Channon & Co. and looked out at the hurrying pedestrians, the cabs, carriages and labouring drays of George Street. It was raining – a steady soft rain driven slant from time to time by the occasional fierce gust of wind – and, under the ponderous pewter light, the sooty facades of the buildings opposite had darkened with the water to a near-black. Like velvet, Brodie thought, or moleskin. He took off his spectacles and wiped the lenses clean on his handkerchief. Looking out of the window again, spectacle-less, he saw that rainy Edinburgh had now gone utterly aqueous. The buildings opposite were a cliff of black suede.

He replaced his spectacles – hooking the wire sides behind his ears – and the world returned to normal. He slipped his watch from his waistcoat pocket. Nearly nine o'clock – better start. He opened up the glossy new grand piano that was on the display dais, propping up the curved lid with its inlaid mirror (only for display purposes – his idea) the better to present the intricate machinery – the 'action' – inside a Channon grand. He removed the fall from over the keys and undid the key-block screws. He checked that no hammers were up and then drew the whole action forward by the flange rail under the front. As it was a new piano it drew out perfectly. Already a passer-by had stopped and was peering in. Drawing out the action always compelled attention. Everyone had seen a grand piano with the lid up but having the action on display somehow altered every easy assumption. The piano no longer seemed familiar. Now all the moving parts were visible beyond the black and white keys – the hammers, the rockers, the jacks, the whippens, the dampers – its innards were exposed like a clock with its back off or a railway engine dismantled in a repair shed. Mysteries – music, time, movement – were reduced to complex, elaborate mechanisms. People tended to be fascinated.

He untied his leather roll of tools, selected the tuning lever and pretended to tune the piano, tightening a few strings here and there, testing them and resetting them. The piano was perfectly tuned – he had tuned it himself when it had emerged, pristine, from the factory two weeks ago. He tuned F a modicum on the sharp side then knocked it in – back into tune – with a few brisk taps on the key. He supported a hammer-head and needled-up the felt a little with his three-pronged voicing tool and returned it to its position. This pantomime of tuning a piano was meant to lure the customers in. He had suggested, at one of the rare staff meetings, that they should have someone actually playing the piano – an accomplished pianist – as they did in showrooms in Germany, and as the Erard and Pleyel piano manufacturers had done in Paris in the 1830s and drawn huge crowds. It was hardly an innovation – but an impromptu recital in a shop window would surely be more enticing than listening to the mannered repetitions of a piano being tuned. *Donk! Ding! Donk! Donk! Donk! Ding!* He had been overruled – an accomplished pianist would cost money – and instead he was given this job of display-tuning: an hour in the morning and an hour after luncheon.

In fact he did attract spectators, although he had been the single beneficiary – he wasn't sure if the firm had sold one more piano as a result of his demonstrations, but many people and not a few institutions (schools, church halls, public house) had slipped into the shop, pressed a calling card on him, and offered him out-of-hours piano tuning. He had earned a good few pounds.

So, he played A above middle C several times, to 'get the pitch', pointedly listening to the tone with a cocked head. Then played a few octaves. He stood, slipped some felt mutes between strings, took out his tuning lever, set it over a wrest pin at random and gave it some tiny turns, just to deliver torque, then eased the pin slightly to 'set the pin' and hit the note hard, to deliver a cast-iron tuning, feeling it in the hand through the lever. Then he sat down and played a few chords, listening to the Channon's particular voice. Big and strongly resonant – the precision thinness of the sounding board (made from Scottish spruce) under the strings was the special Channon trademark, its trade secret. A Channon could rival a Steinway or a Bösendorfer when it came to breaking through an orchestra. Where the spruce forests were in Scotland that Channon used, what trees were selected – the straighter the tree, the straighter the grain – and what sawmills prepared the timber, were facts known only to a handful of people in the firm. Channon claimed that it was the quality of the Scottish wood they used that made their pianos' distinct, unique tone.

Brodie's feigning over, he sat down and started to play 'The Skye Boat Song' and saw that the single spectator had now been joined by three others. If he played for half an hour he knew there would be a crowd of twenty looking on. It was a good idea, the Continental idea. Perhaps, out of that twenty, two might enquire about the price of a baby grand or an upright. He stopped playing, took out his plectrum, reached into the piano and twanged a few strings, listening intently. What would that look like to anyone? A man with a plectrum playing a grand piano like a guitar. All very mysterious—

'Brodie!'

He looked round. Emmeline Grant, Mr Channon's secretary, stood at the window's framing edge, beckoning at him. She was a small burly woman who tried to disguise how fond she was of him.

'I'm in full tune, Mrs Grant.'

'Mr Channon wants to see you. Right away. Come along now.'

'I'm coming, I'm coming.'

He stood, thought about closing the piano down but decided against it. He'd be back in ten minutes. He gave a deep bow to his small audience and followed Mrs Grant through the showroom, with its parked, glossy pianos, and into the main hall of the Channon building. Austere unsmiling portraits of previous generations of Channons hung on olive and charcoal-grey striped wallpaper. Another mistake, Brodie thought: it was like a provincial art gallery or a funeral parlour.

'Give me two minutes, Mrs G. I have to wash my hands.'

'Hurry along. I'll see you upstairs. It's important.'

Brodie went through the back, through a leather, brass-studded door into the warehouse area where the workshop was located. It was a cross between a carpentry shop and an office, he always thought, the air seasoned with the smell of wood shavings, glue and resin. He pushed open the door and found his number two, Lachlan Hood, at work replacing the centre pins on a baby grand – a long job, there were hundreds of them.

Lachlan glanced at him as he came in.

'What's going on, Brodie? Should you no be in the window?'

'I'm wanted. Mr Channon.'

He slid up his roll-top desk and opened the drawer where he kept his tin of tobacco. 'Margarita' was the brand name: an American blend of Virginia, Turkish and perique tobacco, made by a tobacconist called Blakely in New York City and to be found in only one retailer in Edinburgh – Hoskings, in the Grassmarket. He took one of the three cigarettes he had already rolled and lit it, inhaling deeply.

'What's he want you for?' Lachlan asked.

'I don't know. Darling Emmeline says it's "important".'

'Well, it was nice knowing youse. I suppose I'll get your job, the now.'

Lachlan was from Dundee and had a strong Dundonian accent. Brodie made the sign of the evil eye at him, took two more puffs, stubbed out his cigarette and headed for Ainsley Channon's office.

Ainsley Channon was the sixth Channon to head the firm since it had been established in the mid eighteenth century. On the landing was a 1783 Channon five-octave spinet – the first Channon model to be a true success and which began the firm's fortunes. Now it was the fourth largest piano manu-facturer, some said the third, in Britain, after Broadwood, Pate and – possibly – Franklin. And, as if to confirm the length of this lineage, Ainsley Channon dressed in a style that had been fashionable half a century before. He wore luxuriant Dundreary whiskers and a stiff wing collar with silk cravat and pin. His receding grey hair hung down long behind his ears, almost touching his shoulders. He looked like an old musician, like a stout Paganini. Brodie knew he couldn't play a note.

Brodie gave a one-knuckle knock and pushed open the door.

'Come away in, Brodie. Brodie, my boy. Sit ye down, sit ye down.'

The room was large and gloomy – the gas lamps lit even though it was morning – with three tall, twelve-paned windows looking out over George Street. Brodie could make out the high, thin spire of St Andrew's and St George's West Church through the still-falling smear of misty rain.

Ainsley stepped round from behind his partners' desk and pulled up a chair for Brodie, patting its leather seat.

Brodie sat down on it. Ainsley smiled at him as if he hadn't seen him for years, taking him in.

'You'll have a dram.'

It was a statement, not a question and Brodie didn't bother to reply. Ainsley went to a table with a clustered, light-winking collection of decanters, selected one and poured two generous glasses, bringing Brodie's over to him before taking his place behind his desk again.

'Here's how,' Ainsley said and raised his glass.

'*Slangevar*,' Brodie replied and sipped at his amber whisky. Malt, peaty, West Coast.

Ainsley held up a puce cardboard dossier and waved it at him.

'The Brodie Moncur file,' he said.

For some reason Brodie felt a little heart-jig of worry. He calmed it with another sip of whisky.

Ainsley Channon had a somewhat dreamy and disconnected air about him, Brodie knew, and so was not surprised at the meandering path the meeting took.

'How long have you been with us, Brodie? It'll be about three years now, yes?'

'Actually six, sir.'

'Good God, good God, good God.' He paused and smiled, taking this in. 'How's your father?'

'Well, sir.'

'And your siblings?'

'All fit and well.'

'Have you seen Lady Dalcastle recently?'

'Not for a while.'

'Wonderful woman. Wonderful woman. Very brave.'

'I believe she's very well, also.'

Ainsley Channon was a cousin of Lady Dalcastle, who had been a close friend of Brodie's late mother. It was through Lady Dalcastle's good offices that Brodie had been taken on by Channon's as an apprentice tuner.

Ainsley was looking at his dossier again.

'Aye. You're a clever boy, right enough. Very good grades . . .' He looked up. 'Do you parley-voo?'

'Excuse me?'

'Speakee zee French? Ooh la-la. *Bonjour monsieur.*'

'Well, I studied French at school.'

'Give us a wee whirl.'

Brodie thought for a moment.

'*Je peux parler français,*' he said. '*Mais je fais les erreurs. Quand même, les gens me comprennent bien.*'

Ainsley looked at him in astonishment.

'That's incredible! The accent! I'd have sworn blind you were a Frenchie.'

'Thank you, sir. *Merci mille fois.*'

'Good God above. How old are you now, Brodie? Thirty? Thirty-two?'

'I'm twenty-four, sir.'

'Christ alive! How long have you been with us? Three years, now?'

'Six,' Brodie repeated. 'I was apprenticed to old Mr Lanhire, back in '88.'

'Oh, yes, right enough. Findlay Lanhire. God rest him. The best tuner ever. Ever. The very best. Ever. He designed the Phoenix, you know.'

The Phoenix was Channon's bestselling upright. Brodie had tuned hundreds over his six years.

'I learned everything from Mr Lanhire.'

Ainsley leaned forward and peered at him.

'Only twenty-four? You've an old head on your shoulders, Brodie.'

'I came here straight from school.'

Ainsley looked at the dossier.

'What school was that?'

'Mrs Maskelyne's Academy of Music.'

'Where's that? London?'

'Here in Edinburgh, sir.'

Ainsley was still computing numbers in his head.

''88, you say?'

'September 1888. That's when I started at Channon's.'

'Well, we've got a Channon challenge for you now . . . ' He paused. 'Top us up, Brodie.'

Brodie fetched the decanter and topped up their two glasses and sat down again. Ainsley Channon was staring at him over the dome of his steepled fingers. Again, Brodie felt vague unease. He sipped whisky.

'You know we opened that Channon showroom in Paris, last year . . . ' Ainsley said.

Brodie admitted that he did.

'Well, it's not going well,' Ainsley confided, lowering his voice as if someone might overhear. 'In fact it's going very badly, between ourselves.' He explained further. Ainsley's son, Calder Channon, had been appointed manager in Paris and although everything was in reasonable shape, seemed well set up, contacts made, stock warehoused, regular advertisements in the Parisian press placed, they were losing money – not worryingly – but at a steady, unignorable rate.

'We need an injection of new energy,' Ainsley said. 'We need someone who understands the piano business. We need someone with bright ideas . . . ' he paused theatrically. 'And we need someone who can speak French. Calder seems incapable.'

Brodie decided not to confess how rudimentary his grasp of the French language was and let Ainsley continue.

'Here's the plan, Brodie, my boy.'

Brodie was to go to Paris as soon as possible – in a week, say, once his affairs were in order – and become Calder Channon's number two. Assistant manager of the Paris showroom. There was only one thing to have on his mind, Ainsley said: sales, sales, sales – and more sales.

'Do you know how many major piano manufacturers there are in Europe? Go on, have a guess.'

'Twenty?'

'Two hundred and fifty-five, at the last count! That's who we're competing with. Our pianos are wonderful but nobody's buying them in Paris – well, not enough of them, anyway. They're buying trash like Montcalms, Angelems, Maugeners, Pontenegros. They're even starting to make pianos in Japan! Can you believe it? It's a fiercely contested market. Excellence isn't enough. It's got to change, Brodie. And something tells me you're the man for the job – you know pianos inside out and you're a world-class tuner. And you speak fluent French. Good God above! Calder needs someone like you. Stupid old fool that I am for not realizing this.' He sat back and took a gulp of his whisky, pondering. 'Calder was too confident –

overconfident, I now see. He needs someone at his side, help steer the ship, if you know what I mean . . . '

'I understand, sir. But, if the language is a problem, why not employ a Frenchman?'

'Sweet Jesus, no! Are you losing your reason? We've got to have one of our own. Someone you can trust absolutely. Member of the family, as it were.'

'I see.'

'Can you do it, laddie?'

'I can certainly try, sir.'

'Try your damnedest? Try your utmost?'

'Of course.'

Ainsley seemed suddenly cheered and assured him he'd have a significant increase in salary, and his position – and his salary – would be reviewed in six months, depending on results.

Ainsley came round from behind his desk and poured them two more drams, the better to toast the new Parisian enterprise. They clinked glasses, drank.

'We'll meet again, afore you go, Brodie. I've a couple of wee tips that might be useful.' He took Brodie's glass from him and set it on the desk. The meeting was over. As he showed Brodie to the door he squeezed his elbow, hard.

'Calder's a good boy but he could do with a staunch lieutenant.'

'I'll do my best, Mr Channon. Rely on me.'

'That I will. It's a great opportunity for us. Paris is the centre for music, these days. Not London, not Rome, or Berlin. Apart from Vienna, of course. But we could be number one in Europe – see them all off: Steinway, Broadwood, Erard, Bösendorfer, Schiedmayer. You'll see.'

Back in the workshop Brodie smoked another cigarette, thinking hard. He should be pleased, he knew, incredibly pleased – but something was bothering him, something indeterminate, naggingly vague. Was it Paris, the fact that he'd never been there, never been abroad? No, that excited him: to live, to work in Paris, that would be—

Lachlan Hood sauntered in from the shop.

'Still here?'

'Not for long,' Brodie said.

'I knew it. Tough luck, Brodie. Hard cheese, old pal.'

'No. I'm to go to Paris. Help Calder with the shop there.'

Lachlan couldn't conceal his shock, his disappointment.

'Why you? Fuck! Why not me? I've been to America.'

*'Mais est-ce que vous parlez français, monsieur?'*

'What?'

'Exactly.' Brodie spread his hands, mock-ruefully. 'The benefits of a good education, sonny boy. I happen to speak excellent French.'

'Liar. Fucking liar. You speak opera French.'

'All right, I admit it. The key thing is I speak *enough* French. Which is about one hundred per cent more French than you do.' He offered Lachlan a cigarette, and smiled patronizingly.

'If it all goes well, maybe I'll send for you.'

'Bastard.'

# He just wanted a decent book to read ...

Not too much to ask, is it? It was in 1935 when Allen Lane, Managing
Director of Bodley Head Publishers, stood on a platform at Exeter railway
station looking for something good to read on his journey back to London.
His choice was limited to popular magazines and poor-quality paperbacks –
the same choice faced every day by the vast majority of readers, few of
whom could afford hardbacks. Lane's disappointment and subsequent anger
at the range of books generally available led him to found a company – and
change the world.

*'We believed in the existence in this country of a vast reading public for intelligent*
*books at a low price, and staked everything on it'*
**Sir Allen Lane, 1902–1970, founder of Penguin Books**

The quality paperback had arrived – and not just in bookshops. Lane was
adamant that his Penguins should appear in chain stores and tobacconists,
and should cost no more than a packet of cigarettes.

Reading habits (and cigarette prices) have changed since 1935, but
Penguin still believes in publishing the best books for everybody to
enjoy. We still believe that good design costs no more than bad design,
and we still believe that quality books published passionately and responsibly
make the world a better place.

So wherever you see the little bird – whether it's on a piece of
prize-winning literary fiction or a celebrity autobiography, political tour
de force or historical masterpiece, a serial-killer thriller, reference book,
world classic or a piece of pure escapism – you can bet that it represents
the very best that the genre has to offer.

**Whatever you like to read – trust Penguin.**